THE EMPIRE
OF GLASS

DOCTOR WHO – THE MISSING ADVENTURES

Also available:

THE EMPIRE
OF GLASS

Andy Lane

DOCTOR WHO

THE MISSING ADVENTURES

First published in Great Britain in 1995 by
Doctor Who Books
an imprint of Virgin Publishing Ltd
332 Ladbroke Grove
London W10 5AH

ISBN 0 426 20457 3

Cover illustration by Paul Campbell
Internal illustrations by Mike Nicholson

Typeset by Galleon Typesetting, Ipswich
Printed and bound in Great Britain by
Mackays Paperbacks

To the original CLLG – Rhea Antoniades, John Austen, Steve Boyce, Helen Grant, Larry Langford, Anne Micklethwaite, Terry Mitchell-Smith and (especially) Julia Wortley.

Acknowledgements

With grateful thanks to Craig Hinton, Justin Richards, Rebecca Levene, David A. McIntee and Andrew Martin.

'If we could believe with any probability
that there were living beings and
vegetables on the moon or any planet,
different not only from terrestrial ones
but remote from our wildest imaginings, I
should for my part neither affirm nor deny
it, but should leave the decision to wiser
men than I.'

Galileo Galilei having his cake and eating
it in his *Letters on Sunspots*, 1613.

. . . 'It is a tale
Told by an idiot, full of sound and fury,
Signifying nothing.'

William Shakespeare:
Macbeth, Act V, Scene 5.

Prologue

One month.

Mary Harries gazed out across the sparkling blue ocean at the departing ship. From her position on the cliff she was looking down upon its deck – freshly scrubbed and glistening in the hot summer sunlight. Its sails were swollen with the breeze, and it listed slightly to one side as it began its long tack out of the harbour and its longer journey home. Gulls swooped low around its bows and, higher in the sky, the black squiggles of larger birds were wheeling and soaring. She couldn't tell what sort of birds they were, but there was a lot about New Albion that she couldn't recognize.

Turning her attention back to the ship, she could see sailors scurry across the rigging like spiders on a cobweb. One of them turned around and gazed back toward the coast, shielding his eyes with his hand. His chest was bare, and he wore a bandana around his head. Seeing her, he waved in big, sweeping gestures. She waved too, choking back a sob. It was Jim: even at that distance she recognized his sun-bleached hair, drawn back in a tarred pig-tail and bouncing against his back as his powerful arms moved. Those arms, which had pulled her close and held her tight. Those arms, in whose embrace she had slept on many a night. Those powerful, tender arms.

One month.

She blinked, and the ship was blotted out by tears as if by a sudden squall. They spilled, hot and salty, down her

1

cheeks and across her lips, and it was like tasting the salt on Jim's skin again as her mouth explored his body. A sudden sob made her shoulders convulse. Grief and loss twisted her stomach, and she hugged herself despite the heat that made her dress stick to her body, wishing that her arms were Jim's arms and her tears were his lips. But it would never be so again.

One month.

That's how long she and Jim had been given together. That was how long it had been since the ship docked and the colonists had emerged, blinking and unsteady, into the heavy heat and the ever-present humidity. The voyage from England had taken three months, and of the seven score and ten colonists who had started the journey, the inspirational words of Sir Walter Ralegh still ringing in their ears, almost two score were now held in the bosom of Jesus. The rest had followed Governor White onto the soil of New Albion. While he sketched the strange new plants and the strange, rust-skinned primitives, they had built their cabins and planted their crops. The sailors – who, on the ship, had laughed at them and called them 'puke-stockings' – watched at first, amused, but after a few days some had joined in, lending their expertise and their strength. Mary had been cooking one night when Jim had walked over and told her that she was beautiful. He had a sailor's directness and a sailor's weatherbeaten face, but he had the eyes of an angel, and nobody had ever told her that before.

She had been happy, for a while. So happy that she hadn't minded rising at dawn and working until long after the sun had set, trying to put the colony on a firm footing. Then the fever came, and the crops showed no sign of growing, and some of the sheep that they had brought with them from England sickened and died, and Governor White had decided to return to England when the ship left and ask advice. And the perfect idyll of hard days working and long nights spent in Jim's arms were at an end.

The ship was smaller now, and Mary's eyes were

half-blinded by the sparkle of the sun on the water, but she could still see Jim's arm waving. It would be six months at least before Governor White returned, and it might not even be on the same ship. Perhaps the colony would survive, or Good Queen Bess might decide that it was not worth sustaining. Wherever she ended up, Mary knew that it would not be with Jim.

A movement in the sky caught Mary's attention. Glancing up, she noticed that the large birds were swooping lower, almost as if they had been waiting for the ship to leave. She dismissed the notion as fanciful: even in the New World, birds were just birds. Casting one last glance at the departing ship — just a piece of flotsam, dark against the blue of the waves — she turned away toward the trees that hid the settlement. No doubt there would be half a hundred things to do when she got back. There always were. Governor White's daughter was almost seven months with child now, her belly stretched like the canvas of the ship's sails, and she was almost unable to work. That meant more for the rest of the women to do. More to do and nothing to show for it, not even a pair of strong arms in the night.

The birds were plunging down behind the treeline now, and it occurred to Mary that they were larger than any birds that she had ever seen before. Their bodies looked more like the shells of crabs, and their wings were the red of fresh blood. Perhaps the tears gumming her eyelashes together were magnifying things, or perhaps her grief at losing Jim was unhinging her reason, but surely no bird that ever flew looked like *that*.

Mary began to move faster through the underbrush towards the trees, and the path that led to the settlement. Bushes whipped at her legs, scratching her as she broke into a stumbling run. Someone in the settlement had started to scream like a pig about to be slaughtered, and behind the screams Mary could hear the flapping of huge wings. What was happening? What in God's good name was happening?

3

She was barely ten feet from the trees when the demon settled to the ground in front of her, furling its wings across its hard, red back. Eyes on the end of stalks, like those of a snail, regarded her curiously.

And as its claws reached out for her, she screamed. And screamed.

And for all the years following that moment, after everything that was done to her, in her head she still screamed.

August, 1592

Matt Jobswortham pulled back on the horse's reins, slowing his dray down by just a jot. The streets of Deptford were crowded with people going about their business — some in fine clothes, some in sailors' garb, some in rags — and he didn't want any of them going under his wheels. The barrels of cider on the back of the dray were so heavy that the wheels were already cutting great ruts in the road. They would cut through a limb with equal ease and what would happen to him then, eh? He'd be finished for sure, banged up in prison for months until someone bothered to determine whether or not there was a case to answer.

He glanced around, impressed as ever with the bustle of the place. Deptford was near London, and the houses reflected that proximity. Why, some of them were three storeys or more! All these people, living above each other in small rooms, day in and day out. It wasn't natural. He liked coming to London, but he wouldn't like to live there. Give him his farmhouse any day.

It was a hot day, and he could smell something thick and cloying on the back of the wind, like an animal that had been dead for weeks. It was the river of course. He'd crossed it a good half hour before, but he could still smell it. Raw with sewage it was, raw and stinking, like a festering wound running through the centre of the city. He didn't know how people here could stand it.

Matt had been on the road since dawn, bringing the barrels up from Sussex. He'd been dreaming of the cider: imagining the sharp, bitter taste of it as it cut through the dirt in his mouth and the sewer smell at the back of his throat. Surely the landlord of the inn couldn't begrudge him a drop, not after he'd come all this way. It was a long way back, after all. Just a flagon, that's all he asked.

'Mary! Mary Harries!'

Preoccupied with thoughts of drink, he jumped when the voice cut across the rumble of the wheels. It was a cultured voice, full of surprise, and he looked around for its owner. The man wasn't hard to find: he was ten yards or so ahead of the dray, young and fine-featured, and he wore a black velvet jacket slashed to show a red silk lining. He was of the nobility, that much was certain, and yet he was standing outside a Deptford drinking house with a flagon in his hand. 'Mary!' he called again. 'I thought you were *dead*!'

Matt followed the young man's gaze. He was calling to a woman wearing plain black clothes on the same side of the road but nearer to the dray. She gazed at the man with a puzzled expression on her face, as if she recognized him from somewhere, but wasn't sure where.

The young man started to run toward her. 'I thought you *all* died at Roanoake,' he cried, 'and I was the only one left. What happened?'

A spasm of alarm crossed the woman's face. She took a step backward, one hand raised to her head.

'Mary!' the man called. 'It *is* you.'

She turned and ran stiff-legged out into the road, oblivious of the traffic. Her odd gait took her straight in front of Matt's dray. He cried out incoherently but she didn't seem to hear him. He caught one last glimpse of her face — calm and expressionless — before she fell beneath the horse's hooves. By a miracle, the horse managed to step over her as she tried to get to her feet. Matt heaved desperately on the reins to pull the horse in, but the momentum of the heavy barrels pushed the dray

5

onward, carrying the horse with it. Matt glanced down as he passed the woman's body. She looked up at him, and there was nothing in her eyes at all: no concern, no fear, nothing.

And then a sound cut through the air, stopping conversations and making heads turn. It sounded like a sapling, bent to breaking point, suddenly snapping. It was a wet, final sound, and it occurred just as the dray's front right wheel passed over the woman's leg.

The young man stopped, his face ashen with horror. Matt hauled on the reins, trying urgently to stop the dray before its second set of wheels compounded the damage. He kept waiting for her to scream, but there was nothing but silence from beneath the dray. Everything seemed to have stopped in the street: faces were frozen, voices stilled. Time itself had paused.

The horse neighed loudly, jerking back onto its hind legs as the reins bit home. The dray lurched to a halt. Matt quickly scrambled down to the rutted, dusty road, dreading what he would find, but the sight that met his eyes was so bizarre, so unbelievable, that he just stared uncomprehendingly for a moment, unable to take it in and make sense of it.

The woman was getting to her feet. She frowned slightly, as one might when bothered by a mosquito. Her left leg was crushed to half its width beneath the knee, and her calf slanted at a crazy angle to her thigh. Shards of bone projected from the wound, startlingly white against the red-raw flesh. She started to walk, lurching wildly like an upside-down pendulum, and she was across the road and into a side alley before anybody could think to stop her.

One

The first thing that Vicki saw when she walked into the TARDIS's control room was Steven Taylor's hand hovering over the central, mushroom-shaped console.

'Don't touch those controls!' she snapped, her voice echoing around the room.

Steven's shoulders hunched defensively, and he glanced towards her. Gradually the echoes of her voice faded away, leaving only the deep hum that meant the TARDIS was still in flight.

'Why not?' he asked truculently, brows heavy, jaw thrust forward. 'I'm a qualified space pilot, aren't I? These switches and levers may look complicated, but I'm sure I can figure them out. And the Doctor's been gone for hours. He may never come back. We need to be able to fly this thing.' His fingers closed around a large red switch on one facet of the control console. His fingers caressed it hesitantly. It was obvious to Vicki that he hadn't got a clue what he was doing, but didn't want to admit it. 'This thing must make us materialize,' he added. 'Once we've landed, we can take a look around, find out where we are.' He sounded as if he was trying to convince himself as much as her.

'I think that's the door control,' she said quietly.

He hesitated, his indecisive frown quickly replaced by one of exasperation. 'Look, if you've got any better ideas, let me know. Otherwise, trust me for once.'

'Why can't we just wait?' she said, already knowing the answer. Because Steven was incapable of waiting for anything, that was why. Because he'd spent so long

7

impotently pacing around his prison cell on Mechanus before the Doctor had rescued him that his patience had been used up. Not that he would ever admit it, of course. Not even to himself. It was odd, Vicki thought as she gazed at Steven's older yet somehow more innocent face, that her time spent stranded had been perhaps the most idyllic of her life. She'd only had Bennett and Sandy the Sand Monster for company on Dido, but she'd been content. Now, although she was learning so much by travelling with the Doctor, that contentment had been lost. Every moment of her life, every person that she met, demanded something of her.

'We can't just wait,' Steven explained, breaking her chain of introspection, 'because the Doctor might be in trouble. The way he just . . . just vanished, right in front of us . . .' He hesitated, and rubbed a hand across his face. He was tired. Tired and scared, Vicki realized. He'd been alone for so long that he found the prospect of taking responsibility terrifying. 'It was like the Doc had been kidnapped.'

'But we haven't explored the TARDIS completely yet,' she said, trying to inject a note of calmness into her voice. Getting angry with Steven didn't work – he just grew more stubborn and defensive. 'The Doctor could still be here.'

'Where?' Steven challenged, hand still on the switch. The door control switch, Vicki reminded herself. She didn't know what would happen if he pulled it while the TARDIS was in flight, but she suspected the results wouldn't be pleasant. 'We've checked the bedrooms, the food machine alcove, the lounge –'

'What about the locked doors?' she interrupted. 'The Doctor won't tell us what's behind them. There might be more rooms, rooms that the Doctor didn't want us to see.'

Steven slammed his fist against the console. 'Look, we have to do something! And I still think that if we can just materialize somewhere, we can find a trail, or a clue, or . . .'

'And what are you young people doing to my TARDIS?' a peremptory voice demanded from the other side of the console. Steven and Vicki whirled around and gaped at the blurred, fractured bubble of darkness that had appeared — apparently inside the wall — and at the elderly figure within it.

'Doctor!' they cried together.

He appeared to be sitting in a triangular framework, and he was frowning at them. Standing, not without some effort, he walked forward. Behind him, both the frame and the dark bubble were pulled apart into a coruscating web of lines which retreated into the far distance until they were lost from sight, leaving only the solid walls of the TARDIS behind the old man's figure.

'Doctor, we were —' Vicki began.

'Where have you been?' Steven demanded.

The Doctor fixed the space pilot with an imperious gaze. 'Never mind where I've been,' he snapped, 'you were about to meddle with the ship's controls, weren't you?'

'No!' Steven protested. 'I . . . I was just trying to —'

'Steven was trying to help,' Vicki said calmingly. 'You vanished without telling us where you were going. We were worried about you: we thought . . . Oh, I don't know what we thought. What happened?'

The Doctor's stern expression softened, as she had known it would. The one thing he couldn't resist was wide-eyed concern. 'My dear child,' he said, 'of course you were worried, and I have no right to scold you, hmm? If you must know, I've been . . .' He frowned. 'Well, that's most extraordinary. I can't remember *where* I've been. The memory has gone. All I can remember is a dandy and a clown. A dandy and a clown.' Ignoring the puzzled looks that Vicki and Steven exchanged, he raised a hand to caress his lapel, and appeared surprised to find that he was holding a small white envelope. 'Hmm. Perhaps this will tell us something.'

As Vicki and Steven watched, he opened the envelope

9

and took out a slip of cardboard. He peered at it for a few moments, then took his pince-nez out of his waistcoat pocket and slipped them on. 'Most extraordinary,' he repeated, and proffered the card to Steven, who took it warily. Vicki had to pull his arm down to see.

The card was small and white. On it, in very small letters, were the words:

INVITATION
Formal dress required.

R.S.V.P.

'An invitation to what?' Steven asked.

'An invitation to a mystery,' the Doctor replied, frowning and looking away.

Vicki took the card from Steven. 'Who gave it to you?' she asked the Doctor.

'I don't . . . I don't remember,' the old man admitted.

'It's a trap,' Steven said firmly. Vicki watched with some amusement as he narrowed his eyes, squared his shoulders and generally tried to look heroic.

'Don't be stupid, Steven,' she said, and placed the card carefully upon the top of the translucent cylinder in the centre of the control console. 'How can it be a trap if it doesn't even tell us where to go?'

With a low hum, the collection of fragile objects in the centre of the translucent column, the things that had always reminded Vicki of a cross between a child's mobile and a butterfly collection, began to revolve around their central axis. The column itself began to rise and fall rhythmically, whilst lights flashed on the console and the deep vibration of the TARDIS in flight slowly spiralled down towards the grinding, clashing noise of landing.

'Well,' the Doctor said, 'it would appear that *someone* knows where we are going.'

* * *

There was a rat on the stairs again.

Carlo Zeno came face to face with it as he rounded the corner. He was standing on the tiny landing that lay between his own rooms on the second floor and his tenant's rooms on the third. The rat was seven steps higher than he was, on a level with his face. Bright afternoon sunlight streamed through the holes in the rotted window shutters, illuminating it: fat and fearless, its black hair matted and its tail coiled like a pink worm. Zeno could even see the avaricious, calculating gleam in its eye.

'Back to the Devil, you garbage-eating fiend,' he snarled, and started up the stairs towards it, stamping his boots on the wood. The rat watched for a moment, then calmly turned and scuttled towards a hole in the plaster-covered laths of the wall. As Zeno advanced past the stair, he thought he saw its whiskers twitching in the darkness. God and the Doge alone knew how many rats infested his house. Hundreds perhaps. The scrabbling of their claws kept him awake at night as they ran across the floor, scuttled behind the walls and scrabbled between the joists of the ceiling. Rats were the bane of Venice. Rats and Turks.

The door to the top floor of the house was closed, and Carlo pounded on it. 'I've come for the rent!' he shouted, but there was no sound from within. Perhaps his tenant had gone out for a walk, or to buy some food, although Carlo hadn't heard him on the stairs. Perhaps he was asleep. Grimani the barkeeper said that the man drank until he could hardly stand up some nights, and the widow Carpaccio across the alley said she often saw his lamp shining until sunrise. Carlo hadn't asked what the widow Carpaccio was doing awake at that time: it was well known in the district of San Polo that she entertained gentlemen in order to pay her bills. Carlo, on the other hand, was forced to depend on those temporary visitors to Venice who wanted more freedom than that offered by a hotel.

11

'The rent!' he shouted again, slamming the heel of his hand against the wood. 'Do you hear, you lazy slugabed?'

The door was suddenly pulled open. The room was dark, and smelled of sour wine, old fruit and unwashed bedding. The scant light from the window down on the landing barely illuminated the sullen figure of Carlo's tenant. His shirt was undone, and his breeches were creased as if he had been sleeping in them.

'You fat oaf,' he said in his haughty Florentine accent. 'Unless you've come to tell me that the Doge has finally granted me an audience, or that the lagoon is flooding, I'll have your tongue for a garter.'

Carlo stared blankly at his tenant's plump, bearded face for a few moments. He could barely stop himself from picking the man up and throwing him bodily down the stairs. What incredible arrogance! He'd been occupying Carlo's top floor and the roof platform for two weeks now, and Carlo had yet to receive a pleasant word from him. Or any money.

'You think you frighten me with your talk of the Doge?' Carlo snapped. 'If you think I'm going to waive the rent you owe me just to curry favour then your brain is addled and your wits have run away.'

'You'll get your money when I've got mine,' the man said, running a hand through his tousled hair. 'The Doge will reward me well for what I can give him.'

'If I could spend your promises then I'd be eating peacock tonight. If I don't get the money owing to me by sundown, I'll throw you and your belongings into the canal!'

Carlo turned to go, but a hand descended on his shoulder, stopping him. He turned, ready for an attack, but his tenant had twisted his mouth into what he probably hoped was an ingratiating smile. The expression didn't look at home on his face: the fleshy lips beneath that beard were more suited to a sneer.

'I . . . please, I apologize for my manner,' the man said.

'I find myself embarrassed by a temporary shortage of funds, not a position that a gentleman of noble birth and breeding, such as myself, is used to —'

'Not too embarrassed to drink your weight in wine every night,' Carlo grumbled, slightly mollified by the man's tone. 'Or do you pay Grimani in stories too?'

'— but, as I was about to say, I have just enough left to pay you what I owe.' He turned away and disappeared into the gloom of his rooms. He was muttering something beneath his breath: elaborate Florentine curses, no doubt. Carlo heard him rummage among his possessions for a moment, then he was back, appearing suddenly in the slice of light from the landing like a demon on stage. 'Here,' he said, handing over a small leather bag with obvious reluctance. 'It should —' he winced slightly '— suffice, until the Doge pays me for my services.'

Carlo weighed the bag in his hand. The coins chinked comfortingly, and he ran through all the things he could do with the money. He'd go and pay his own bill at Grimani's tavern, then perhaps the widow Carpaccio might be willing to accept a few coins in exchange for an hour or two of pleasure.

'That'll do,' he said gruffly. 'For now. But mind you pay me promptly next week, otherwise I'll have the police call round.' He spat to one side, making sure that his tenant knew he didn't believe these stories about audiences with the ruling authority of Venice, then turned and clattered down the stairs. Turning at the landing, he saw the man's eyes gleaming in the dark gap between door and jamb. The thought put him in mind of the rat he had seen earlier. Shivering, he crossed himself and continued round the corner and down, past his own rooms, to the door.

As he walked out into the narrow alley that separated his house from the widow Carpaccio's, he glanced upwards. The lip of the roof platform jutted over the edge of the roof towards a similar platform on the widow's house. He could still remember the way she used

13

to sit up there for hours bleaching her hair in the bright sunlight. That was when she had been young and beautiful, and Carlo had been younger and full of life. He used to watch her from his bedroom window, waiting for the wind off the Adriatic to skim the roofs of the houses and lift her skirts a few inches. Ah, the follies of youth.

He squinted for a moment. Was there something on the platform? Something long and tubular, shrouded in a velvet cloth?

He shook his head. He had coins and Grimani had a new consignment of Bardolino wine from the mainland. By the end of the evening, he hoped that their respective positions would be a little more equitable.

Steven Taylor stood in the TARDIS doorway and looked around. They had landed on a beach of mixed sand and pebbles that fell steeply to a blue sea. A few hundred yards away, a mist hovered over the waves, hiding the horizon and turning the low sun into a dull circle. The mist thinned overhead to reveal a purple sky. Steven couldn't tell whether it was naturally that colour or whether it was a temporary meteorological condition.

He took a cautious sniff of air. It smelt . . . well, it smelt like nothing else he had ever smelt. That was one of the problems about being a space pilot. He'd gone from living in a cramped apartment in the middle of an Earth Hiveblock to living in a cockpit in the middle of deep space, with only the occasional night in a space station to relieve the monotony. Even his time imprisoned on Mechanus had been spent in a small, sterile metal room. The first new thing he had smelt since childhood had been the burning forests during the Dalek attack, and since then he had been plunged from new world to new world, each one of which didn't smell like anything he had ever smelt before. Things always looked like other things he'd seen, things even sounded like things he'd heard, but smells were unique. Individual. Incomparable.

'What can you see?' Vicki asked from behind him. 'Oh, get out of the way Steven.'

He stepped out of the TARDIS, feeling the sand crunch beneath his boots. It was hot and humid, and he could feel sweat prickle beneath his tunic and across his scalp.

Vicki pushed past him and walked a couple of steps towards the water. 'I love oceans,' she said cheerfully. 'There weren't any on Dido – not within walking distance, anyway, and I used to dream about them.'

'Don't touch that liquid, my dear,' the Doctor fussed as he left the TARDIS and carefully locked the door behind him. 'It might be acid, or . . . or all manner of things.' He slipped the key into his waistcoat pocket, and cast a quick glance at Steven. That key had been the source of several arguments between them. Steven felt that he should have his own key, just in case anything ever happened to the Doctor. The Doctor dismissed the idea, claiming that Steven was just scaremongering. The truth was, of course, that he didn't trust Steven an inch.

The one thing they were both agreed on was that Vicki shouldn't have one.

'What a wonderful place,' the Doctor said, gazing around. He sniffed the air in the same way that Steven had seen him sniff fine wines. 'Salt marshes, I think you'll find. Ah, yes, and wood smoke. There must be a settlement of some sort nearby.' He walked a few steps down the beach and bent down to pick up a dried out strand of seaweed. 'No sign of tides,' he said, examining it carefully. He moved towards the water's edge. Taking a small strip of paper from a pocket, he bent forward and dipped it in the water. 'And the neutral pH indicates that this liquid is safe. You may go paddling if you wish.' He turned to find Vicki already standing ankle-deep in the water. She smiled apologetically. He frowned and wagged a finger at her. 'Foolish child,' he chided. 'You might have got yourself into all sorts of trouble, and then where would you be, hmm?'

'Sorry, Doctor.' Vicki looked genuinely crestfallen.

The Doctor turned to Steven. 'Salt water but no tides. What does that suggest to you, my boy?'

'No moon?'

The Doctor nodded judiciously. 'Yes, or . . . ?'

Steven shrugged. 'Or a lagoon. Is it important?'

'Most instructive, hmm? A lagoon. Yes.' A breeze ruffled the Doctor's long, white hair. Steven stared at him, wondering what the old man was getting at. Sometimes, just sometimes, it occurred to him that the Doctor possessed a laser-sharp intelligence that he chose to hide in vague mutterings and abrupt changes in mood and conversation, but most of the time he just thought that the Doctor was a senile old fool.

'Doctor! Steven!' Vicki's voice cut through his thoughts. He turned, crouching, ready to protect her from whatever threat had sprung from hiding, fight any monster that was lurking in the vicinity, but the beach was empty apart from the three of them and the TARDIS. Vicki was pointing out to sea, into the mist. Or, rather, into where the mist had been. The breeze had thinned it out and shredded it, revealing sketchy details of the waterscape beyond. Near at hand there were islands, some barely more than sandbanks with sparse vegetation, some rocky and covered with bushes. Beyond them, scarcely more than a darker grey shadow against the grey mist, there was a city: a fabulous city of towers and minarets, steeples and domes, all seeming to float upon the water like a mirage.

'Ah,' the Doctor said, 'just as I thought – we've arrived at Venice.'

'Venice?' Steven and Vicki chorused together.

'A city built on sandbanks and wooden pilings, just off the Italian coast. It sank beneath the waves centuries before either of you were born. Well, I rather think I know where we're meant to go, hmm? Vicki, my dear, why don't you go back inside the TARDIS and retrieve the dinghy from the store cupboard by the food machine?'

16

Vicki nodded and, taking the key which the Doctor proffered, vanished inside the time and space machine. As soon as she was out of earshot, Steven turned to the Doctor. 'I don't like this. It smells like a trap to me.'

'And to me, dear boy.' The Doctor nodded. 'A trap, indeed. I am in complete agreement.'

'And you're just going to walk into it?' Steven said, aghast.

'Whoever gave me that invitation had me in their power, and let me go,' the Doctor mused. 'If this *is* a trap, and it has all of the classic signs, then perhaps we aren't the intended victims.'

'No?' Steven frowned. 'But if we're not the victims, then what are we?'

The Doctor's bright blue eyes twinkled. 'Perhaps we're the bait!'

Galileo Galilei, ex-tutor to Prince Cosimo of Tuscany, Professor of Mathematics at the University of Padua, equal of scholars and natural philosophers and heir to the mantle of Bruno and Brahe, burped and took another swig of wine from the bottle.

Light trickled between the curtains, casting a bruised purple illumination across the strewn clothes, piles of manuscripts and half-eaten plates of food that filled the space in the room. Nearly sunset, then. Nearly time to start work.

That damned landlord had irritated him to the point where he had almost struck the man down. Venice should be paying *him* to be there, not the other way around. Things would change soon. Oh yes, things would change. All he needed was five minutes with the Doge on top of the bell tower in St Mark's Square, and his fortune would be made. All of Italy – no, all of Europe – would defer to him. The name of Galileo Galilei would resound through the ages.

He staggered across the rotting, creaking floorboards towards the tiny stairway that led upwards, towards the

17

platform on the roof. This place was a deathtrap, what with the galloping rot and the rats both competing to see who could gnaw their way through the timbers fastest. One good sneeze could bring the place down around his ears.

Things had been different on his previous visits. He was used to whoring and drinking with Gianfrancesco Sagredo in his palace on the Grand Canal, or debating natural philosophy with Friar Paulo Sarpi in the Doge's Palace. Sagredo was in Syria now, drawing a diplomat's salary and, no doubt, raking commissions off crooked merchants and rapacious pirates. Sarpi, by contrast, was still recovering from the fifteen stab wounds he had suffered during the attempt on his life by agents of the Pope. Galileo had seen the wounds, and was amazed at his old friend's survival. One of the stilettos had entered Sarpi's right ear, passed through his temple, shattered his jaw and exited through his right cheek. Sarpi had claimed that God was smiling on him that day. Galileo couldn't help thinking that if that was God smiling, what must his wrath be like?

He hauled himself up the ladder and on to the platform. The air was cold, and the platform gave slightly beneath his bulk. Just his luck if a strut snapped, sending the greatest philosophical mind in Christendom tumbling into the alley below. Thus did God check the excess pride of man.

He walked to the edge of the platform, past the velvet-shrouded object in the centre and the chair beside it, and gazed out across the city. The sky was the deep purple of grapes, and tinged with fire along one edge where the sun had descended beneath the line of houses. Soon it would be night. The moon had already risen like a plate of burnished pewter sent spinning across the sky. *His* moon. The object given to him by God for his own personal glory. The flambeaux that burned across the city, illuminating the distant campanile tower with fitful light, mirrored the searing ambition in his heart.

18

He reached out and tugged the velvet cloth off the shrouded object, throwing it carelessly across the chair. The spyglass beneath — brass half-covered with scarlet cloth — shone in the last few glimmerings of sunlight. About the length of his arm, it sat on a tripod inscribed with calibrations, symbols and Latin inscriptions. He had constructed it in his own workshop in Padua, based on what his friends and his spies had heard of Hans Lippershey's work in Germany, but he wouldn't be telling the Doge that. No, as far as the Venetian nobles were concerned, he had invented the whole thing himself. What to look at? He could turn it North, towards the Italian coast, and onwards towards Padua and beautiful Marina. Or he could turn it South, gazing out into the Adriatic Sea and the incoming fishing boats.

He smiled to himself. Marina would be asleep and the fishing boats would wait. No, there was only one choice. He swivelled the spyglass upwards and aligned it roughly towards the silvery disc of the moon. By eye he could make out the mysterious shapes that lay across its surface like veils, but with the spyglass he could make out rough circles and lines that changed their appearance as the sun moved in relation to them and its rays struck them at different angles. Nobody else had seen what he was seeing! The knowledge almost made him drunk with delight.

He removed the leather cap from the glass lens and sat down in the chair. Leaning forward, he gazed through the glass. Perhaps tonight God would inspire him to discover what these shapes were, and why they changed.

The moon's surface was startlingly white — bone white — with fuzzy grey shapes marring its perfection. Galileo forgot the cold, and forgot the uncomfortable position that he had to adopt, as his eye scanned the surface, looking for —

He jerked back suddenly, almost upsetting his chair. That couldn't be right. Surely not. He bent down and gazed through the lens again, then blinked a couple of times. Perhaps what he had seen was a mote in his eye, or a bird passing across his field of view. He looked again. It was still there: an object, too small to recognize but too large to ignore. Its shape was circular, like a discus, and it spun rapidly while moving in a straight line. It was moving at an angle, but there was no doubt that it was heading away from the surface of the moon and towards him.

Two

'Would you like me to row for a while?' Vicki asked. 'Or are you just resting for a moment?' Steven tried to detect some note of sarcasm in her voice, but she was too good for that. He tried to mutter a sarcastic rejoinder, but he was panting too hard to get the words out.

'Yes, put your back into it, my boy,' the Doctor said. 'I want to make landfall before breakfast, you know.'

Steven had been rowing the inflatable dinghy for what seemed like hours, and he was tired. No, he was worse than tired: he was exhausted. Bone-wearingly, mind-achingly exhausted. His arms had progressed from fatigue through burning pain to a distant numbness, and his mind had become fixated on details like the texture of the material that the dinghy was made out of, and the way the Doctor's ring glowed in the darkness.

The sun had set some time ago, and the moon hung overhead like a tossed coin frozen at its apogee. The distant lights of Venice glimmering on the water had seemed to Steven to be receding just as fast as he rowed, but now, as he looked over his shoulder he saw a long stone embankment with low wooden piers projecting from it into the water. Flaming torches on poles lit up a large square, thronged with people. He was too tired to care.

'What is this place, Doctor?' Vicki asked.

'A strange little republic,' the Doctor replied, 'that lasted for several thousand years with little more than superficial change. The city was originally founded by refugees from the Roman mainland who were fleeing the various and frequent invasions by Goths, Huns, Avars, Herulians and Lombards —'

'I didn't know that there were any attempted alien invasions this early in Earth's history,' Vicki said, frowning.

'They weren't aliens, child,' the Doctor said reprovingly, 'they were tribes. Dear, dear: your knowledge of your own history is sadly lacking! They were savage, rapacious tribes. The refugees fled their depredations and settled here in the lagoon, on the many islands and sandbanks. They built houses on wooden piles driven deep into the mud of the lagoon. Gradually they linked those houses by paths and by bridges. That was over a thousand years ago. Now they have a city built on wood and mud. Just wood and mud. Imagine that!' he cackled.

Steven found that he could. Only too well, in fact. He had just spent a chunk of his life imprisoned in one city on stilts, and the last thing he wanted to do was visit another. He still had nightmares about the Mechanoid city crashing in flames to the jungle floor, the sound of its supporting struts snapping echoing like cannon fire through the night air. And what had the Doctor said earlier on about Venice sinking some time in the future? Just how far in the future? he wondered.

He glanced again over his shoulder, half-expecting to see the entire city slide beneath the waters of the lagoon, then he shrugged. If it happened, it happened. There was nothing he could do about it. Turning his back on the city, he continued rowing.

The Doctor was still telling Vicki about the history of Venice, and how the city had made itself into the most important trading centre in Europe, but Steven found his attention slipping. The island behind them had long since vanished into the mist and the darkness, and the moon glittered on their wake like a thousand watching eyes. The noise of shouting and laughter from Venice itself, somewhere just over Steven's shoulder, blended into a

22

hypnotic murmur, and Steven realized that for several minutes his eyes had been fixed on a log, drifting along behind the dinghy. It was just a darker spot against the waves, but it was the only point of interest in the ever-changing, ever-similar backdrop of the waves. In his half-hypnotized state, he could almost imagine that it was the head of something swimming behind them, following them from island to island.

And then it vanished abruptly beneath the waves, almost as if it had realized Steven had seen it.

The hubbub in the Tavern of St Theodore and of the Crocodile almost deafened Galileo as he carried his flagon of Bardolino wine away from the bar and towards an unoccupied bench. The place was large and sprawled over several rooms connected by low doorways. It was popular with the local gondoliers, and he had to detour around large groups of them as they argued raucously, scuffled affably, fell over drunkenly and generally comported themselves in the ebullient Venetian manner that he had come to know well.

Venice, city of opposites: mystery and misery; excess and penury; hard marble and soft water. No matter how often he visited, he was never sure whether he loved it or hated it.

Galileo took a long swig from the flagon, and almost choked. The wine was sour and left a bitter aftertaste in his mouth; he kept forgetting how bad the wine was here compared to home. It was evidence of God's wit that when he was in Padua he wished he was in Venice, and when he was in Venice he wished he was in Padua. When he was in Rome, of course, he couldn't decide *where* he wanted to be, so long, of course, as he didn't have to be in Rome.

His thoughts turned to Marina. Fiery, lusty Marina. Although they had been together for ten years, and she had borne his children, they had never married. Even the notoriously easygoing Venetian authorities would have

23

drawn the line at the Professor of Mathematics at Padua University marrying a common strumpet, and his mother would have died of shame! He hadn't been faithful to Marina – she had never expected him to be – but he loved her none the less. Most of the time. Wine could slake one kind of thirst, women another, but Marina satisfied some spiritual yearning in him to which he couldn't put a name. They argued – did they argue! – but he always returned to her. Eventually.

He spat on the tavern's sawdust-covered floor and wiped his sleeve across his mouth. Enough of this puerile thinking. He had a problem to solve. That bizarre apparition that he had seen through his spyglass still occupied his thoughts, crowding out all rational argument with its incontrovertible presence. He could formulate no theory to account for it. It had a man-made look, and it had moved in an unnaturally direct manner, like a cart on a road, but he had never before seen or heard about phenomena that travelled between the Moon and the Earth. And it *had* made that journey: he had observed its progress, swivelling his spyglass to track it as it moved and grew larger in his sight, until he lost it somewhere over the rooftops of Venice. It seemed to him that it had come to rest somewhere in the Adriatic, just off the Lido. Was it a delusion of celestial vapours, like the one Johannes Kepler had written to warn him of five years before, or was it some messenger of God – an Angel sent to walk the Earth?

He took another mouthful of wine and swallowed it before the taste could make him retch. Natural science was full of such puzzles, and God had set him the task of unravelling them. It was his curse and misfortune to be the greatest genius in Europe, if not the world.

As he was about to set his flagon down, a passing figure jogged his elbow. The base of the flagon hit the edge of the bench, spilling most of its contents in a crimson tide over the sawdust-strewn boards. To tell the truth, he wasn't sorry to see it go, but the figure looming over him

24

said, in English-accented Italian, 'My pardon, good sir. Please allow a clumsy foreigner to refill your flagon.'

Before Galileo could argue, the man had gone. He watched the man shoulder his way through the crowd. Fine clothes, if old – a lace-collared shirt beneath a scuffed leather jerkin. An English noble, down on his luck perhaps? There were a thousand stories in the city. Nobody came to Venice without the baggage of their past.

As his thoughts drifted, he became aware that there were a lot of foreign voices in the Tavern of St Theodore and of the Crocodile that night. Most of them seemed to be speaking English. Venice attracted visitors from East and West, of course, but, as he thought about it, it seemed to him that there had been more Englishmen than usual since his arrival. Perhaps it had something to do with the accession of the Scottish King, James, to the English throne.

The crowd parted again as the Englishman returned, and Galileo was struck both by the width of his shoulders and the way he moved, cat-like and sure-footed, through the thronging mass. They seemed to part for him, as a shoal of fish would part for a shark, then seal up again behind him. 'Your drink, kind sir,' the man said, placing a fresh flagon before Galileo. 'And my renewed apologies.'

Galileo stared up into his weather-beaten face and his grey eyes, the same shade as his profusion of prematurely grey hair, and felt a chill of unease. A scar ran from the man's forehead across one eye and down his cheek, like a fissure in baked earth.

'My thanks,' he said gruffly, but the man had gone, pushing past a group of young noblemen who were clad in silks and satins. The noblemen, disturbed and angered at his careless effrontery, gazed after him, then turned their attention to Galileo.

Galileo was about to take a swig of wine, hoping that it was of better quality than the last lot, when a voice said, 'By my lights, it is the Florentine Galileo Galilei, is it not?

25

The man who denies God pre-eminence in the heavens.'

He sighed. 'I am Galileo,' he confirmed, glancing up. 'What of it?'

The group of noble ruffians had moved to stand before him. One of them, a youth with long black hair and a sparse beard, was smiling cruelly. 'Do you not repeat at Padua,' he sneered, 'the heresy taught by Giordano Bruno that our world revolves around the sun?'

'It is no heresy, but simple fact,' Galileo growled. The youths were obviously spoiling for a fight, but he couldn't help himself. He had to respond. 'God has arranged his heavens such that the sun provides light and warmth to all its children and, like a hearth fire, it is the centre around which everything is arranged.'

'But that is plainly foolish,' the young man replied, gazing around at his companions, who nodded their heads in agreement, 'as everyone knows that all celestial bodies circle *us*. No other star is pre-eminent.'

'Foolishness,' Galileo snapped, 'lies in denying the evidence of one's senses. If you saw a tortoise would you call it a rabbit? If you saw a ship, would you call it a cart? Why then should I see what I plainly see and call it something else?'

Some part of him noticed that the smiles on the faces of the youths had soured somewhat, and that their hands were hovering around the hilts of their swords, but he felt a wave of black anger pass across his thoughts, clouding him to all but the fact that he had been publicly doubted. 'And are you an astronomer then,' he continued, 'that you can question my observations? If so you disguise your experience well under the mantle of a callow youth. Or better yet, are you a bishop that you can talk to me of heresy? Where are your robes and your cross?'

'Do you know who I am?' the youth snapped, his face suffused with blood.

'But that you are arrogant beyond good sense, I neither know nor care who you are,' Galileo rejoined.

'I am Baldassarre Nicolotti!'

26

He said the name as if he expected Galileo to recognize it, and unfortunately Galileo did. He gritted his teeth. The Nicolottis were one of the more illustrious and widespread families in Venice. Their name appeared in the Golden Book – the list of Venetian aristocracy who were eligible for election to the various councils that ran the Serene Republic. He seemed to remember that they were involved in a long-running feud with the Castellani family. If the Doge got to hear that he was brawling in a tavern with one of them, Galileo's chances of gaining an audience would be about the same as his ever becoming Pope. He couldn't back down, though. Not once his professional expertise had been questioned. 'Strange,' he growled, 'you look more to me like the arse of a horse, and your words match its excrement for consistency and usefulness.' It wasn't elegant, but then again neither was cannon fire against a fortification, and that worked well enough.

'I'll have your liver on a plate!' Baldassarre hissed through clenched teeth. He pulled his sword from its scabbard. His friends cleared a space for the fight, pushing back the other patrons and knocking benches away to form a rough circle. The noise in the tavern dimmed slightly, then rose again to its previous level. Fights were nothing if not frequent in Venice.

Galileo stood slowly, tankard clenched in his hand. He'd been in situations like this too often not to know what the best course of action was. 'Did your mother never wean you from her milk?' he said. 'You don't appear to be able to handle your drink like a man.'

The tip of Baldassarre's sword waved back and forth in front of Galileo's nose. 'I can handle any drink you throw at me,' he sneered.

'Then let's put that to the test.' Galileo suddenly threw the contents of his tankard at Baldassarre. The crimson liquid caught the youth full in the face. Spluttering, he tried to wipe his eyes with his sleeve, almost skewering one of his companions with his sword as he did so. The rest of the youths rushed forward to help.

Galileo took advantage of the distraction to take a couple of steps backwards, out of the nominal circle of the fight. Time to make his excuses and leave. He turned towards the door, but a choking noise from behind stopped him.

Baldassarre's body was twitching like a man in the grip of St Vitus's Dance. Foam frothed from his lips and splattered the floor around his contused head. His eyes were starting from their sockets. One hand rose up, clenched as if to grasp something that only he could see, and then he slumped back lifelessly to the floor. It was all over in a handful of seconds.

Instinct took over, and Galileo was out of the door and halfway down the alley before anybody thought to turn around and look for him.

'Keep going. Only a few moments more,' the Doctor encouraged. 'Perhaps those people on the embankment are waiting to meet us.' As Steven turned to glance at the approaching fire-lit scene he noticed the way the flames emphasized the cruel smile on the Doctor's face.

There was a sudden jar as the dinghy hit wood, and the Doctor and Vicki were scrambling past him and onto the nearest jetty.

'Don't mention it,' he muttered as he levered himself up on paralysed arms. 'Glad I could help.'

Stone steps led up the side of the embankment to the promenade on top. Even Steven, tired as he was, felt something stir in his chest at the scene that greeted him. The travellers were standing between two stone pillars. Before them, the light from the flaming torches illuminated a square that was halfway between a market and a carnival. Women in long dresses and men in elaborately brocaded costumes paraded between stalls that sold food, clothes, animals, statues and all manner of other objects. The smells of wood smoke, cooked meat, over-ripe fruit and rotting vegetables made Steven's stomach rumble. The people and the stalls were set against a

28

backdrop of elaborately arched and colonnaded stone buildings, each a masterpiece of architecture jostling with its neighbours for attention. To their left was a small building attached to a tall tower of red brick. Shouts and laughter echoed back and forth between the buildings, the individual words blending together to form a *mélange* of sound.

'St Mark's Square,' the Doctor proclaimed. 'Birthplace of my old friend Marco Polo, and the gateway for trade and travel between Europe and the mysterious Orient.'

Vicki nudged Steven's arm. 'Somebody's seen us,' she whispered, pointing towards a knot of men who were approaching them.

'Don't worry,' the Doctor said, 'I'm sure they mean us no harm.' He stepped forward as the men approached. 'I am the Doctor,' he proclaimed. 'Perhaps you are expecting me.'

One of the men stepped forward. He was small but broad-shouldered, and he was bald. His face held a cynical expression. 'By the power invested in me by the Doge of Venice and by the Council of Ten,' he growled, 'I arrest you as Turkish spies.'

'Wait!' the Doctor cried imperiously. He raised one hand in admonition. Behind his back he was making urgent gestures to his companions. 'Is this how you treat visitors to this great city? Well, is it? I mean, what's the world coming to when travellers cannot come and go freely, as and when they wish?'

What did those gesticulations mean? Steven wondered. Run? Hide? Attack the guards? Perhaps the Doctor's earlier companions, Ian and Barbara, would have understood instantly, but Steven hadn't known the Doctor for long enough to be able to interpret him.

The bald guard frowned. 'Step forward,' he said, 'into the light.'

The Doctor did as he was instructed, and the frown on the guard's face was replaced by an expression of confusion, and embarrassment.

'Cardinal Bellarmine!' he cried, kneeling on the stone esplanade. 'We didn't . . . I mean, we weren't . . .'

The Doctor's face froze for a moment. 'Expecting us?' he said finally, smiling. 'No, that is perfectly apparent, isn't it? Well, the journey from . . . the journey went quicker than we had expected. And this is how you greet us!'

'Who's Cardinal Bellarmine?' Vicki hissed from beside Steven.

'I've got no idea,' he whispered. 'And I don't think the Doctor has either. I just hope he knows what he's doing.'

'And do you know why I'm here?' the Doctor continued, waving the guard to his feet. 'What is your name, by the way?'

'Speroni, your eminence. Sperone Speroni. I am the Lord of the Nightwatch for St Mark's Square and the local area.'

'Of course you are, of course you are.' The Doctor turned and waved Steven and Vicki closer. At least, Steven reflected, that gesture was unambiguous. 'And these are my travelling companions, Steven Taylor and Vicki . . . ah, yes . . . Vicki. Now, you were about to tell me what you were told about my mission.'

'Indeed.' Speroni looked dazed, like a man who had been suddenly overtaken by events and couldn't catch up. 'I was informed that you would be arriving as representative of the Vatican to question Galileo Galilei on the invention he claims to have made, but I wasn't . . . I mean, I assumed — we all did — that you would be travelling in your robes and accompanied by a full retinue of guards —'

The Doctor gazed questioningly at him. 'Galileo's invention?'

'The spyglass,' Speroni prompted, frowning. 'The device with which distant objects might be made closer.'

'Vatican? Galileo? Spyglass?' A smile crossed his face, and he turned briefly to Steven and Vicki. 'Ah, then this must be the year of our Lord, 1609,' he said for their benefit, nodding as if he had known this all the time. He turned back to Speroni. 'Perhaps you could escort us to our rooms. I presume that they are ready?'

Speroni caught the eye of one of his men, and jerked his head. The man ran off, his boots clattering on the stone. 'They are,' he confirmed, flushing slightly. 'Perhaps we could aid you with your baggage, your eminence?'

'My . . . Oh. Ah, yes. We don't have any baggage. Lost at sea, dear chap, along with my robes and the rest of my retinue. Lost at sea.' He smiled paternally at Speroni, who was scratching his head in puzzlement at these strangers and their antics.

'Aren't we all,' Steven muttered.

Carlo Zeno tottered out of the Tavern of St Theodore and of the Crocodile and into the narrow alleyway. Turning left, he staggered towards his house. What an evening! Young Baldassarre, struck down in front of his eyes. Poison, they were saying. Judging by the way his eyeballs had protruded and the colour of his tongue, Zeno wasn't about to contradict them.

The alley was bisected after a few feet by a narrow canal. A stone bridge arced across to the other side, where the alley carried on. Zeno staggered up the steps to the top of the bridge, trying not to lose his balance and fall into the silted, foul-smelling liquid that flowed sluggishly beneath. Too often before he had arrived back at his lodgings soaking wet and covered in excrement. He couldn't afford to ruin any more clothes.

He paused for a moment at the top of the bridge, thinking. They were saying in the tavern that it was Galileo Galilei who had thrown the poisoned wine into Baldassarre's face. Zeno wasn't so sure. He didn't like his lodger, that much was certain, but Galileo's burly form was more suited to a bludgeon than to poison. And he wasn't Venetian, either. Poison came naturally to Venetians. When the Pope's agents had struck down Friar Sarpi and left a dagger sticking out of his cheekbone, the doctors had plunged it into a dog to test what type of poison had been used. So surprised were they when the dog showed no sign of poisoning that they plunged it into a chicken as well. When the chicken didn't die, they knew it couldn't have been a Venetian that carried out the attack. And what about that writer — the one who was fed a poisoned communion wafer by the priest of the church of the Misericordia? Poison was a Venetian weapon, for sure.

A sudden, urgent pressure in his bladder interrupted his thoughts. Damn that Grimani: his wine went through a man's guts faster than a stream down a hill, and probably didn't taste much worse going out than it had done going in. He wasn't sure that he could wait until he got home.

Taking a quick look either way along the canal for moving boats, he quickly tugged at the lacing on his breeches and began to urinate over the edge of the bridge and into the canal beneath. Within seconds a feeling of blessed relief spread through his body.

Something made a wet choking sound beneath the bridge. Zeno cursed to himself. Just his luck if a pair of lovers had parked their gondola beneath the bridge for privacy. 'Your pardon!' he called out. 'I didn't see you there!'

His hands fumbled with the laces of his breeches as he stumbled to the far side of the canal. He thought he could hear noises from the water line. Perhaps whoever had been on the receiving end of his emissions had taken offence, and wished to inflict punishment. Turning, he saw a dark shape rising from the water and onto the side of the canal. 'I beg your pardon, sir,' he said, extending his hands in supplication. 'I didn't mean to give offence.' His drink-befuddled brain wondered why the figure was so silent. And so thin. 'Whatever is within my power to do to make amends, I will —'

The words died in his throat as the figure stepped forward into the pool of moonlight. As slender as a branch, its skin was blue and rough, and its head, no bigger than a knot of wood, tapered into a single horn that erupted from the centre of its forehead and swept up and back to a sharp point. It turned its knob-like head and gazed at Zeno from a tiny red eye.

'What manner of demon *are* you?' gasped Zeno. The demon said nothing. Zeno took a step backwards as its head lowered until the point of its horn was pointed directly at his chest. 'Begone, spawn of the Devil!' he shouted, more in desperation than in hope, but the demon sprang forward. Zeno tried to dive to one side, but he was too slow. The demon's twig-like claws were grasping his shoulders, pushing him back against the brickwork of the nearest house. There was a terrible grinding, tearing sensation in his chest, and he felt the jar as its horn ground against the brick behind him. He was still trying to work out what had happened, where his life had suddenly turned off the path he thought it had been following and into the shadows, when he felt a pressure on his shoulders as the demon's claws pressed him back. The thin horn, slicked red with his blood, pulled free from his flesh, and the pain was sudden and terrible.

He fell to his knees, his life-blood splattering and steaming on the cobbles in front of him. As he looked up imploringly at the demon that stood before him, it shimmered for a moment, as if he was seeing it in a puddle of water, and then he was looking at a man, an ordinary man, of medium height and unremarkable appearance. And he died happy, knowing that his soul had not been taken by a demon, and that he had somehow mistaken an ordinary murderer for a monster.

Three

'Well, I wish that we were always greeted like this,' Steven said, gazing around the room at the ornate carpets, the life-sized frescoes of biblical scenes and the furniture with its carved legs and delicately embroidered upholstery.

Vicki dived onto a silk-cushioned sedan. 'Isn't it wonderful!' she cried. 'I could happily live on this thing forever.'

'It's acceptable, I suppose,' the Doctor sniffed. He crossed to a long wooden cabinet and opened a door at random. 'But I've been to planets where furnishings this basic would be considered an insult.' Reaching inside, he brought out a bottle of wine. 'Then again, I suppose it does have its advantages.'

'I'm not complaining,' Steven said. He walked over to the window. Beyond the leaded glass he could see the wooden jetty that they had landed beside, and the square across which they had been escorted. 'What's this place called again, Doctor?'

'The city is called Venice, my boy, and this building is called the Doge's Palace. We have been mistaken for persons of high rank.' He reached into the cupboard again and retrieved a wine glass.

'So who is this Cardinal Bellarmine, then?'

Behind him, a soft snore could be heard. Steven and the Doctor both turned, to see Vicki curled up on the sedan, fast asleep.

'Poor dear,' the Doctor said. 'It's been a long day for her. She deserves her sleep.' He turned his face back

34

to Steven. 'Now, where was I? Oh yes – Cardinal Roberto Francesco Romolo Bellarmine, general of the Jesuit Order, Consultor of the Holy Office and Master of Controversial Questions at the Vatican. I assume that is who I have been mistaken for. Although many believe him to have been behind Guy Fawkes's attempt to blow up the English Parliament, he will be made a Saint in, oh let me see, some three hundred years time.' The Doctor frowned. 'Hmm, I must admit to a slight worry. Being mistaken for an emissary of the Pope in Venice in 1609 is, perhaps, not the safest thing that could have happened.'

'Why not?' Steven asked.

The Doctor shook his head. 'Religion is never an easy thing to explain. Where do I start. Let me see . . .' He furrowed his brow, thinking, then raised a finger aloft. 'Yes, I do believe that it began three years ago when two priests visiting Venice were charged with various things, including murder, by the Venetian authorities. They were locked up in the dungeons in this very building –'

'Dungeons?' Steven asked, but the Doctor kept talking.

'– and the Doge of Venice threatened to have them put on trial in a secular court, rather than an ecclesiastical one. Tried by the people, not by the Church, if you like.'

'And what happened?' Steven asked, more because he knew the Doctor wanted him to than because he wanted to know the answer.

'What happened? Why, the Vatican couldn't let its ecclesiastical authority go unchallenged, could it?'

'Couldn't it?' Steven couldn't see why not, but he assumed that the Doctor knew what he was talking about.

'Why no, of course not. The Pope had to have the final say on everything. So he excommunicated Venice: lock, stock and barrel.' The Doctor rubbed his hands together. 'Caused quite a furore, I believe. No baptisms or burials could be carried out, no masses could be held, all marriages were dissolved and all children were declared illegitimate.'

'And what happened then?' Steven was becoming interested in the story, despite himself.

'For a few months it looked as if war might break out. Spain allied itself with the Vatican and France allied itself with Venice. England, which had split away from the Catholic Church some seventy years before, made advances to Venice as well. The whole poisonous boil seemed about to erupt, but thanks to a little fancy diplomatic footwork, the two sides came to a face-saving arrangement. Honour was satisfied on both sides, and Venice was brought back into the fold.'

'Oh,' said Steven, disappointed. He'd been hoping for a good scrap.

'But that is why Papal emissaries are not necessarily the most welcome visitors, even now,' the Doctor continued. 'Still, there are worse people to have been mistaken for. Cardinal Bellarmine is no religious fanatic, but a deeply philosophical thinker. He has a formidable mind, sharp as a pin, and he is an astronomer to boot. I'm not surprised that he's interested in Galileo's spyglass. It's right up his street, hmm?'

'And who's this Galileo that you're supposed to have come to see?' Steven said. He was getting a little lost amongst all the names and the history. 'And what's a spyglass?'

'Your education has been woefully neglected, my boy. We're fortunate to have arrived at such a time in your history.' The Doctor frowned for a moment and patted the pocket in which he had placed the mysterious invitation. 'Or perhaps luck had nothing to do with it,' he added.

Irving Braxiatel stood in the centre of the room and gazed around with some pleasure at the books that lined the walls, their spines facing inward as was the custom. The collection was complete. In this room he had every single book that was on the Index of the Catholic Church. They were banned knowledge, books considered too dangerous to read, but such books were, in the end, the most precious. Censorship illuminated perfectly the directions in which any civilization would advance. And knowledge was power, of course.

He smiled to himself. Knowledge was his speciality. He collected it assiduously. It was his most profound desire to have all of the knowledge in the Universe in one place at one time: a huge Library that any member of any intelligent race could consult without let or hindrance. A dream, of course, but an achievable one. His own race collected knowledge, but as an end in itself, and they never shared it, not even if by doing so they could avert catastrophe and save lives.

Braxiatel believed that perfect knowledge led to peace, and so he had left his people and travelled, seeking out obscure facts to add to his vast and comprehensive database. His presence on Earth, in Venice, was on other business, but he hoped to make a small start here by collecting together works of fact and fiction that would otherwise be burned. Perhaps, at some stage in the planet's future, he might return and see what had become of the Braxiatel Collection.

He took off his bifocal spectacles and polished them with a handkerchief. What was it that Friar Sarpi had called the Index earlier that evening, when he brought the last of the books along? 'The first secret device religion ever invented to make men stupid.' Sarpi didn't agree with the existence of the Index, but he was a Friar when all was said and done, and couldn't be seen to disagree with the Pope's edicts. That was why Sarpi obtained the books in secret and passed them to Braxiatel. To preserve them. To keep their knowledge alive.

'Excuse me, sir.'

Braxiatel turned. Cremonini, his manservant, was standing in the doorway. 'Yes, what is it?'

'A visitor, sir.'

'I'm not receiving anybody tonight. Send them away.'

Cremonini coughed discreetly. 'No sir, you have a *visitor*.'

'Ah.' Braxiatel nodded. 'I'll come straight down.'

Sperone Speroni bent close to Baldassarre Nicolotti's contorted face, close enough to have kissed the corpse's cold lips, and sniffed.

'That's poison, right enough,' he said, pulling back from the body and gazing up at the imposing form of Baron Tommaso Nicolotti. 'Your son was murdered.'

Around them, the Tavern of St Theodore and of the Crocodile was empty of patrons. Its buttressed timbers, and the smell of damp wood that underlay the smell of spilled wine, reminded Speroni of the inside of a ship's hull. For a moment he felt a twinge of nostalgia for the Arsenale, and the career he had lost when he was chosen as a Lord of the Nightwatch, but only for a moment. The simplicity of that life was a fading memory now.

'Are you sure?' the Baron snarled, his voice like gravel shifting at the bottom of some deep well. 'Is there no doubt in your mind?'

'None, my lord,' Sperone replied. He stood up and brushed at his trousers. Despite Tommaso's saturnine glower and expensive clothes, Speroni was polite but not deferential. 'The smell is unmistakable. It's a common compound distilled from the leaf of the laurel bush. Death can occur within seconds or hours, depending on the dosage.'

'Common,' Tommaso sneered. 'The word sums up my son's short and unproductive life. He drank with common gondoliers, consorted with common whores and died from a common poison.' He gazed down at his son's face for a moment, then fastidiously turned the body over with the toe of his boot. 'And what of his murderer? Was this attack against my son or against my family? Was the murderer a jealous lover, a distressed moneylender or an assassin in the pay of the Castellanis?'

'Too early to say,' Speroni said, shrugging. 'I could have someone tortured, but what would that give us apart from one more corpse?'

'In the hands of even a passable torturer,' Tommaso agreed, 'the victim will give any answers you want, and none of them are reliable.' He turned his gaze upon Speroni. 'The only function of torture is to provide an example to others. What of this Paduan teacher? I hear that he was present, and argued with my son. He would make a fine example.'

'Galileo Galilei?' Speroni grimaced. 'He's a violent man, but poison isn't his tool.'

'He threw wine into my son's face. The wine may have contained the poison.'

'So could anything your son ate or drank in the past twelve hours.'

The corner of Tommaso's mouth turned up in the closest Speroni had ever seen him get to a smile. 'Never the less, this Galileo would do well to leave Venice immediately, lest he find himself missing certain vital elements of his being. His heart, for instance.'

'My lord,' Speroni said as hard as he dared, 'there is no reason to believe that Galileo is involved in this matter, beyond his proximity to your son when he died.'

'My family honour demands vengeance,' Tommaso said levelly. 'It matters little to me whether we get the right person or not. Everybody is guilty of something.'

'I shall hold you and your family responsible for Galileo's life,' Speroni warned. 'Nicolotti or not, Lord or not, there are laws here in Venice.'

'Laws?' Tommaso's lips twisted as if he had bitten into something sour. 'Laws are for the peasants. The families of the Golden Book make their own laws.'

'Suffice it to say,' the Doctor continued, 'that 1609 is one of the pivotal years for scientific history. Galileo Galilei is

39

about to present the Doge of Venice with the first telescope, and thus open up the stars to mankind's inspection. There is a direct line between this moment in time and the spaceship which you were unfortunate enough to crash on the planet Mechanus.'

Steven was about to make some protest about this cavalier dismissal of his heroic struggle with the controls of a dead spacefighter, but through the window he suddenly caught sight of something hanging from a pillar in the square and lost his train of thought. 'Is this Doge the leader of Venice then?' he said, trying to make out what the object was by the flickering light of the flambeaux.

The Doctor nodded sagely. 'The Doge heads the Council of Three, which heads the Council of Ten, which heads the Great Council.' From a pocket he withdrew a corkscrew, with which he proceeded to open the wine.

'Powerful man, then?' Steven asked. The object hanging from the pillar was swaying slightly in the fresh breeze that was blowing in off the lagoon. People were passing it by without paying it any attention.

'That's a difficult question,' the Doctor observed judiciously. 'Suffice it to say, that at this time in its history, Venice itself is one of the most influential states in the world. Most, if not all, of the trade between Europe and the Orient passes through its ports. Every commodity known to man of this century — silks, spices, precious stones, slaves, marble, ivory, ebony, fabulous animals . . . It is the greatest sea power of the age, unrivalled in firepower, tonnage and efficiency. During the recent wars against the Turks a new galley left its shipyards — the Arsenale — every morning for one hundred days. Imagine that! A new warship every morning!' He poured himself a glass of wine. 'And that, incidentally, is what Speroni and his men were so worried about — that we might be Turkish spies.'

'Why are they worried, if they can build ships that

quickly?' Steven asked. That dangling object was worrying him. The more he looked at it, the more it looked
like a body, hanging by a chain.

'The approach into the lagoon from the Adriatic
is almost impossible to navigate, except by skilled
Venetians,' the Doctor replied, and took a sip of his wine.
'Hmm, most acceptable. Yes, most acceptable. There are
sandbanks under the surface that would rip the keel from
any ship that didn't know the way through the maze. The
Venetians are paranoid about Turkish spies sneaking into
the lagoon in small boats and mapping out the
sandbanks.'

One of the flambeaux flared suddenly as the wind
caught it, casting its light across the pillar and the
puffy, bird-pecked face of the body that hung from it,
suspended by a metal chain around its throat. The flesh of
the neck had swelled so much that the links of the chain
had become buried in it.

'Doctor . . .' Steven whispered, his mouth suddenly
dry, 'there's a dead body out there.'

'I wouldn't be at all surprised,' the Doctor said,
nodding. 'Not at all. Three hundred or so years ago
Marco Polo described Venice to me as being one of the
most repressive states he'd ever known – and he had
travelled a bit – with one important difference.'

Steven swallowed. 'What's that?' he asked.

The Doctor sipped at his wine again, and sighed
happily. 'Most repressive states exist to ensure that the
leader holds on to his power. In Venice, the entire power
of the state is dedicated to ensuring that nobody has any
power at all.'

'Not even this Doge?' Steven asked.

'Especially not the Doge,' the Doctor replied. 'He's
virtually powerless, forbidden to talk to foreigners alone
and unable to write an uncensored letter to his wife,
should he have one. The Venetians are so terrified of a
dictator taking over the state that they go through the
most ridiculous rigmarole to elect a Doge. Nine members

41

of the Great Council select forty people, twelve of whom are then chosen at random to select twenty-five people. Nine of these twenty-five are again chosen at random to select forty-five people. Eleven of these forty-five are then chosen at random to select another forty-one, and these forty-one then elect the Doge. And, as if that wasn't enough, they ensure that the man they elect is in his seventies so that he won't have time to amass too much power.'

Steven turned away from the window, forgetting in his amazement the body hanging from the pillar. 'What a ridiculously complicated system.'

'Complicated it may be,' the Doctor replied seriously, 'but it makes absolutely, perfectly certain that there can be no favouritism, no influence and no vote-rigging.'

Steven's gaze was dragged back to the swaying body. 'So who has the real power, then?'

'It's spread out through the various members of the various Councils. No one person can ever make a decision. It *has* to be agreed by majority.'

'But personalities will always win through over committees,' Steven protested. 'Individuals will always take control. I may not know much about history, but I know *that*.'

'Of course,' the Doctor said, walking over to join Steven by the window. 'Let one man have power, and it goes to his head. Government by an unelected, unaccountable group of shadowy figures is, when you look at it dispassionately, quite an elegant solution.' He gazed out across St Mark's Square, the light from the flambeaux flickering across his angular, lined face. 'A typically Venetian solution. Never let anybody become too popular with the people.'

'And if they do?' Steven asked.

The Doctor turned to gaze at Steven. His eyes were a sharp, penetrating blue. They seemed much younger than the rest of his face. 'There is a Venetian saying,' he murmured, nodding his head towards the body hanging

42

from the pillar. 'The Council of Ten send you to the torture chamber; the Council of Three send you to the grave.'

Steven swallowed. 'I think,' he said, 'that I'm going to go out for a breath of fresh air.'

The salon was the only room in the house save the kitchen that contained no books. It was plain, its walls furnished only with a tapestry showing a golden lion confronting a group of robed merchants. As Braxiatel entered, an ordinary man, of medium height and unremarkable appearance turned from the window that overlooked the canal.

'What news, Szaratak?' Braxiatel asked.

'The Doctor has arrived,' Szaratak replied. 'He landed on an island out in the lagoon with two companions. I followed them to the city. The last thing I saw was them making friends with the local guards.'

'Good, I was beginning to worry that our people hadn't passed the invitation on to him.' Braxiatel smiled slightly. You could always count on the Doctor to arrive in the right place, give or take a few miles, at the right time, give or take a few days. His approximateness was one of his few endearing qualities. 'Have you made contact?'

'Of course I didn't make contact!' Szaratak snarled. 'You said you would rather do it yourself. If you wanted me to make contact then why didn't you say so?'

'Calm down. You did right: there's no sense worrying the poor chap unduly.' Braxiatel turned towards the door, then turned back. 'Oh, and you may as well turn the hologuise projector off. We don't want to waste the batteries.'

The man reached down to his hip and fiddled with something hidden. As Braxiatel watched, the man's body shimmered and faded away. Within seconds, a stick-thin alien with a rapier-like horn and mottled blue skin covered with bumps was standing before him.

43

'You weren't seen, were you?' Braxiatel said. 'It would scupper our plans completely if anybody saw you in your true form.'

'No,' Szaratak snarled, 'I wasn't seen.'

Steven had never seen anything like Venice before. He walked its alleys as if he were in a dream, trying to forget the rotting body dangling from the pillar, letting his feet take him where they would. The Doctor had assured him that it was impossible to get lost in the city. All one had to do was to ask any passer-by the way to St Mark's Square. He hoped that the Doctor was right. There were certainly enough people to ask. Crowds thronged the place, dressed in everything from rags to silk robes.

The haphazard arrangement of the alleys amazed him. They followed no plan or pattern, running in random directions and narrowing or widening for no apparent reason, terminating in taverns, restaurants, houses or just dead ends. Sometimes they crossed dark, glittering canals that stank of sewage, sometimes they ran parallel to them. The canals seemed to form an alternate means of transportation: a second Venice that lived beside the first. Black gondolas with gilded prows floated along them, curtains fluttering at the windows of their cabins. They looked like chrysalises for coffins.

Steven marvelled at the bright colours and exotic smells as he walked along narrow thoroughfares, down winding streets and through leaning arches and across bridges made of wood or stone. He ended up, out of breath, sitting on a flight of stone steps which had been smoothed into curves by generations of feet. He felt dazed by the labyrinthine geography, and he had lost all track of time. Venice didn't seem to sleep.

A cat sprawled on the steps above. Venetians and travellers from other countries ignored him as they walked past, as if he occupied a different but parallel universe to theirs, perhaps.

He shook his head. All he needed was a good night's

sleep in a soft bed, and he'd be as right as rain. This place was no more alien than the other places, times and planets he'd visited.

He patted the cat on the head, pulled himself to his feet and caught hold of the sleeve of a passing woman. 'Excuse me,' he said, 'but which way is St Mark's Square?'

The woman pointed down a narrow and empty alley. 'Merely straight ahead,' she said, and pulled herself free of his grip. Within moments she had vanished into the crowd.

Steven shrugged, and pushed his way across the flow of pedestrians and into the alley. It was unlit. He wasn't sure about this. He wasn't sure at all. For a moment he considered turning back and following the tide of people, but then the Doctor's advice came back to him. Sighing, he headed on down the alley.

After five minutes the alley had narrowed to the point where he had to walk sideways. He was about to turn back in disgust when he was disgorged onto the bank of a canal washed white by the light of the moon. The mouth of the alley behind him was just a narrow slit in the wall, almost indistinguishable from the brick if he hadn't known what to look for. Across the canal rose a sheer cliff-face of houses, their windows shuttered against the night. To his left was a bridge over the canal, and to his right –

He caught his breath and glanced around. There was nobody in sight: the embankment on both sides of the canal was empty. He listened hard, but he could hear nothing. No talking, no movement, nothing apart from the sigh of the faint lap, lap, lap of water against stone and the moan of the wind getting lost in the canyon-like alleys.

Steven looked again to his right, where a body was lying crumpled up on the stone embankment. Ribbons of blood curled away from it, seeking out the cracks between the stones and trickling towards the canal.

Catching his breath, he crouched down beside the body and cautiously felt for a pulse, but the skin was cold and his hand came away sticky and dark with blood.

'Brilliant,' he sighed. 'I knew we shouldn't have accepted that invitation.'

Something scraped against stone behind him.

Four

———————

Sandy's scales were rough under her hands, but Vicki loved the way he growled as she stroked him. His blunt little body wriggled when she tickled him under the chin, and his little antennae stood perfectly upright. He was the only thing left that loved her. The only thing left that she loved.

She stood up, Sandy nestling at her leg, and gazed out across the Didonian plain. The sun was just setting behind the mountains, sending plumes of scarlet and gold up into the atmosphere. Beautiful. She took a deep breath. The air was so clear and so cold that her lungs tingled. It was all so different from Earth. Bennett hated it here, but she had got used to it. So quiet, so peaceful. So undemanding.

It wouldn't be long before it was dark. She should be getting back to the ship. Bennett didn't like her to be out after sunset. He said that the Didonians were savages who would cook her and eat her, and he wouldn't be able to lift a finger to help. Besides, it was time to prepare dinner. He'd get angry if she didn't have it on the table on time. It wasn't as if he could do anything to her – he'd been paralysed in the crash – but his tongue was sharp, and his voice was loud, and she could not manipulate him with flattery and smiles the way she could manipulate every-body else: he didn't react in predictable ways. Sometimes she had to run all the way to Sandy's cave before she couldn't hear him shouting and cursing.

Vicki took a few steps away from the cave and towards the ship, but the smell of cooked meat stopped her. It couldn't be dinner – she hadn't even put it in the rehydrater yet. Surely Bennett couldn't have got to the kitchen by himself?

There was a noise behind her: a pitiful, mewling noise. She turned, and took a step backwards. Sandy was lying there in the cave mouth, his chest burned to a cinder. His foreclaws scrabbled in the sand as he crawled towards her, crying her name.

Screaming, she jerked awake.

She was lying on an upholstered couch in a room with lots of paintings, and someone had covered her with a blanket. For a moment she didn't know where she was, but then the memories fell back into place. Her name was Vicki, she was in Venice in Earth's past, and Sandy was dead, killed by Barbara Wright. Bennett was dead too, killed by the Didonians, who hadn't been savages after all. And Bennett hadn't been paralysed: he'd only been pretending. Things had been so simple before she met the Doctor, and sometimes she wished that they could be that simple again. But they never would.

'Unhappiness like smoke above this sleeping city rises your,' a strangely musical voice said from the window. 'No one as beautiful unhappy should be as you.'

Her head jerked around so fast that she felt a tendon pull to its limit. That hadn't been the Doctor's voice. Or Steven's.

A dark shape sat on the window ledge. The flickering light from the square outside haloed its edges, and all she could make out were its claws on the wood of the window ledge and the faint suggestion of wings.

'Who are you?' she asked. For some reason she was perfectly calm. She tried to work up some fear, but there was nothing there. Nothing at all.

'Name Albrellian is my,' the creature said. Its voice was like a flute playing.

'I'm Vicki,' she said automatically, still worried by the fact that she wasn't worried. Perhaps she was still asleep, just surfacing briefly into semi-consciousness as she slipped from one dream into another.

48

'Universe a better place is now that met you have I,' Albrellian said, shifting slightly in the window. She thought that she could make out eyestalks emerging from some sort of carapace, and a ruff of hair. 'Your language well speak I, think do not you?'

'Er . . . yes, you're almost word-perfect.' Vicki opened her mouth to say something else, but yawned instead. 'Excuse me,' she murmured, then continued: 'How long have you been sitting in the window watching me?'

'Presence awake is keeping you my,' Albrellian hooted in concern. 'Apologies like water flow. Perhaps, if allow me to you, might to speak with you again return will I.' He seemed to fall backwards out of the window, his wings opening to fill the space, and then he was gone and the stars were shining down upon her. Moments later, something soared against the pocked face of the moon, but it could have been anything.

Vicki shook her head and laughed. Dreams! You never knew what you were going to get.

She snuggled down beneath the blanket and closed her eyes. What next, she wondered? A handsome lover? A fairy-tale palace?

She dreamed. Again.

Steven tried to spring to his feet, or even just to turn his head, but he couldn't move. All he could do was gaze in horror at the crushed, mangled chest of the corpse on the ground in front of him. Whatever caused that incredible, charnel-house damage was standing behind him. Right behind him. He could hear it shuffling closer, ready to pounce. Its breath was hot against the back of his neck. He tried to will his legs to move, but the muscles were rigid and quivering with tension.

Taking a deep, shuddering breath, Steven pounded his fist against his thigh, trying to provoke some reaction, even if the muscle just spasmed and sent him sprawling on the cobbles. Nothing. Just hot breath on the back of his neck.

'I wouldn't punish yourself,' a voice said from behind him. 'The man's dead.'

The paralysis left as unexpectedly as it had appeared, and Steven slumped to his knees. Turning, he saw a middle-aged man dressed in faded velvets. He had a bushy beard and watchful eyes.

'Who are you?' Steven asked, standing upright.

'My name is Galileo Galilei,' the man replied, as if he expected Steven to recognize the name. To his own surprise, Steven did.

'The astronomer?'

Galileo nodded. 'The very same. And you are?'

'Steven Taylor.' Suddenly remembering the body at his feet, he blurted, 'I didn't do it, you know,' before he could stop himself.

'I know,' Galileo said, walking around to Steven's side to gaze down on the corpse. He seemed strangely unmoved by the sight. 'The wound was obviously made by something sharp and long – a sword, I would presume. You possess nothing of that shape about your person, and no scabbard to indicate that you ever had one. Logic would dictate, therefore, that unless you have supernaturally caused the weapon to vanish, you are innocent.' He smiled, causing his bushy beard to twitch. 'Of course, had you the power to cause a murder weapon to vanish into thin air, then you would not have required one to begin with, for you would have been able to strike the man dead with a word, or perhaps reach into his very bosom and crush his heart without so much as breaking the skin.' He cocked his head to one side and gazed at Steven, frowning. 'You are silent. Do you find some fault with my reasoning?'

'No!' Steven exclaimed. 'Far from it! I'm innocent, and I'm not about to argue with anybody who believes me.' He gazed wildly along the sides of the canal, but there was nobody but the two of them around. The crowds he had walked amongst earlier seemed to stick to well-defined tributaries, leaving little undisturbed

Venetian backwaters such as this. 'Shouldn't we call the police or something? I mean, there's been a murder. Someone should be told. I think —'

Galileo raised a hand. 'I think not. I have but recently left the scene of another suspicious death. The local police may not believe me to be as innocent as I believe myself to be.'

'Why not?' Steven asked. 'I get the impression that death by violence isn't anything special around here.' He caught the flash of expression on Galileo's face, and quickly added, 'Sorry, I didn't mean to insult your home, but even so —'

'This isn't my home.' Another twitch of the beard. 'Although there have been times when I wished that it were. No matter, you are right that death is no stranger to this island, but the police would not be impressed with the fact that I insulted the one victim and knew the other.'

Steven glanced askance at him. 'Which one's this?' he asked, nodding down at the corpse.

'My landlord. I had no argument with him, but the police may wish to make something of the fact that I regularly owed him money.' He snorted. 'If the fact that I owe money were grounds for murder, then much of Padua and Florence would be free of human life by now.'

'So, do you think the two deaths are connected?' Steven asked. 'Apart from by you?'

Galileo shrugged. 'Possibly. We do not have enough evidence to say, as yet. I would suggest, my friend, that we repair to my lodgings, where we can recover our wits with a few glasses of wine.' He gazed down at the body, then up at Steven. 'No doubt, as a man of obvious breeding and intelligence, you will have already appreciated the logical corollary to my problem.'

Steven nodded. 'You can't afford for the body to be found. Even if someone else reports it to the police, they'll come looking for you because you owed him money.'

'Exactly. Might I recommend . . . ?' He nodded towards the murky waters of the canal. Steven looked from Galileo's face to the body and back. Dump it in the canal? Hide the evidence? His mind flinched at the thought, but there was no denying that if he were found by the police, standing over a dead body, there would be questions. A lot of questions. And with the Doctor impersonating a powerful cleric and abusing the Doge's hospitality . . .

Steven remembered the body hanging from the pillar in St Mark's Square and felt a shiver, like the tiny patter of rats' feet, across the flesh of his back. He bent down to the body. Galileo bent down as well, and together they rolled it towards the edge of the stone paving.

'Shouldn't we say something?' Steven asked.

Galileo shrugged. 'I am no priest. If it makes you happy . . .' He closed his eyes and, in a deep and sonorous voice, said, 'Dear Lord, we know not how this man came to lose his life, but we commend his immortal soul to your eternal care.' Opening one eye, he winked at Steven. 'And we ask your protection over the following days for what may befall us,' he added, then tipped the body over the edge. It bobbed without noise and floated for a moment before the dark, scummy water rolled over it.

Galileo stood up and brushed his hands against his breeches. 'Are you still interested in that wine?' he asked.

'Lead the way,' Steven replied. 'Is it far?'

'We should be able to get there unseen. Follow me.'

He moved away. Steven, after a last glance at the still surface of the water, followed.

Vicki was woken by the sound of water lapping against stone. She gazed up at the ceiling for a while, drifting through thoughts and memories. The early morning sun reflecting off the lagoon illuminated the ceiling with patterns of light that rippled and reformed themselves: always the same and yet different second by second.

More sounds intruded through the open window.

Merchants were hawking their wares with shouts in various languages. Bells tolled briefly in the distance, calling the faithful to church, and far, far away she thought that she could hear a man's voice yodelling a similar call to the mosque. A brief volley of trumpets caused everything else to quieten for a few moments. Smells began to register: seaweed, ripe vegetables, spices.

Drifting, her mind alighted on the dreams of the previous night. She smiled as she remembered the dark winged shape at the window, and the polite way it had talked to her. What did that one mean? She drew the blanket tighter about her. That creature had such a deep, soothing voice. She could remember every word that it had spoken. None of her other dreams were that clear.

Eventually she threw the blanket to the floor and stood up. She felt amazingly awake and happy: better than she had for weeks. There was something about sleeping in the TARDIS that she hated: perhaps it was the dryness of the air, or the ever-present background hum, but she always woke up tired. For a while she had thought that she was ill, but all she had needed was a good night's sleep.

Pulling her clothes into some semblance of order, she wandered across to the window. The square outside was bustling with activity: people shopping, talking, drinking, walking or just standing around, singly or in groups. The costumes were gaudy: the faces full of character. This place was more alive than anywhere she had ever seen. Everybody looked like they were living the most important moment of their lives right in front of her.

She rested her hands on the windowsill, ready to lean out and look to either side, but something stopped her. There were ridges beneath her fingers: rough, splintery ruts in the wood. She moved her hands and looked down at the sill. The wood had been crushed in two places, one on either side. The splintered areas were about the size of her hands, but they didn't look like they'd been caused by hands.

53

They looked like they'd been caused by claws.

'Good morning, my dear,' the Doctor said from the doorway. 'Did you sleep well?'

'Doctor!' She turned, smiling at the familiar elderly face. 'I had a wonderful night!'

The Doctor beamed at her. He looked no different from the last time she had seen him: just as distinguished and just as sprightly. 'Good, my child. This place seems to agree with us all. I spent a very instructive night in the Doge's library, and Steven seems to have "hit the town", as Chetter — *Chester*ton used to say.'

'Doctor, come and look at this.' Vicki gestured him over to the window. 'I had the oddest dream last night. I dreamed that there was something sitting on the windowsill, talking to me. It wasn't human, and when I woke up this morning, I found these marks.'

The Doctor examined them closely. 'Hmm. Are you sure that they weren't there last night?'

'Well. . .' She thought for a moment. 'I don't remember them.'

'No, and more to the point, neither do I.' He ran a hand across his chin. 'I cannot explain it, not yet, but when added to the mysterious invitation, it begins to fit a pattern of sorts, doesn't it, hmm?'

'Does it?' Vicki frowned.

'However, my dear, we have a far more pressing problem on our hands.'

'Do we?'

He nodded. 'Apparently the Doge wishes to see us this morning. Now, I don't know whether he has ever met Cardinal Bellarmine or not. If he hasn't, then I have to try and pretend to be a confidant of the Pope. If he has, then I'm afraid all of our geese are cooked.'

Vicki was about to say something when the door opened again and a haggard, unshaven figure entered. 'Steven!' she cried. He looked terrible, and he was wearing different clothes to the ones he had left in — velvet trousers and a brown velvet jacket, embroidered with a maze-like pattern and with a laced shirt beneath.

'Where have you been?' the Doctor snapped. 'We've been worried sick.'

Vicki glanced over at him. The Doctor hadn't seemed worried when he entered the room. Catching her questioning glance, he winked at her. Obviously he wanted to teach Steven a lesson.

'I've been . . .' Steven hesitated for a moment. '. . . researching the parts we're supposed to be playing.'

'And how precisely have you been doing that, hmm?'

Steven winced at the harshness of the Doctor's voice. Even from where she stood by the window, Vicki could smell the alcohol on Steven's breath. 'I've been out drinking with Galileo Galilei,' he said finally.

The Doctor had the good grace to look abashed. 'Well, that's different,' he said. 'You appear to have made more progress than we have. What sort of person is he, by the way?'

Steven shrugged. 'He can drink like a fish and he thinks he's God's gift to science,' he said. 'But why not find out for yourself? He's invited us round to dinner tonight.'

The Doctor beamed. 'You see how it's all beginning to fit together?' he said. 'We'll get to the bottom of this mystery before you know it, and,' he glanced over at Vicki, 'along the way we'll find out what was squatting on your windowsill.'

Steven looked puzzled, but a knock at the door distracted him. He was closest, so he opened it. Three guards in half-armour were standing outside. Their faces were bland, their expressions fixed.

'We've come to escort you to the meeting,' one of them said.

'Excellent,' the Doctor said, striding towards the door. 'Come on, you two. We don't want to keep the Doge waiting.'

'Look,' Steven said, 'I'm feeling a bit rocky. Mind if I duck out and get some sleep?'

The Doctor fixed Steven with his piercing gaze. 'Don't

make a habit of it. There are races who would quite cheerfully kill you if you insulted them by missing an important meeting like this.' He strode off out of the door, leaving Vicki to follow on.

'How much did you two drink?' she asked as she passed him.

'I lost count after the fifth bottle,' he said. Close-up, his eyes were bloodshot and the skin around them was puffy.

As she reached the door, she turned back and said, 'The couch is very comfortable.'

'At the moment,' Steven rejoined, 'I could quite happily sleep on the flagstones outside.'

As Vicki closed the door, Steven was already stretching out on the couch. She ran along the tapestry-clad corridor to catch up with the Doctor and the guards. She was just in time to hear him say, 'How long have we got, my good man?'

'All day, I think,' one of the men said. 'That's just today, of course. The whole thing will last for a week.'

The Doctor frowned, and turned to Vicki. 'I'm not sure I can keep up this masquerade for a week,' he whispered. 'I had assumed we would only be in there for half an hour or so.'

'Perhaps he isn't serious,' she said. She turned to the guard to clarify his answer, but he had already turned to say something to the man beside him. She strained to hear what they were saying, just in case it gave her some clue as to what was going to happen.

'Did they find Envoy Albrellian?' the man was saying. Vicki felt a cold shiver run through her body. Albrellian? For a moment her mind floundered as she tried to remember where she had heard the name before, and then the memory hit home hard enough to make her head spin. It was the name the alien in her dream had used.

'Yes,' the second man said, 'he went for a late night fly around the city. Said he needed to stretch his wings. Braxiatel was furious.'

They laughed. Vicki clutched at the Doctor's coat

56

sleeve. 'Doctor, there's something funny going on here.'

'Funny how, child?'

She shrugged. 'I'm not sure, but they're talking about something that happened in my dream.'

The Doctor glanced at the two men out of the corner of his eye. 'They look human to me – or, at least, humanoid. Hmm . . .' He thought for a second. 'I'm not sure I want to go where they're taking us, not until I know more about what we're doing here, at least. If they're the real thing, they will expect me to be Cardinal Bellarmine. If they're not, and if they are associated with that invitation, then they will know me as the Doctor. Can you say something to them, something that will make them react to my name?'

Vicki nodded, thinking quickly. 'Pretend to be ill,' she said.

The Doctor nodded slightly, and reached out to take her hand. For a few seconds he squeezed it comfortingly, then he let it drop, stopped abruptly in the middle of the corridor and bent double in a coughing fit. He was so convincing that Vicki almost panicked. Taking a deep breath, she said, 'Cardinal Bellarmine is ill!'

The first man just looked at her. 'Who?' he said.

'Cardinal Bellarmine!' she said, pointing.

'She means the Doctor,' said the second guard. 'Quick, get a medkit!'

The Doctor straightened up and shoved the first man in the chest. He staggered back into his colleague. The Doctor took Vicki by the wrist and pulled her back along the corridor. 'Come on, my dear. We'll make for our rooms!'

Stone walls and tapestries flew past in a blur as they ran. For an old man, the Doctor was capable of an amazing burst of speed when he tried. It was all Vicki could do to keep up with him. His hand was clamped so hard around her wrist that she was getting pins and needles. Her breath was rasping in her chest, coming in short gasps. She hadn't run this fast for years. How far were the rooms? She was sure that they hadn't walked that far away from them.

And then she recognized a tapestry as it flashed past, and knew that they were only a step or two away.

Something closed over her free wrist. She jerked to a halt. The Doctor ran on oblivious until her hand was wrenched from his. As he stumbled to a halt and turned around, trying to work out what had happened, Vicki looked back over her shoulder. One of the guards was grasping her wrist, while the other lumbered up behind. Desperately she tried to lever his hand away from her wrist, but her own fingers closed over something alien, like bumpy twigs. She lashed out at the guard's face, but her hand passed through empty air where his cheek should have been. Whatever he was, he wasn't human.

Five

Steven Taylor rested his head in his hands and groaned. He was sitting in a shadowed recess in a nearly empty hostelry with a name something like the Tavern of the Angel, and he had a large glass of a vile liquid named grappa in front of him. It was cloudy, it was fiery and it made his head swim, but it was calming his system down and, at that moment, he didn't care what else it did so long as his stomach stopped churning.

After tossing and turning for what seemed like hours, he had eventually realized that he wasn't going to get any sleep. The TARDIS did that to him — ever since leaving Mechanus he seemed to have been suffering from on-going time- and space-lag. He'd gone for a walk, and eventually stumbled into this tavern beside some large bridge called the Rialto. It was small, and its walls were lined with boating mementoes — oars, nets, floats, the occasional badly stuffed fish — but it was a haven of sanity and cool air compared to the madness of the crowds outside. The bridge was arched, and lined on both sides with shops and stalls, and the shouts and laughter of the various people that were crossing it was driving slivers of pure pain into Steven's temples.

What *had* he been drinking last night? Watery and sour, it had tasted like adulterated vinegar, but after a couple of bottles he'd found he'd developed a taste for it. Whatever it was, it was strong. When he woke up beneath Galileo's table, with the sun shining in his eyes and the astronomer snoring heavily on the couch, his head felt like someone had half-filled it with water. It took twice as much effort as usual to move it, and whenever he did the outside seemed to move a second or two before the inside caught up. Turning it, even slightly, made him nauseous and unsteady on his feet – even more unsteady than he already was.

It was almost worth it, though. Last night had been fun – the most fun he'd had for longer than he cared to remember. He and Galileo had talked for hours. The man was a witty and entertaining companion, full of stories and barbed jokes against his academic contemporaries. He was also a good listener, encouraging Steven to talk about . . .

Oh no. Steven's head sank lower in his hands as he vaguely remembered babbling on about the Doctor and the TARDIS. Had he talked about the future and alien worlds? If he had, and Galileo remembered, he didn't know *what* the man's reaction might be. At best history might be changed, at worst Steven and his friends might be betrayed to the Inquisition, if they had that here as well. The few days that the TARDIS had spent in Spain during the time of Torquemada would haunt Steven for some time to come, and he wasn't keen to come that close to any hot irons again.

The cloying, penetrating smell of fish drifted across from the Rialto market, and Steven nearly threw up. Quickly he gulped down a mouthful of the grappa. The fumes burned his throat, but a blessed warmth spread across his stomach as the alcohol hit it. There was probably something in the TARDIS that could help him, but even if he had a key he couldn't remember which island it was on.

Trying to distract his mind from thoughts of vomiting, Steven glanced around the tavern. Small groups of people were sitting around, beneath the nets and the oars, talking and sipping drinks. Judging by what he could hear, many of them appeared to be English. One or two were dressed differently from the rest – less colourfully, in plain black cloth with white collars and large black hats.

He caught the eye of a young, bearded man standing in

60

a group near the doorway. The man frowned, and Steven quickly looked away. The last thing he wanted to do was to attract attention to himself. The *first* thing he wanted to do was turn time back about eight hours, but unfortunately that wasn't possible. At least, not without the Doctor's help.

Steven realized with a sudden jolt that the young, bearded man and his friends were standing over him.

'Good morning,' he said, with some effort, 'can I help you?'

'It is we who can help you,' the man snarled, 'to an early grave.' His face was young and lean, but his eyes betrayed an inherent uncertainty that his swagger was meant to cover.

For a moment the words were meaningless, and Steven rolled them around in his mind until they slotted together to make some kind of sense. 'Sorry?' he said. 'I'm not sure I follow.'

'My name is *Antonio* Nicolotti,' the man said. 'I am the elder brother of Baldassarre Nicolotti, whom you poisoned yesterday.'

'I didn't poison anyone,' Steven said. 'Not yesterday, and not ever. I've never even heard of you or your brother.' His mind, lagging a few seconds behind his words, suddenly alerted him to the fact that he did know the name. Hadn't Galileo said something about a Baldassarre Nicolotti? Something about a bar, and a poisoned tankard of wine?

'You are Galileo Galilei,' Antonio said firmly.

'No!' Steven protested, faintly discerning the potential shape of the next few minutes through the haze of his hangover. 'I'm not Galileo!'

'It wasn't a question,' the man said. 'You meet his description, despite having shaved your beard off to avoid being recognized, and you're wearing his clothes. One would think,' he added, turning to his friends, 'that a noted natural philosopher would be able to think of a more convincing lie.'

Steven looked down at his clothes, momentarily non-plussed to find that he was dressed in faded velvet breeches, a threadbare linen shirt and an embroidered jacket. A memory surfaced in the murky, stagnant canal of his thoughts: Galileo ridiculing his clothing some time after the third bottle of wine, and offering to lend him a more fitting costume.

Antonio's friends laughed dutifully as he turned back to Steven, hand reaching for the dagger at his side. 'Make your peace with the God you deny,' he snarled. Everything seemed to be moving in slow motion as Steven pushed his chair back and tried to stagger to his feet. As his horrified gaze wavered between the man's face and his dagger, he saw the dagger leave its sheath and . . .

And vanish. Antonio's hand groped vainly for the hilt, but it had disappeared. His face was almost comical in its confusion.

'Your sword should not play the orator for you,' a gravelly voice said in English, then switching to Italian it added, 'Forgive me, but I have an aversion to brawls in taverns, and I find those that do more childish valorous than manly wise.'

Antonio whirled around. Behind him, Steven caught sight of a man with a fine-boned face, a mane of grey hair and a scar running down one cheek. 'Hand me back that dagger, cur!' Antonio snarled.

'Not until you learn some better manners,' the man replied. His gaze quickly switched to Steven and he jerked his head slightly. Never one to ignore a hint, Steven quietly began to back away from the group of people.

One of Antonio's companions pulled his knife from its sheath and took a step forward. The stranger's free hand shot out and hit him just beneath his rib-cage. He bent over, choking, and the stranger plucked the knife from his hand.

'What do you think you're doing?' Antonio said as the stranger began to juggle with the daggers.

62

'Using such conceits as clownage keeps in pay,' the stranger replied. 'A most cultured and rewarding pastime, I can assure you.' The daggers were just a blur in the air now, and some of Antonio's friends were beginning to cheer. 'This is too easy: will somebody increase the challenge?'

As Steven backed through the doorway and into the bright morning sunlight, the last thing he saw was the stranger catching a third blade as it was thrown to him – or was it *at* him – and incorporating it into his performance.

Steven shook his head and turned away towards the arch of the Rialto. Venice was turning out to be full of surprises – and not all of them were pleasant.

'Turkish spies!' Sperone Speroni, Lord of the Nightwatch, punched his right hand into his left palm as he spoke. The scowl on his face made the skin wrinkle all the way up his bald head. 'Turkish scum!' he added, and spat on the floor near to where Vicki sat on the couch. She was surprised, and frightened, at the vehemence in his voice. 'Thank the Lord that my guards heard your cries for help and chased them off. I will have their eyes plucked from their heads and thrust down their throats!'

'While I commend your enthusiasm,' the Doctor said drily from his position by the window, 'I would question your identification. Do you have any proof that Turkish spies were involved in our abduction, or is this some blind hope of yours?'

Vicki found herself fascinated by Speroni's hands. They were large and blunt-fingered, and covered in white scars. The hands of a workman, an artisan, not a policeman.

Speroni looked at the Doctor blankly. 'Who else could it have been? Those devious, murdering bastards would do anything to gain access to Venice's wealth.'

'But how would kidnapping us aid their aims?' the Doctor asked. 'I mean to say, the disappearance of –' he seemed to catch himself – 'of a prominent Roman

63

Catholic Cardinal and his travelling companions would hardly further the aims of the Ottoman Empire, would it?'

'You don't know the underhand way their heathen minds work, your Eminence,' Speroni said. 'Their agents will have been reporting the . . .' he flushed slightly, and looked away from the Doctor's gaze '. . . the difficulties between the Holy Roman Empire and the Serene Venetian Republic over the past few years. They will have heard about the excommunication of the city, and of the attempt on the life of Friar Sarpi . . .'

As Speroni listed the various indignities heaped upon Venice by the Vatican, Vicki glanced over at the Doctor and noticed that he was just nodding blandly. Surely, she thought, if he had really been Cardinal Bellarmine, he would have reacted a bit more strongly to that. She fluttered her fingers to attract his attention, and when he glanced questioningly at her she jerked her head at Speroni and frowned.

'And, of course, let us not forget the heresies committed by the Serene Republic,' the Doctor quickly added, taking the hint. 'Sarpi's writings questioning the supremacy of the church have been inflammatory, if not heretical, and –'

'Friar Sarpi merely put into words what –' Speroni stopped in mid-sentence and took a deep breath. 'Your pardon, Eminence, I do not mean to debate theology with a man of your learning. What I was saying was that the Ottoman Empire would dearly love to drive a wedge between Rome and Venice. The disappearance and, dare I even mention it, demise of the Pope's special emissary would serve their purpose very well.'

'A fair point,' the Doctor conceded. He was opening his mouth to say something else when the door opened, revealing one of Speroni's policemen. The man approached the Lord of the Nightwatch and murmured something in his ear. Vicki took the opportunity to slip across to the Doctor.

'What about the guard?' she asked. 'He was an alien, not a Turkish spy.'

'My dear girl,' the Doctor murmured, 'Cardinal or no Cardinal, if I start blabbering about being almost abducted by aliens, the Doge would have me locked away faster than you could say "boiled asparagus"!' He ran a hand through his long, white hair. 'Our position here is precarious enough, without bringing our sanity into question. And besides, I'm still uncertain what connection these aliens have with the invitation I received. Until we know *that*, we had best tread very carefully. Very carefully indeed, hmm?'

Vicki nodded doubtfully. She supposed that the Doctor was right, but the thought that anybody she looked at might really be an alien in disguise made her edgy. 'How do you think they disguised themselves?' she asked, hoping that the Doctor could give her some clue enabling her to tell real Venetians from fake Venetians. Or, if it came to that, a real Doctor from a fake Doctor . . .

'Probably a holographic image generator of some kind,' he said. 'Quite simple technology. If they had been true shapeshifters, then their arms would have felt like human arms. The fact that you could tell they were alien by touching them means that they were just covering their true form with a projected human image.'

Speroni broke off from his discussion to address the Doctor. 'Cardinal Bellarmine? We have just received word from the Doge. He apologizes for the delay, hopes that you are rested and will receive you now.'

They were led along corridors that closely resembled the ones that they had been led along by the fake policemen. It was difficult to tell: the tapestries all looked the same to Vicki. They went up stairs, down stairs and along corridors panelled in heavy wood. The floor of one corridor rang hollow, and she glanced out of a heavily barred window to find that they were crossing a stretch of canal with two black gondolas floating on it.

After an indeterminable time, they ascended an

65

impressive marble staircase and passed through an open pair of double doors into a large room. It was lined with tapestries and filled with people who stared at them as they were escorted towards another pair of doors. Speroni gestured the Doctor and Vicki onward. The doors opened as they approached, and Vicki followed the Doctor into a large room panelled in dark wood and floored with marble slabs. The ceiling was painted with clouds and angels, and enormous canvasses lined the walls, each at least twice as tall as Vicki and many times longer. They all seemed to show groups of robed men staring at the artist with the same expression of wary blankness that Vicki had seen in group holograms from her own time.

And then she realized that one such group of men standing on a raised dais at the end of the room weren't in a painting at all: they were real. As the Doctor walked fearlessly forward to meet them, they moved apart slightly to reveal a tall man seated on a gilded leather chair. He wore white robes embroidered in gold and scarlet, and a hat with earflaps and which rose to a peak at the back.

'Your Eminence, Cardinal Roberto Francesco Romolo Bellarmine,' he said in a dry, quiet voice, 'I am Doge Leonardo Donà. I bid you welcome to the Venetian Republic.'

Steven walked away from the Tavern of the Angel as fast as he dared without attracting attention. His head was still pounding with the after-effects of the worst hangover he'd ever had, and his chest felt as if someone were tightening iron bands around it. Somewhere in the back of his mind, an ever-present flicker of frustration and anger was being fanned into a fire. What was it about the Doctor that meant his companions were always running for their lives? Why couldn't they just have a rest for once? Why couldn't life just pass them by, instead of grabbing them by the scruff of the neck and dragging them along, kicking and screaming, behind it?

Slowing to a halt in a sparsely populated square, he sat

at the base of a well. A group of white cats were sunning themselves nearby. They looked up at him for a long moment, then went back to cleaning their fur. He looked around. There was an inn on one side of the square with a handful of tourists standing outside. Three alleys led off in different directions, vanishing into shadows after a few feet. The rest of the buildings were tall, anonymous houses built in red stone. There was nothing to distinguish the square from the hundreds of others he had walked through since he had arrived. Apart possibly from the colour of the cats.

He sighed, and rested his head in his hands. All he wanted to do at that moment was to sleep until the Doctor decided it was time to leave.

'A close shave, my friend.'

He groaned softly. Would he never be left in peace with his aching head? Glancing up, he winced as a sharp pain arrowed through his skull. The man who had distracted his attackers in the tavern was standing in front of him, one leg up on the pedestal surrounding the well. The sun was behind him, silhouetting his grey mane of hair and his bulky leather jerkin.

'I suppose I should thank you,' Steven said grudgingly.

'That depends what value you put on your life,' the man rejoined. 'But how could I stand idle whilst a beautiful lad such as yourself put himself in the way of a sword's point?'

'I didn't do it deliberately,' Steven explained. 'They thought I was someone else.'

'Mistaken identity may be the very lifeblood of drama, but it makes for poor reality. Whatever end a man should have, it should be dignified, and to die in error for an Italian teacher and occasional heretic is certainly undignified. Far be that fate from us.'

'You know Galileo, then?' Steven asked.

'I know of him. We have moved in the same circles, although we have never met.' A cloud covered the face of the sun, and Steven found himself staring into a pair of

67

granite-coloured eyes set in a face that looked like fine-grained leather. The scar running down one side was a few years old, and twisted one corner of the man's mouth up into a cynical smile. 'My name,' he added, 'is Giovanni Zarattino Chigi. And yours is . . . ?'

'Taylor. Steven Taylor.'

'A fine English name,' Chigi said, extending a hand. Steven took it, and found himself hauled to his feet. 'Or perhaps I should say a fine British name. I hear things have changed since I left our fine country.' He held on to Steven's hand, smiling warmly as he squeezed.

'So I hear,' Steven said carefully, untangling his hand from Chigi's grasp. 'I've been away too.' He was surprised at Chigi's height: the man was so broad-shouldered that he seemed smaller, more in proportion.

'And are you a diplomat, an adventurer, or a seeker after trade?' Chigi was still smiling, but Steven reminded himself that the scar would make him smile no matter what mood he was in.

'I'm . . . accident-prone,' Steven said eventually.

Chigi laughed. 'Very cautious, and very wise. You have the look of a military man. I will assume, for the sake of conversation, that you are a buccaneer. I have a flair for the dramatic: please don't disappoint me by letting me find out that you are a trader in horseflesh.'

'I promise,' Steven laughed.

'And are you here with the other Englishmen?' Chigi asked.

'What other Englishmen?'

'Venice is, at the moment, playing host to many countrymen of ours,' Chigi said. Steven wondered about the 'ours' – Chigi sounded like an Italian name to him. 'They are easily spotted, as they wear clothes of a design that was out of fashion when *I* left England, and that was sixteen years ago.'

'Nothing to do with me, I'm afraid,' Steven said, reflecting ruefully that those words seemed destined to become his epitaph.

Chigi looked away, across the square. 'A shame,' he said. 'They interest me strangely. As do you.'

Steven smiled. Despite himself, he was beginning to like the man. 'You may not want my thanks for saving my life, but I have precious little else to offer, I'm afraid.'

'Perhaps I could buy you a drink?' Chigi looked nonchalantly across the square.

Steven let his gaze wander down that scar, across that weathered skin. 'That sounds good,' he said noncommittally. 'But I can't make any promises.'

'Which of us can?' Chigi murmured, still looking across the square. He seemed almost to be talking to himself.

'That was a bit of a fiasco, wasn't it?' Irving Braxiatel said mildly. He was sitting in his study, idly flicking through a book selected at random from the shelves. Gazing over the top of his bifocal glasses at the two stick-thin Jamarians standing in front of him, he said, 'You and Tzorogol were supposed to escort the Doctor and his young assistant here so I could take them to the Island. Instead you end up chasing him all over the Doge's Palace, frightening him and drawing attention to yourselves from the locals.' Without raising his voice, he made it clear from his tone that he was furious. 'I put you in charge of collecting him, Szaratak, because I wanted to ensure that the Doctor was treated properly. I trusted you to do this with no fuss. Do you have an explanation for this seemingly bizarre behaviour, or shall I just put it down to the inherent stupidity of your race?'

'It's not our fault,' Szaratak snapped. Its thin hands clenched and unclenched by its side.

'He didn't want to come,' agreed Tzorogol.

'Don't be so stupid,' Braxiatel snapped. He took off his glasses and began to polish them furiously. 'He got the invitation, didn't he? He must have done, otherwise he wouldn't be here. And if he got the invitation, he must have known that we would come and collect him. It's really very simple, even for a race like yours.'

Szaratak shot a quick sideways glance at Tzorogol, but not so quick that Braxiatel didn't catch it. 'It's *not* our fault,' it said with barely suppressed fury. 'The Doctor was expecting to be taken to the Doge. He was pretending to be someone called Cardinal Bellarmine. He and his companion ran from us. They didn't know who we were. They weren't expecting us.'

'You were using your hologuises?'

'Of course!' Szaratak growled. 'We're not stupid. We tried to catch up with them to explain. They were running too fast. The Doctor's companion realized I wasn't human. She screamed. The scream alerted the Nightwatch. As soon as we heard them coming, we left.'

'That's the smartest thing you've done all day,' Braxiatel muttered. 'The last thing we need is for one of you to get caught by the Venetians.' He slipped his glasses back on. 'The thing I don't understand is why the Doctor is staying at the Doge's Palace in the first place. The invitation was supposed to ensure that he was delivered straight into our hands. I had suitable accommodation already prepared.'

'Perhaps it's not the Doctor at all,' Tzorogol muttered.

'What do you mean?'

'You keep telling us how necessary it is that you have tight security,' it explained, glaring at the floor. 'You keep telling us about the races who would do anything to disrupt what we're attempting here. Perhaps there's some plot to substitute a false Doctor. Perhaps he's a shapeshifter, or someone in a holographic disguise, or a robot copy.'

Braxiatel was about to make a scathing comment when he caught himself. 'It's . . . possible,' he agreed finally, 'although I can't see how the security of the Island could possibly be compromised by anyone whose biomorphic profile hasn't already been programmed into its defensive systems.' He sighed. Organising anything of this scale was bound to present problems. If only they had been the

70

problems he was anticipating, he would have been happier. 'All I can suggest is that you pass word around the other Jamarians to keep an eye out for *anyone* meeting the description of the Doctor. In the mean time, we must try to establish whether the one we have is the real one.'

The sun was high in the sky when the path split in two ahead of the carriage and the riders that surrounded it. One fork led straight ahead of them, the other curved gradually off to the right. Both had been raised a few feet above the marshy Italian landscape by piled earth, and both had been swept clear of grass by the feet of the hundreds of horses and the wheels of the hundreds of carts that made the same journey every month.

Cardinal Roberto Francesco Romolo Bellarmine leaned out of the carriage window, and winced as a pang of pain shot through his shoulder. The salt in the air and the chill of the wind was causing his arthritis to play up. He offered a quick prayer, not for relief from the pain but for the strength to withstand it. It was, after all, God's way of reminding him that he was not indispensable to the Church, no matter what the Pope might think.

Ahead, he saw the leader of the party of soldiers that had been detailed to accompany him conferring with one of his troops. 'What causes this wait?' the man shouted with some asperity. He was hoping to have arrived by now, by God's grace, and the delay was making him irritable.

The commander of the party of soldiers pulled on the reins of his horse and trotted back to the coach. 'Your Eminence,' he said, bowing as best he could on horseback, 'we are attempting to determine which of the paths is the safest method by which to convey you to your destination. There are pirates and Turks to consider, and –'

'Fie on the safest,' Bellarmine muttered, 'just choose the fastest.' He dismissed the soldier with a curt nod, and gazed across the patchy landscape of partial dunes and salt sea grasses. Above him gulls wheeled, calling to each other in a harsh tongue. He could smell the sea. If he was where he thought he was then the town of Chioggia lay somewhere to his right, out on the edge of a promontory of land. The path that continued onwards must skirt the edge of the lagoon and then curve northwards, towards Mestre and Venice. Somewhere along the coast he would be able to charter a boat to take them all to the city. A day or two to complete his work, and then he could return to Rome, and civilization.

Venice. He laughed aloud, making two of the soldiers turn to see what the noise was. Would it be too much to regard Venice as the sanctuary of Satan? Friar Sarpi's writings could certainly tear the Church apart, if he were allowed to continue, and if everything he had heard about Galileo's spyglass was true then the ghost of Giordano Bruno might haunt them still. Such danger, concentrated in one place. Were they really the tools of the Devil, or just foolish men who were ignorant of the forces they meddled with?

Was there a difference?

His thoughts preoccupied by theological speculation, Cardinal Bellarmine didn't even notice when the coach started to move again, taking him foot by laborious foot closer to Venice.

Six

Galileo Galilei reached across the vegetable stall and rooted amongst the yellow peppers. 'This!' he said, pulling one out and waving it at the stall's proprietor, 'is a ripe pepper. This,' and he waved the one that he had been given moments before, 'is *over*-ripe. Even a dolt such as yourself must be able to tell the difference.'

The stall's proprietor sighed. 'Venetian peppers always look like that,' she said. 'And they taste better that way. Everyone knows that.'

'Then everyone is foolish,' Galileo snapped. 'I will take five more like this.' He waved the ripe pepper at her, just in case she decided to miss the point. 'And I will risk the taste.'

The proprietor shrugged, and raised her eyebrows at her other customers. As he watched her select more peppers that matched the one he had, he shook his head. Thieves! Venice was populated with thieves! Back home in Padua he would have left his cook to choose the food for a meal such as the one he had invited Steven and his friends to that night, but he didn't trust the cook he had hired that morning. All Venetians were in collusion to defraud the rest of the world: everyone knew that. He would choose the food, and present it to the cook as an accomplished fact.

He shuddered, remembering that the cleaners he had hired would be cleaning and airing the rented house even as he wasted his time wandering around the market. He just hoped that they wouldn't disturb any of his manuscripts. Or his spyglass. He had given them full instructions, but Venetians heard what they wanted to hear. They were a race apart.

'Have you heard about Galileo Galilei?' a voice said beside him. The speaker was a woman: a maid perhaps, or a cook's helper. He froze, his attention distracted from the peppers.

'No,' her companion said: a common strumpet by her look. 'What has he done this time?'

'Poisoned a man in the Tavern of St Theodore and of the Crocodile, so they say. Tommaso Nicolotti is furious. Apparently Galileo was attacked in the Tavern of the Angel by Tomasso's other son, but escaped with his life intact, if not his dignity.'

The women laughed as Galileo pondered. Poison a man in a tavern he may have done, if only by accident, but he was sure that he would have remembered being attacked by another Nicolotti, no matter how drunk he might have been. And he'd never been in the Tavern of the Angel, he was sure of it.

He smiled. Of course: Steven Taylor had left his house wearing his clothes! The poor man . . .

The stall-keeper handed over his peppers, and Galileo was so amused by the fact that Steven had been attacked in error that he completely forgot to check them until it was too late to return them. And they *were* over-ripe: every single one of them.

'Doctor, isn't this wonderful?'

Vicki held the dress up against herself and pirouetted. The hem flared out as she spun, and the gold thread glittered in the candlelight, casting little points of light across the tapestries of their rooms.

'Hmm?' The Doctor looked over from where he was adjusting his cravat in the mirror. 'Oh, yes my dear, I dare say it's very pretty. Very pretty indeed.'

'You're not going to Galileo's house as you are?' she asked.

'Yes, of course. I see no need to change.' He ran his

thumb behind the lapel of his jacket. 'I find that these clothes suffice for most occasions, planets and time periods.'

Vicki was about to press the issue when the door to their room opened and Steven walked in. 'Almost ready?' he asked. 'We don't want to keep Galileo waiting.'

'You seem to have recovered somewhat since this morning,' the Doctor observed.

Steven flushed slightly. 'I've been walking it off,' he said.

'There are some fresh clothes in your bedroom,' Vicki said. 'If they're anything like the ones that were laid out for me, then you'll look almost human.'

Steven sneered at her for a moment, then crossed over to the door that led to his bedroom. 'I hope there's some hot water too,' he said.

As he vanished, Vicki crossed over to the window and gazed out across St Mark's Square. 'It's beautiful here,' she said wistfully, gazing at the wavering reflection of the moon in the lagoon.

The Doctor murmured something non-committal from the far side of the room.

Vicki's gaze moved across the crowds of the square to the brick bell tower that the Doctor had called the campanile. It seemed to be reaching up into the star-strewn sky, aiming for the heart of the moon. The air smelled of seawater and spice. Somewhere in the distance, someone was singing a pure, simple song.

Something moved on top of the campanile. Vicki glanced up, and caught a momentary glimpse of a pair of leathery wings stretching out from a hard, shiny body. She rubbed a hand across her eyes and looked again, but the campanile was empty.

'Sir?'

Irving Braxiatel looked up from the book he had been reading. Outside the window the sun was setting in bands of crimson and gold. The light from the candelabra flickered over the bland face of Cremonini, his man-servant, in the doorway. 'Yes?' Braxiatel said calmly. 'What is it?'

'A visitor, sir.'

Braxiatel closed the book. 'Don't tell me: a *special* visitor.'

'Indeed, sir.'

Braxiatel nodded. 'I'll be straight down.' He sighed as he levered himself up out of the chair. The organization of this business was proving to be more problematic than he had expected when he had started out. It had seemed like such a simple idea, but putting it into practice had taken almost twenty human years. To his race that was a mere blink of an eye, of course, but he had found that his time on Earth had influenced him in strange ways. He had come to think like them, even to act like them at times. He hadn't been as polluted by their influence as the Doctor, of course, but if he ever went home he would have to make some changes in his manner.

Twenty years. As he walked down the stairs towards the salon, he remembered the problems, the setbacks and the unmitigated disasters that had befallen him in that time. The whole thing had been on the verge of falling apart at one stage, until he had suggested, albeit reluctantly, involving the Doctor. That had turned the tide. The Doctor was integral to his plans now, and he would not, *could* not stop. Not when he was so close to success. It was a shame that the Doctor's name was so symbolic, but Braxiatel was enough of a realist to accept it, and work with it. He didn't have to like it, though.

Szaratak and Tzorogol, his two Jamarian aides, were standing in the salon waiting for him. As soon as he entered, they turned off their hologuise generators and returned to their thin, horned Jamarian forms.

'What has happened?' Braxiatel asked immediately. 'I wasn't expecting a report until tomorrow morning.'

'We have located the Doctor,' Szaratak grunted. 'The *real* Doctor,' it added, flicking its head back so that its horn whistled through the air. 'He's making his way by coach around the coastline. He'll be in Venice within a few hours.'

'By coach?' Braxiatel frowned. 'Are you sure?'

'Of course we're sure,' Tzorogol snapped. 'He's exactly the way you described him: an old man with sharp features and white hair.'

'This is the only other person for miles around who fits the description,' Szaratak added. 'We did a full scan. How many people do you want around here who look like the Doctor before you decide which one you want?'

'All right,' Braxiatel said, irritated by Szaratak's near-insolence, 'send a welcoming committee of as many envoys as you can round up. Explain the situation to them first. Is the Doctor alone?'

Szaratak and Tzorogol both shook their small heads. 'He has company with him,' Szaratak growled.

'Hmm,' Braxiatel mused, 'he does travel with companions, we know that, and his companions are used to dealing with aliens. Tell the envoys there's no point in using their hologuises. I don't want any misunderstandings on the Doctor's part, and besides, those things drain energy like nobody's business.' He stared at the two Jamarians. 'Was that it, or is there something else?'

They glanced at each other. 'That's it,' Szaratak growled.

'Then get going,' Braxiatel snapped. The two Jamarians glared at him for a moment, then turned to leave. 'And don't forget to turn your hologuises on before you leave the house,' he shouted after them.

Jamarians. He shook his head sadly. To think that he was reduced to using a race too paranoid to develop anything more than a rudimentary civilization. He'd have been better off using Ogrons.

'This is excellent,' the Doctor said, waving his hand across the table. 'A repast fit for a king.'

Vicki smiled enthusiastically as Galileo nodded his

acknowledgement. 'It's wonderful,' she said. 'What *is* everything?'

Galileo took a swig of his wine, and wiped the back of his hand across his mouth. 'Red and yellow peppers in olive oil,' he said, indicating a gaily coloured dish, 'tomatoes stuffed with anchovies, squid and a salad of mozzarella, aubergine and olives. A simple first course. There will be soup and potato dumplings to follow, then calves brains and tongue.'

Vicki looked over to where Steven was gazing morosely at the plate in front of him. Behind him, Galileo's dining room was in semi-darkness, with only the light from the candelabras illuminating the table and the food. In the shadows beyond, Vicki gained the impression of faded velvets and threadbare tapestries. 'Isn't it nice, Steven?' she said brightly, just to see his reaction. She wasn't disappointed: he flinched, startled, then looked around the table.

'Er . . . that's right,' he said, and slumped down again.

'You seem distracted, my boy,' the Doctor said, spearing an olive with his knife. 'Is there something you want to tell us?'

Steven glanced up and flushed guiltily. His eyes flickered towards Galileo. 'No, I . . . What I mean is . . .'

The Doctor's steely gaze fastened on Steven. 'We have all had strange experiences since we arrived here in Venice,' he chided. 'Vicki and I were almost abducted by . . .' He paused, and coughed. 'By persons in disguise, and Vicki has had a dream that turns out to have been more than a dream. When this is added to the invitation we received, well, it makes one think, does it not?' He leaned forward. 'If you have anything to add, and I would be surprised if you didn't, then I suggest you add it now. The more we know about whatever is happening here, the better off we will be!'

Steven opened his mouth to answer, but Galileo beat him to it. 'Don't blame your friend, Doctor,' he said. 'I am the one he is protecting.' He looked from the Doctor

78

to Vicki and back again. 'But before I begin, I assure you that I am blameless in every way.'

The Doctor nodded. 'I will accept that assurance — for the moment.'

'Very well.' Galileo took a deep breath. 'The first "occurrence" as you put it was . . . No, let me tell you about the second one. I will demonstrate the first after dessert. The second was when my wine was poisoned in a nearby tavern.'

'How do you know it was poisoned?' the Doctor queried sharply.

'Because when I threw it into the face of some oaf who insulted me, he died of poisoning,' Galileo replied.

'Seems fairly convincing to me,' Steven murmured to Vicki.

'The third occurrence,' Galileo continued, 'was when your friend Steven and I discovered a dead body not far from here.'

'Poisoned?' Vicki asked.

'No, my dear lady,' Galileo replied with a smile, 'stabbed through the heart with a long, thin blade. A rapier, perhaps, although the ribs were crushed, indicating that the blow was a forceful one.'

'Did you know either of the murdered men?' the Doctor asked.

'The first, no. The second, yes.' Galileo waved a hand at the shadowy room around him. 'He was the owner of this fine house, and thus my landlord.'

'To be at the scene of one murder can be accounted a misfortune,' the Doctor said with a slight smile. 'To be at the scene of two begins to look like carelessness. Do you have any suspects?'

'For the first death — the poisoning?' Galileo shrugged. 'Only the man who bought me the wine. He was an Englishman with long grey hair and a deep scar running down the side of his face —'

Steven, who had just picked up his flagon of wine, suddenly jerked in his chair, spilling wine over his lap.

'Sorry,' he muttered. 'Sudden chill.'

'– Although I suspect that he may have been employed by my enemies, of whom I have many.' Galileo smiled, rather proudly. 'Not only among my contemporaries at the University of Padua, but also among the wider philosophical community. I have proved the valued theorems of many distinguished thinkers to be less worthy of consideration than the maunderings of a village idiot, and they do not thank me for it. I think it would be fair to say that I have many enemies.'

'You surprise me,' the Doctor murmured. 'Is there any more of this fine wine, by the by?'

The crickets were rasping in the bushes and the grass as Cardinal Roberto Bellarmine's coach halted. Disturbed, Bellarmine paused in his reading of the Bible and glanced out of the window. Ahead of him the soldiers were conferring and examining a map. The moon glittered on the waters of the Adriatic and, from their position on top of the rolling hills that swept down toward the shore, Cardinal Bellarmine could just make out the dark bulk of Venice on the horizon, pinpricked with the red spots of torches. To Venice's left the island of Murano lay sleepily: to its right the long line of the Lido separated the lagoon from the sea. Down near the beach, Bellarmine could see a ramshackle collection of huts and, a few yards into the water, the bobbing hulls of fishing boats. There was a fire lit, and a group of fishermen were sitting around it singing and eating. His mouth watered as the smell of cooking fish drifted up the hillside towards him. Perhaps in the name of God these simple fishermen would offer them food and shelter for the night, and carry them across the lagoon to Venice in the morning.

Then again, given the well-known Venetian feelings about the Pope, perhaps not.

As the soldiers conferred, Cardinal Bellarmine took up his reading where he had left off: chapter two of the Book of Hosea. 'Rebuke your mother, rebuke her,' he intoned, 'for she is not my wife and I am not her husband. Let her remove the adulterous look from her face and the unfaithfulness from between her breasts.' He paused for a moment, turning the words over in his mind, searching for meanings within meanings, hidden symbols, links with passages elsewhere in the Bible. Bellarmine firmly believed that the answer to any question was hidden within the Bible, couched in obscure language and poetic imagery. It was the task of theologians such as himself to tease out these answers and apply them to the secular world.

A noise from above made him pause – a great roaring, as if the mother of all lions were showing its wrath. He glanced out of the coach's window, and gasped as he saw a red star falling from the sky to the Earth, casting its fiery light all around. Smoke rose from it like the smoke from a gigantic furnace, and the sky and the stars were blotted out by its passage. A torrent of noise like a trumpet blast blotted out the wild neighing of the horses and the shouts of the soldiers, and made him cover his ears and cower.

His coach suddenly began to shake as the horses jerked in their harnesses. Bellarmine shouted to the driver to calm them down, but the man did not answer. Perhaps he hadn't heard over the roaring. Perhaps he had fled, or fainted. Bellarmine shot a concerned glance out of the window to where the red glare illuminated the hillside and the now deserted beach with the light of hell. If the horses took it into their heads to plunge down that grassy slope then the coach would certainly tip over and smash into firewood. Bellarmine gathered his robes up and, throwing the door open, jumped out just as the coach began to move. The door caught his foot as the horses pulled away, pitching him to the hard ground. As his shoulder and knees hit the earth simultaneously a wave of nausea passed through him. His bible slipped from his grasp and spun away.

The noise and the light ceased. The rasp of crickets in the underbrush gradually began afresh: one at first but soon too many to count.

The coach was receding into the distance and the soldiers had fled; he could see their horses galloping frantically along the path, the riders clinging to the reins. Or perhaps the horses had bolted and the riders were attempting to regain control. Either way, he would receive no help from that direction. Slowly, fearfully, he turned his eyes to the nearby hillside, and a prayer rose unbidden to his lips.

On the hill nearby, on the side away from the beach, sat a glowing wheel, twenty feet across, set around with small hubs that looked like eyes. Bellarmine's legs suddenly gave out, and he sank to his knees. Confusion filled his mind. Surely this was the very object that Ezekiel had written about – the chariot sent by God? What could this mean? Was he being called to Heaven to meet his Maker, or was this one of Satan's tricks?

A section of the great wheel slid aside like a curtain. White light spilled out, so bright that Bellarmine had to shield his eyes. In the midst of the light, four creatures emerged from the wheel. One was taller than Bellarmine, heavily muscled, and had the face of a lion. Another walked on all fours, with a heavy, anvil-like face that bore two short horns. The third had a face like a man, but was taller and thinner than any man had ever been that walked the Earth. The fourth was feathered and winged like an eagle. They were familiar to him. They were like old friends. How often had he turned to those passages in Ezekiel and Revelations, seeking out their secret meanings? Why had he never suspected that the passages might have been literal truth, and that God's Angels bore those forms?

'We have come for you,' the Angels said in unison. 'You are expected.'

And Cardinal Bellarmine broke down in tears.

'An excellent meal,' the Doctor said. 'My compliments to your cook.' He reached out and speared a chunk of cheese from the plate in the centre of the table. 'I always say you can tell the quality of a civilization by the food it eats, don't I, my boy?'

'Yes, Doctor,' Steven dutifully responded. In fact, there were so many things that the Doctor always said that he was beginning to lose count.

'This dessert is wonderful,' Vicki said, spooning more of the thick yellow liquid into her mouth. 'What is it?'

'Zabaglione,' Galileo replied. 'A confection made with eggs, sugar and marsala wine. I am humbled that it meets with your approval. My modest fare is exalted by your glorious beauty. In fact –'

Steven coughed warningly and, when Galileo glanced over at him, Steven shook his head. He'd seen what Galileo was like when he had a few bottles of wine inside him, and he'd had quite a few over dinner. So had Steven. In fact, his head was beginning to swim.

'You said earlier on,' the Doctor mused, 'that there was an unusual occurrence that you would demonstrate after dessert. Am I permitted to know what it might be, or do you intend keeping me in the dark for a while longer?'

Galileo gazed thoughtfully at the Doctor. Despite his prodigious consumption of wine, his gaze was still sharp and watchful. 'Before I do,' he said abruptly, 'I must break one of my personal rules, and discuss religion. You and your companions are, I presume, English: you have that look about you. That may indicate Protestant leanings. However, your perfect grasp of Italian may suggest a long residence in our fair land, leading one to believe that you have Catholic tendencies. But then again, what is Catholic in Venice has been considered heresy in Rome, and vice versa. So, you see, I can come to no firm conclusion concerning at which altar you worship.'

'In a long and eventful life,' the Doctor said eventually, 'I have experienced nothing that I could not account for by the laws of physics, chemistry or biology. If a God or Gods exist, and I cannot rule out the possibility, then I can only presume that He, She or They take no active

83

part in the lives of the many and various creatures that populate this extensive and wonderful universe of theirs.' He picked a crumb of cheese from his plate and swallowed it. 'In addition, I have seen countless races worship countless Gods with attributes which are mutually incompatible, and each race believes itself to be following the one true faith. While I respect their beliefs, I would consider it arrogance for any race to try and impose their beliefs on me, and if I had a belief of my own then it would be equally arrogant of me to impose it on them. In short, sir, I am currently an agnostic, and by the time my life draws to its close, and I have travelled from one side of the universe to the other and seen every sight there is to see, I firmly expect to be an atheist. Does that answer your question?'

'That and several others,' Galileo said. 'You and I have more in common than I had thought.' He stood up. 'Follow me. I have something that might interest you.'

He led Steven, Vicki and the Doctor away from the table, strewn with the remains of their meal, and out into the stairwell. For a moment Steven thought he was going to take them down into the alley outside, but instead he headed upstairs. At the top he climbed up a ladder and threw a trapdoor open. The others followed him up onto a wooden platform which crowned the house. The sky above them was so bright with stars that Steven could have read a book by them, most of them lying in the thick band of the galactic disc. From far below he could hear the lapping of water.

'Careful,' he muttered to Vicki, 'don't lose your footing.'

'Don't worry,' she said. 'I'm as sure footed as a — Oh!' He caught her arm as she stumbled. She pulled her arm free. 'I can look after myself, thank you,' she said.

'You couldn't get much wetter if you *did* fall in,' he whispered to himself as she moved closer to the Doctor.

Galileo and the Doctor were standing beside a shrouded shape. Galileo pulled the covering sheet off with a flourish. Steven couldn't see what the fuss was about: all that was underneath was a crude, low power telescope on a tripod. It looked as if it was made out of brass covered in red leather.

'With this spyglass,' Galileo said proudly, 'I can bring objects sixty times closer. The principle is complex and difficult to explain, and I laboured mightily to produce it. The Doge will pay heavily to obtain it.'

'The principle of refraction is simple enough,' the Doctor said. 'The power is limited, of course, by the distance between your lenses. If you can reflect the light from a concave mirror at the end here —' he indicated the eyepiece, '— and then reflect it out of the side of the spyglass using an inclined plane mirror halfway up, then you could almost double the length and greatly increase the magnifying power. I could suggest other —'

Galileo's face was thunderous. 'There are no improvements to make to this spyglass,' he interrupted. 'I have perfected it.'

'If you say so.' The Doctor smiled at Steven.

'Is this piece of glass meant to be broken?' Vicki said. She was peering into the far end of the telescope.

'What?' Galileo pushed her out of the way. 'What have you done, girl?' He peered at the end of the telescope. 'The lens has been smashed! It took days to produce one to the right specifications, and now it's ruined!'

'I didn't do anything!' Vicki protested. 'It was like that when I found it!'

Galileo whirled around as if he expected to find the saboteur on the platform with them. 'Whoever did this will rue the day that their paths ever crossed that of Galileo Galilei,' he shouted.

'Yes, yes, that's all very well,' the Doctor fussed, 'but I presume that you wanted to show me something through this simple device. Can you not at least tell me what it was that you saw?'

Galileo sighed, and turned back to the Doctor. 'I can do better than that,' he said, still angry, 'I can show you a sketch I made.' From beneath his coat he brought out a roll of parchment and handed it to the Doctor. As Steven watched, the Doctor unrolled it and glanced at whatever illustration it contained.

'I saw it last night,' Galileo said. 'It was travelling between the moon and the Earth. I swear so.'

'I believe you,' the Doctor said. He turned the parchment toward Steven, who drew in his breath sharply. The sketch on the parchment was rough, done in charcoal, but showed a disc like a flattened egg with circular holes along the side.

'Do you recognize it?' the Doctor asked quietly.

Steven met his worried gaze. 'It's a spaceship,' he said tersely.

Seven

William Shakespeare licked the salt from his lips and gazed forlornly at the distant horizon. There was still no sign of Venice, no blemish upon the junction of sea and sky that might indicate the presence of land. The translucent blue sea stretched all around them, as if they were mired in glass. For all Shakespeare knew, they might not have moved for days. He wasn't sure how much more of this he could take. He wasn't a good traveller at the best of times, and this was not the best of times. Not by any reckoning.

The deck beneath his feet rocked with a predictable rhythm as the ship fell forward into each wave and rode up again upon the wave's back, dragging its bulk forward, yard by precious yard. A gust of wind blew spume into his eyes. The salt stung, and he wiped his sleeve angrily across his face. Damn Walsingham! Damn both the Walsinghams. Damn both the Walsinghams and thrice damn the King!

Rope creaked alarmingly against wood in the rigging, and the cries of the sailors were almost indistinguishable from the cries of the birds that flew alongside the ship, waiting patiently, mindlessly, for the slops to be thrown overboard. The slops! Shakespeare's stomach rebelled at the thought of food. He'd forced down some wormy meat and hard biscuit that morning to blunt the edge of his hunger, but it had just come straight back up again. He hadn't kept anything down since leaving Southampton. He wasn't sure if he would ever be able to eat again.

He leant upon the rail and rested his head in his hands. Below him, past the line of portholes, the water slapped against the curve of the hull. And beneath that, what? Fathomless depths. Darkness and silence. How easy it would be to miss one's step, to pitch when the ship was tossing, and to tumble, alone and unnoticed, into that murky abyss. What was the nightmare that he had put in Clarence's mouth in *The Tragedy of King Richard the Third?* 'Lord, Lord, methought what pain it was to drown: what dreadful noise of water in mine ears, what sights of ugly death within mine eyes! Methought I saw a thousand fearful wracks; a thousand men that fishes gnaw'd upon; wedges of gold, great anchors, heaps of pearl, inestimable stones, unvalu'd jewels, all scattered in the bottom of the sea. Some lay in dead men's skulls; and in those holes where eyes did once inhabit, there were crept as 'twere in scorn of eyes, reflecting gems that woo'd the slimy bottom of the deep, and mocked the dead bones that lay scatter'd by.'

He pulled his mind away from those morbid and some-what flowery words, and found them migrating toward the play that they came from. Sudden anger surged up within him – or, at least, he thought it was anger. It might have been the last fragments of his breakfast. Not only had that zooterkin Christopher Marlowe stolen some of his themes for *Edward II*, but that coney-catching mounte-bank Francis Pearson had produced his own inferior copy and called it *The True Tragedie of Richard the Third*. Marlowe was dead, thank the Lord, and Pearson was a talentless hack who would never amount to anything, but there was no saying what was happening in London with Shakespeare gone. He could return to find his entire body of work being performed under other titles by inferior actors, with some upstart writer getting all the credit. Worse still, *Macbeth* was in rehearsal, ready to be performed before the King at Hampton Court Palace. What travesties might Richard Burbage and the rest of the King's Men commit upon it in his absence?

Perhaps he should think about returning to Stratford, his family and his grain-dealing business. Writing was a fool's game. Long hours, low pay and little praise.

Just like spying, really.

'All right, Mr Hall?'

Shakespeare almost didn't acknowledge the sailor walking past, but at the last moment he remembered his false identity – the one that Walsingham had persuaded him to take on for this mission. 'Feeling a little unsteady,' he replied.

'Get some victuals down your neck,' the sailor shouted back over his shoulder.

'Thank you,' Shakespeare muttered. 'I'll try.' He turned to stare across the damp boards at his fellow passengers, trying to distract his mind from the warring sensations of hunger and nausea. There were other Englishmen aboard, but they seemed to be avoiding him as assiduously as he was avoiding them. Their dress was old fashioned and much patched, and despite their gaiety he discerned some darker feeling within them, some hidden mood that could only be glimpsed in their eyes.

Or perhaps he was just being foolish. What had possessed him, agreeing to this absurd mission? His work as an informant and courier for Francis Walsingham, the Secretary of State whose network of agents and informers had been set up to protect the Queen from Catholic plots, had been fulfilling and financially rewarding. The work had taken him across Europe, from Denmark to Venice, and provided the raw material for many of his plays, but when Walsingham died Shakespeare had thought that he was free of the life of intrigue, free to return to grain dealing and acting. No such luck. Thomas Walsingham had taken over where his cousin had left off. Shakespeare was still an agent of the crown, as were Ben Jonson and half the other playwrights in London. If any of them needed to be reminded of the risks, all they had to do was remember Christopher Marlowe, stabbed in a tavern in Deptford. Marlowe, of course, had been one that loved a cup of hot wine: drunkenness had been his best virtue, and it was handy-dandy whether that or his spying had led to his death.

Shakespeare shuddered as he recalled Walsingham's ascetic face, floating on a foam-like ruff above his raven-black robes, his hair hidden by a skullcap. And that voice! That cold, dry voice! 'You will travel to Venice. You are familiar with the city? Good. A reliable agent tells me that the Doge is negotiating with a previously unknown Empire – probably in the East – for lucrative trade concessions. The King wishes you to determine the truth of this matter and engage in preliminary negotiations on his behalf with this Empire. While you are gone, we will put about the rumour that you are secluded, writing a new play. It is an explanation that has served us before – it will work again.'

Walsingham's planning was impeccable, his logic unassailable, his force of personality unquestionable. And so Shakespeare, playwright, grain merchant and sometime spy, found himself the prisoner of circumstance, bound once again for Venice – home of Shylock and of Othello – without a clue as to how to accomplish his mission.

He looked up into the ship's rigging: a tangled mass of ropes and wooden spars suspended like some solid cloud above his head. A sailor swung one-handed from it as he climbed up to the crow's nest. Despite his sea-sickness and his terror of heights, Shakespeare would happily have swapped lives with him. Quite happily.

'Sleep well, my dear.' The Doctor smiled and patted Vicki's arm as they entered their salon. Somewhere out in St Mark's Square, a clock tolled twice. 'Although I'm sure that you won't have any problems after that marvellous meal.'

'*I* certainly won't,' Steven muttered. He was weaving slightly as he crossed the ornate carpet towards his bedroom.

'Not considering the amount you drank.' The Doctor's

tone was reproving, but Vicki could see a twinkle in his eye. 'Good night, my boy. Breakfast at eight sharp. Don't be late.'

The sound of the door slamming behind him cut off Steven's grunted reply.

The Doctor took a step towards his own bedroom. Vicki felt a panicky sensation swell up in her chest. She didn't want to be left alone. Not that night. Not if she might wake up to find something . . . something *alien* . . . sitting on her windowsill. 'You're in a good mood,' she said rapidly.

The Doctor stopped and nodded. 'I found Mr Galileo to be a most congenial companion. Most congenial indeed. It is so seldom that I get a chance to converse with somebody almost on my own intellectual level.'

Vicki couldn't help but smile to herself. The Doctor was so blithely unaware of how conceited he sometimes sounded. 'Better not let Steven hear you say that,' she said. 'He might take offence. He thinks he's the intellectual equivalent of everyone.'

'That,' the Doctor said drily, 'is his main problem.' He turned to face her. 'You don't seem to mind an old man's ways, however,' he said, his voice unusually hesitant. 'Do I seem arrogant to you, child?'

Vicki opened her mouth to reply, then caught herself. For once the Doctor was asking her a serious question. The least he deserved was a serious answer. 'No,' she said finally, 'because you're not an old man.' She took a deep breath. 'In fact, you're not a man at all, are you?'

His clear blue eyes gazed at her for a moment, then he nodded slightly, more in acknowledgement of a point scored than in answer. Crossing to the divan he busied himself with plumping up cushions and sitting down. 'And what makes you think that?' he said finally.

'A lot of things.' Vicki crossed her arms and walked over to the window. Outside, the throng of revellers and traders was no different from when she had woken up. Only the faces had changed. 'Barbara and Ian were

91

suspicious of you . . . I don't mean that they thought you were evil or anything like that – just that you weren't what you seemed. Barbara confided in me one night, shortly before they left. Since then I've been watching you, and . . .' She shrugged. 'You look like a man, you talk like a man, but you're not. There's something about the way you watch people sometimes, like I used to look at Sandy.'

'Sandy?' he prompted.

'My sand monster, back on Dido. I loved him, but not in the same way I loved my mother and my father. And that's the way you love us, isn't it? Like we're pets.'

She waited, feeling as if she was standing on the edge of a cliff, and it was too dark to see where the bottom was. The Doctor's face didn't change, but she could sense a certain re-evaluation going on underneath the surface.

'You're very . . . sensitive,' he said finally. 'That is your greatest strength. That, and your ability to play up to the image that people have of you.'

'Then . . .?'

He smiled. 'Then what am I? A wanderer, my dear. A wanderer and a survivor. I am not of your race. I am not of your Earth. I am a wanderer in the fourth dimension of space and time, a refugee from an ancient civilization, cut off from my own people by aeons of time and universes far beyond human understanding.'

'And was Susan a wanderer too?'

His face suddenly clouded over. 'Susan? Who told you about Susan?'

'Barbara did.' Vicki suddenly felt as if she had been thrown on the defensive. 'She said that Susan was your granddaughter, and she left the TARDIS to get married.'

The Doctor stood. 'Yes, Susan was my granddaughter, if such terms can be applied to beings like us. I loved Susan. I loved her very much. And now that she has gone, I miss her more than you will ever know. I feel that I am . . .'

'Alone?' Vicki suggested gently.

The Doctor nodded. 'Alone,' he confirmed. 'When I left, she came with me. She could have stayed, but she felt that I needed looking after.' The Doctor's face was suddenly haggard. 'Although she was sweet, and guileless, and innocent, she was the closest thing to a conversational partner of my own level. There were things that we could talk about that would be meaningless babble to . . .' He shot Vicki a guilty glance. '. . . to anybody else. She was the only person who understood.'

'Understood what?' Vicki whispered.

'Who I am,' the Doctor said, not meeting her gaze. 'Why I left. Where I was going. And now . . .'

Vicki was about to say something trivial and comforting when there was a flurry of wings outside the window. For a moment she thought that a flock of pigeons were landing on the ledge outside, but when the shadow of a huge pair of wings blotted out the firelight from the square below she gestured to the Doctor to back away, out of the line of sight of the window. He did so, quickly and silently. The windowsill creaked as something heavy settled upon it. The bright light of the moon cast a squat shadow across the carpet.

'Vicki?' The voice was as musical and calming as she remembered.

'Yes?' she said, her throat suddenly dry.

'Alarmed do not be. Albrellian it is. Souls briefly last night touched did ours.'

'I thought you were a dream.'

Albrellian laughed: a high-pitched trilling. 'Happy a nightmare not considered am I. Afraid that forgotten might have you me.'

'How could I forget,' she said, 'a charming alien perched outside my window.'

There was a pause. 'That not of this Earth am I know you. So, one of the Doctor's companions are you. That means . . .' Albrellian trailed off, as if it was thinking things through.

'Yes,' the Doctor said, stepping forward into the light. 'And *I* am the Doctor. The definitive article, so to speak. Might I ask you to step into the room, sir, and show yourself to us, rather than skulk outside the window like a common Lothario.'

Albrellian drew his breath in sharply. For a moment, nothing happened, then the bulky shadow on the windowsill moved forward into the light of the torches. The first thing to emerge from the shadows was a strangely formed limb like a length of bamboo terminating in something like the claw of a crab but with four opposable sections of different sizes. A second claw followed, and then the creature's body. Albrellian was an arthropod the size of a human, but much broader and shorter. He had three pairs of powerful walking legs and two pairs of the more delicate crab-like manipulatory appendages that Vicki had first seen. His hard shell was dark red in colour, covered in irregular maroon blotches, with a ruff of maroon hair sprouting from the top. Four stalked eyes emerged from the hair – two of which were fixed upon the Doctor and two upon Vicki. As Vicki watched, entranced, a pair of leathery wings folded themselves up and slid beneath a section of shell that hinged back to cover them.

'Thank you,' the Doctor said. He slipped his thumbs beneath the lapels of his coat. 'It seems that introductions are in order. As I have said, I am the Doctor. My companion, with whom I believe you have already talked, is Vicki. And you are . . . ?'

'Albrellian, of the Greld, am I.'

'The Greld?' The Doctor frowned. 'Forgive me: I am unfamiliar with your race.'

'Dealers in . . . technology are we. Home around the star that humans call Canopus make we.'

'Then you are a long way from that home.' There was a querulous, aggressive tone to the Doctor's voice. 'I hope that you do not intend extending the Greld commonwealth in this direction.'

94

'Home is indeed far away my,' Albrellian said, maintaining eye-contact with the Doctor, 'but further away still from *your* home, lord of time, are you.'

The Doctor raised his eyebrows. 'You know of me?'

Albrellian bowed its great shell until the rim was touching the carpet. 'Deeds the stuff of legend are your.'

The Doctor glanced over at Vicki and raised his eyebrows. She shrugged helplessly. There was a definite subtext to the conversation, but she was at a loss to know what it was.

'What did you mean,' the Doctor asked, 'when you recognized Vicki as one of my companions and started to draw a conclusion from that fact?'

'Thoughts were bewildered my,' Albrellian admitted, straightening itself up. 'Arrival with awe and trepidation awaiting have been your we. Only this evening informed that on the mainland and taken to Laputa you and your travelling companions were met was I. Surprised was I, for when last night to Vicki talked I, convinced that with you she was was I, and both in Venice here were you. Somewhere along the line, a message has been garbled.'

'I don't understand what you are talking about,' the Doctor snapped. 'Your grammar could do with some practice. What or where is Laputa?'

'The island.' Albrellian turned to Vicki. 'Surely understand you?'

Vicki shook her head. 'All I know is that we were invited here for some reason, but we don't know why.'

'Laputa,' the Doctor murmured to Vicki, 'was a fictional island in Jonathan Swift's *Gulliver's Travels*, but that book won't be written for another hundred years. Is something happening here that Swift will write about, or does someone else here have knowledge before its time?'

'Show Albrellian the invitation, Doctor,' Vicki urged. 'Perhaps he might be able to tell us who sent it.'

The Doctor slipped his hand into his coat and pulled out the impossibly white slip of material. 'This was given to me under mysterious circumstances,' he said. 'Perhaps you can shed some light on its meaning.'

Albrellian reached a claw into a crevice in its shell and drew out a similar white slip. 'All have them do we,' it said simply. 'That is why here are we.'

The Doctor reached out and took the invitation from Albrellian's claw. He turned it over and looked at it, then wordlessly held it out to Vicki. The words were the same as the ones she remembered from the invitation that the Doctor had bought back with him from . . . from wherever it was that he had been taken.

INVITATION

Formal dress required.

R.S.V.P.

'An invitation to what?' she asked helplessly.

'Games do not play Doctor,' Albrellian whooped. 'The invitation a formality is. By the messenger who delivered it to you fully briefed must have been you.'

The Doctor handed the slip of paper back to the Greld. 'If I was briefed,' he said, 'then I have forgotten the briefing. There is a small period of my life that I cannot recall. Perhaps, if I could, then all would be clear to me.'

'And the information within the invitation itself what about? How else did get here you?'

The Doctor shrugged. 'My travelling machine took care of that. The invitation itself guided us.'

Albrellian shifted all four of its eyes to the Doctor. 'Difficult your assurances to accept find it I,' it said. 'Some kind of artifice this is off balance to get us all. Concessions from us want you.'

'Don't be so foolish,' the Doctor snapped. 'How can I want concessions when I don't even know what's being conceded, or in what forum?'

'When the Convention only hope of peace is our, how games can play you?' Albrellian shouted.

'Convention?' The Doctor was frowning. 'What convention? Where?'

'The Convention on Laputa!'

The Doctor and Albrellian were eyeballs to eyeballs now, and both were shouting so loud that they could probably be heard from the Square below. 'I have no intention of going to any convention, on Laputa or otherwise, until I know exactly what is going on!'

'But needed are you! Without you proceed cannot we!'

The Doctor shook his head firmly and folded his arms across his chest. 'I will not be manipulated any further,' he said. 'Here I am and here I stay until someone explains to me precisely what is going on.'

'If prepared to games play are you, then so am I.' Albrellian sprang across the room. Before she could move, Vicki found her arms and legs pinioned in a firm but gentle grip by all four of his manipulatory appendages. 'On Laputa friend will be your, when bothered to turn up can be you.'

'Doctor –' Vicki cried, but Albrellian's claws tightened on her limbs. She cried out, more in surprise than in pain, and struggled, but it made no difference.

The Doctor made as if to intercept Albrellian, but the alien moved towards the window.

'Where she'll be, know you,' the alien whistled, and jumped out of the window.

In his library, Irving Braxiatel sighed in relief. Everything was going to be all right. 'And you say that the Doctor is sleeping happily?' he asked, just to hear the good news again.

Szaratak nodded its thin, knobbly head. 'The envoys brought him in an hour or so ago. Apparently he was so tired that he fell asleep on the ground in front of them. They carried him into a skiff and took him straight to Laputa.'

'And his companions?'

Szaratak shrugged, although with a Jamarian's build it was more of a ripple. 'It would appear that they haven't been with the Doctor for very long. The sight of the envoys frightened them. They ran off.'

Braxiatel ran a hand through his hair. 'You've done well, Szaratak. Which envoys did you send, by the way?'

'The first ones I could find – Ontraag, Jullatii, Dentraal and Oolian.'

'Nothing too frightening there,' Braxiatel said. 'And the imposter?'

'Imposter?'

'The person wandering around Venice pretending to be the Doctor. The one who ran away when you approached him in the Doge's palace.'

'He's probably still there. Shall I deal with him?'

Braxiatel thought for a moment. He couldn't afford to have an imposter wandering around – not with the Convention about to start. It might prove – disruptive. 'I have to leave for Laputa,' he said. 'Get him out of the way.'

'Permanently?' Szaratak asked softly.

Braxiatel's mind was already occupied with agendas and arrangements. 'Yes, of course,' he said.

Behind him, Szaratak snickered. Braxiatel thought little of it as he left the library and walked down the flight of stairs to the ground floor. His staff – Jamarians, most of them, but with their hologuises on almost all the time – were at the front door unloading vegetables from a boat tied up on the canal. He passed by them without a word and walked through to the back of the house. Checking to ensure that he wasn't observed – he had deliberately kept security on the house light because he didn't want to make the locals suspicious – he stopped by a particularly ornate tapestry and pulled it back from the wall. There was a metal door set into the bricks behind it, and he keyed his personal code into the security lock in its centre. The door slid back into the wall and he walked down the revealed steps into the new watertight room that the Jamarians had built beneath the house.

The room was essentially a white metal box with a path around the edge of a pool of water. A small control panel was set into one wall. The pool was at the same level as the canal outside, and in its centre floated an ambassadorial skiff, smooth and ovoid, like a rather fat metal egg. Braxiatel glanced back, checking that the security door had closed behind him, then walked to the edge of the pool.

'Open,' he muttered. An opening appeared in the side of the skiff. He stepped into the cool, dark interior. 'Shut.' A constellation of multi-coloured lights sprang to life around the circumference of the skiff as the door closed. Braxiatel sat in the form-fitting central seat and ran his hands across the lights: adjusting course, speed and power. Laputa and the Armageddon Convention were waiting for him.

Galileo's hand began to ache — a deep-seated grinding pain in the bone that he was all too familiar with — so he switched the paddle from one side of the Doctor's strange boat to the other. 'I still say we should have paid a gondolier to take us,' he grumbled.

'I didn't want to involve anyone else in this business,' the Doctor said, shading his eyes from the rays of the early morning sun which slanted across the flat surface of the lagoon. In his other hand he held a long tube capped with glass lenses — a spyglass, but one larger and better finished than Galileo's.

The island with the blue box from which the Doctor had retrieved the spyglass had vanished into the mists behind the Doctor, and Galileo had his back to Venice as he rowed. He felt as if they were cocooned in a white shroud. 'You mean that you don't trust anybody,' he said.

'That too.'

'Then what about your friend — Steven? He's built like an ox. Couldn't he have rowed us?'

The Doctor squinted and peered ahead, over Galileo's

shoulder. 'No sign of Venice yet, my boy,' he said. 'No, I asked Steven to take a look around for Vicki. I don't hold out much hope that she's still there, but I prefer not to make unwarranted assumptions. Best to rule the city out of our consideration. I'm far more certain that if we can trace that spaceship you saw to this place Laputa that Albrellian talked about, we'll find Vicki.'

'Ships that travel through the void of space, beings from other worlds, boxes that are barely larger than a coffin and yet can swallow you up for ten minutes while you look for your spyglass . . .' Galileo shook his head in bewilderment. 'You ask a lot of a man's imagination, Doctor. By rights I should call you a heretic, if not a lunatic, but I find you strangely convincing, and your words strike chords in my own thoughts.'

'You are a man of unusual breadth of vision, Galileo.' The Doctor gazed into his eyes. 'If anybody in this time is prepared to believe in life on other worlds, it is you.'

'Twenty years ago,' Galileo grumbled, 'in the Academy of Florence, I gave a learned discourse on the exact location, size and shape of Dante's Inferno and, using pure logic, I proved that the Devil himself was two thousand arm-lengths in height.' He gazed levelly at the Doctor. 'That doesn't mean that I actually *believe* that the Devil is two thousand arm-lengths in height. I apply logic to everything and I believe nothing.'

'An admirable, if somewhat narrow, outlook.' The Doctor's gaze switched over Galileo's shoulder again. 'I think we're bearing a little to port. You'd best switch back to your other hand.'

'I get arthritis in my other hand,' Galileo snapped. 'Besides, I'm an astronomer, not a sailor. Perhaps you would like to take a turn?'

'The exercise will do you good,' the Doctor said with a slight smile. 'Besides, have you no respect for my age?'

'Not much,' Galileo admitted. 'There are older professors at the University of Padua who I hold in great contempt. Age can lead to stupidity as well as wisdom.'

'Then perhaps if I point out that I'm doing this for you . . .'

'How so?' Galileo asked, then swore as a splinter jabbed into his palm. He let the boat drift for a moment while he carefully pulled it out, then took the opportunity to glance over his shoulder. The dark, low bulk of one of Venice's many islands was just visible through the veils of mist.

'The objective lens of your spyglass was smashed,' the Doctor said as Galileo began to pull on the oars again. 'It would take time for the Venetian glass-makers to make a new one – time we do not have. This particular model –' he waved the metal tube '– has somewhat greater magnifying power.'

Galileo was about to make a cutting rejoinder when he felt the boat rock beneath them. 'I think we've hit a sandbank,' he said, pulling back on the oars.

'I don't think so.' The Doctor frowned. 'I can't see anything.'

'Well, there's *something* beneath us.' Galileo glanced over the side.

And saw mad, red eyes looking up at him.

Before he could shout a warning to the Doctor, the entire boat heaved to one side. The last thing Galileo saw before his head went beneath the waves and water forced its way into his mouth and nostrils was the Doctor's despairing face, and the bony hand that was pulling him down.

Eight

Steven cursed beneath his breath as he pushed through the crowds. Damn Vicki for getting herself kidnapped like that. It wasn't as if he didn't already have enough to worry about without having to track her down as well. The Nicolottis probably still thought he was Galileo Galilei and, judging by what they were going to do to him last time, the last thing he wanted to do was show his face in the alleys of Venice. The Doctor, however, had virtually ordered him to wander around the city and listen out for any odd stories of large flying creatures. Steven had argued, but arguing with the Doctor never did any good.

He paused for a moment on a wooden bridge that arced across a particularly scummy canal. There was no balustrade – just a wooden rim a few inches high, and he rested one foot on it as he gazed along the waterway. Wooden stumps projected out of the water like rotting teeth, and the houses were multi-coloured and festooned with climbing plants. The top two storeys of the walls to his right glowed as the sunlight slanted in across the roofs to illuminate them. A figure moved on a platform attached to one particular roof: a woman wearing a hat with a hole cut in the top. Her hair cascaded out of the missing crown, and she was running her hands through it, spreading it out along the brim of the hat and angling her head to catch the sun's rays. Steven wasn't sure if she was drying her hair or bleaching it, but the artless, unselfconciousness of her actions caught his attention and brought a strange lump to his throat. He looked away,

102

aware of tears prickling his eyes. Every time he thought he'd got over it, something would remind him of his imprisonment.

How many years had he been locked up in that cell on Mechanus? After a while, every day had come to resemble the one before and the one after. Sometimes he had woken up, panicky and sweating, unsure whether he had been asleep for minutes, hours or days. He had come to hate the unfaltering beat of his heart, knowing that it was ticking away his life. He had always been under observation by the Mechanoids – or, at least, he *could* have been, and he had lived out his incarceration assuming that he was. He could do nothing without wondering what the Mechanoids were thinking as they watched. And now, to see a woman so obviously luxuriating in the warmth of the sun on her skin without worrying who was watching her, reminded him of what he had been missing all those years. Sunlight. Privacy. Female companionship.

Steven sighed. This wasn't getting him any closer to finding Vicki. He'd listened in to conversations in shops and taverns, in alleys, on bridges, in churches and shouted between windows, but nobody had mentioned seeing anything odd at all. Mostly they had been talking about taxes, the Pope and who was sleeping with whom. The only conversation that was even slightly out of the ordinary concerned the unusual number of Englishmen in old fashioned clothes who had recently arrived in Venice, and Steven didn't think that had any relevance to Vicki's disappearance.

A hand caught his shoulder and spun him around. He raised an arm to knock it away, but his wrists and elbows were suddenly pinioned by two burly men in half-armour, one on either side. Between them was a man their equal in size but dressed far more elaborately. His eyes were a cold, pure blue in colour, and his face was set into lines of disdain and contempt.

'You have a choice,' he said, his voice a deep growl.

'You can tell me where to find Galileo Galilei, or you can die.'

'Who the hell do you think you are?' Steven shouted, confused at the speed of events. He tried to catch the eye of someone in the passing crowd, but the four of them were isolated in a little bubble of privacy in the centre of the throng.

'I am Tommaso Nicolotti,' the man said. 'Galileo killed my son. I will kill him. That is the way of things.' His voice was as toneless and dispassionate as his face. 'My eldest son, Antonio, tells me that you are a friend and confidant of Galileo: so much so that Antonio mistook you for Galileo yesterday. That being so, you will tell me where he is.'

'I don't know!' Steven snarled. 'And if I did, I wouldn't tell you!' He tugged at the arms that were holding him, but they were as immovable as iron bands.

'Foolish,' Tommaso chided. He pulled a thin, needle-like knife from a hidden sheath. 'Very foolish. You will tell me, of course, and soon. I do not have time for elaborate games, so I will merely remove your ears and your nose. Then your eyes. You *will* tell me.'

Steven's heart was racing so fast and so hard that he could feel his eyeballs bulge slightly with each beat. Desperate, he sagged forward as if he was going to faint, and fluttered his eyes upwards. The armoured guards relaxed their grip slightly as his weight bore down on them, and he suddenly flung himself backwards. His heel caught the wooden rim of the bridge and he toppled backwards. One of the guards reached out for Steven's hair, and Steven twisted, turning his fall into a dive. The last thing he saw before he hit the water was Tommaso Nicolotti's face twisted into a snarl of pure rage.

The shock of hitting the cold water drove the air from Steven's lungs. His heart hammered in his chest. He struck out beneath the surface, desperately trying to put some distance between him and the Nicolottis. There was so much murk suspended in the water that he couldn't see further than a few inches. He was close to one of the walls, and he reached out for the crumbling, weed-encrusted bricks, but his fingers just slid helplessly off. Roaring sounds deafened him, and his lungs burned as he tried to keep from gasping for air. Another ten seconds: he could manage that. Nine more seconds, then he could surface and breathe again. Eight more seconds before he dare –

Something smooth and metallic emerged from a large, dark opening and brushed past his body. Steven's hand caught on a projecting bump on its surface and his body was pulled along behind it before his mind could even catch up with what was happening. The enormity of what had happened filled his thoughts to the extent that he forgot that he needed to breathe, forgot that his heart was about to burst, forgot that his lungs were crying out for oxygen. All he knew was that there was something artificial down there with him, something the size of a small spacecraft that vibrated with pent-up power, something that suddenly twisted sideways, turning into an intersecting canal, taking him with it.

And then it accelerated away, pulling out of his hand and vanishing into the murk. The eddies of its passage sent him spinning, and just as his tortured lungs over-rode everything else and he opened his mouth to breathe, his head emerged from the water. Coughing and spluttering, he floated for a moment in the murky waters of the canal. All thoughts of Tommaso Nicolotti had vanished from his mind, expunged by the undeniably artificial shape that he had felt beneath his hand. What was going on?

White on blue: that was all she could see. That was all there was. Blue skies and blue seas, with an almost imperceptible horizon between the two. White clouds hanging against the backcloth of the sky, and white crests to the waves so far below. White on blue, and sometimes she didn't know which was sky and clouds, and which was waves and sea.

And red. The glossy redness of Albrellian's claws holding her arms and her legs and his great wings scything through the air.

White and blue and red.

Vicki closed her eyes and tried to quell her nausea. She didn't know how long they had been flying for, but the pointed roofs and church steeples of Venice had vanished behind them long ago, and the sky had shaded up from black through cobalt blue to violet before the sun had appeared above the horizon. Now the sun was hidden behind Albrellian's body, sending their shadows skipping over the waves far below.

Vicki had given up asking Albrellian where they were going. He had said nothing since flinging himself out of the window and carrying her away. His claws were cutting into her flesh so tightly that her hands and feet had gone numb. She had tried asking him to loosen up a bit, but it was as if he couldn't hear her. Because of the way he was gripping her she couldn't even try to prise them open. Not that it would do her much good if she could. All Albrellian had to do was open his claws and she would fall, tumbling and screaming, all the way down to the distant waves.

Vicki sighed, and let her head hang down. Keeping it straight so that she could look ahead was just causing the muscles in her neck to spasm. How much longer was this going to go on? She wasn't sure whether to be bored or terrified.

The waves rolled ceaselessly beneath them. Wind buffeted her hair into her eyes. She looked up again, hoping that there would be some change to the dull, monotonous view.

And there was.

Far ahead, just breasting the horizon, an island had appeared. Vicki squinted, trying to make out more details. It was a vibrant green against the calm sea, like an emerald set on blue velvet. As they got closer, Vicki could make out a fringe of golden beach and buildings half-hidden by the foliage: geodesic domes and smooth-walled cones, upside-down pyramids and slender towers supporting oval caps. To one side of the island there was a cleared expanse of ground that had been covered with a flat, grey surfacing material. Vicki gasped as she caught sight of ranks of egg-shaped metal objects that glinted in the sun, lined up on the grey surface. They looked suspiciously like short-range spaceships.

Albrellian said something, but the wind snatched it from Vicki's ears. 'Pardon?' she yelled, and chuckled slightly at her politeness.

' "Laputa" said I,' Albrellian said.

'The island?'

'Yes, the island.'

Vicki craned her neck, trying to see Albrellian's face. 'So we're talking again, are we?' she shouted.

'What –' Albrellian hesitated. 'What to say was not sure I. On impulse acted did I, away like that taking you. Angry at the Doctor was I, and . . .'

Vicki wasn't sure whether Albrellian had trailed off or whether the wind had whipped his words away again. 'And what?' she prompted.

'And wanted to you to talk did I.'

'We were talking, weren't we?'

'Properly wanted to you to talk did I, with care to your words to listen, into your eyes deeply to look.'

That, Vicki reflected, didn't sound very promising. She was about to say something else when they began to lose height, descending towards the island. She couldn't help noticing that despite the idyllic landscaping, the island was ringed with towers on which weapon batteries were mounted. The closest battery was tracking them as they approached Laputa.

'We *are* safe, aren't we?' Vicki asked.

'Do not worry,' Albrellian said. 'Biomorphic code recognize will they my.'

'Are you sure?' She hoped that her voice didn't sound as nervous to Albrellian as it did to her.

'Before it has worked. Of leaving the island us disapprove do they, but when we do, shoot down us can hardly they.' Albrellian sounded smug. 'After all, do not a war to start want they.'

'Want who?'

'Braxiatel and his Jamarian cronies.'

Before Vicki could ask who Braxiatel was, Albrellian folded his wings and dived towards a balcony halfway up one of the towers. Vicki suppressed a scream as the bland, curved surface rushed towards them. At the last moment Albrellian flung his wings wide open to brake their descent. A flurry of air forced Vicki to close her eyes. She felt Albrellian release her legs and then, as her feet swung to touch the ground, her arms. She opened her eyes to find him settling calmly on the balcony in front of her. Behind him was an opening screened by a transparent shield through which Vicki could see a luxuriously appointed apartment with glowing computer screens and control surfaces.

'Home to welcome my,' Albrellian said.

Vicki folded her arms. 'And do you want to tell me why you've brought me here?'

'Would have realized by now hoped I would you,' Albrellian said. 'It is because love you I.'

A rat swam straight at the view screen of Braxiatel's skiff as the vessel left the Grand Canal, peering at the tiny camera lens as if it could actually see inside. The vessel accelerated past the creature, knocking it aside, and Braxiatel caught a last sight of its little legs scrabbling away ineffectually as it tumbled in the skiff's turbulent wake.

At least, he hoped it was a rat. It might have been the Devgherrian Envoy out for a night on the town. Braxiatel had left instructions with his Jamarian staff that none of the envoys were allowed off the island, but the envoys knew full well that the Jamarians had no power to stop them. Some of them respected Braxiatel's instructions, but others — and Albrellian was a prime example — were out every night.

Braxiatel couldn't blame them. After all, he was living in Venice rather than on Laputa because he didn't like being cooped up.

A quick check of the monitor screens showed no gondolas or fishing vessels around, so Braxiatel accelerated through the murky water of the lagoon. Up on the surface a wake would be forming, but there was no one around to see it, apart perhaps from some foolhardy swimmer. Braxiatel waited for a few seconds, just long enough for the ever-present mists to draw in and hide the land, and then he ran his hands across the controls. The skiff's course changed, angling up toward the surface. The water grew lighter, bluer, until, in a sudden flurry of foam, the skiff broke the surface and continued smoothly upward into the sky. Within moments the waves had vanished into the mist below, and the skiff was cruising at seagull height.

Braxiatel sighed and leaned back in his chair. It was a lovely day out there. Best make the most of it: things were bound to go rapidly downhill once he got to Laputa.

Galileo's mouth and nostrils were full of salt water, and his lungs were burning with the desire to breathe. The sudden plunge into the cold lagoon had disoriented him completely: he didn't know which way was up and which was down. His arms and legs flailed wildly, involuntarily, churning up the water and confusing him even more as bubbles and sediment roiled in all directions. The desperate urge to breathe was like a huge lump in his throat, and his heart was pounding against his ribs hard enough to break them. He could feel the wild pumping of blood in his ears and his neck and his temples. Red-flecked darkness crowded around him, pressing insistently upon his ever-weakening thoughts. He could feel his movements becoming weaker, his arms beating more slowly through the resisting water, moving like weeds with the current. He was dying. He was already dead.

His right hand suddenly met with less resistance as it thrashed. Blindly he pushed himself in that direction. Moments or eternities later, his head broke water. Desperately he whooped in great gulps of air, and it was the sweetest, most precious thing he had ever tasted. He would have swapped all the wine in his cellars for it, and never regretted the transaction.

As his senses calmed, Galileo became aware of his surroundings. The mist had closed in, and he could only see for a few feet, but there was no sign of either the Doctor or the boat. Over the rushing of blood in his ears he could make out a commotion in the water nearby. Weakly, he swam towards the sound, and within moments he could see, through the mist, two figures. One – an unnaturally etiolated figure with a prominent horn – was holding the other's head under the surface of the lagoon. Around the head of the submerged figure, a halo of white hair floated on the water.

Beyond them, scarcely more than a dark blot against the mist, was the overturned shape of the Doctor's boat.

For a moment, but only for a moment, Galileo considered swimming around the struggling figures. The Doctor was old and feeble, and the other creature was like nothing Galileo had ever seen or heard about before. He never really knew why he didn't leave them, but suddenly he found himself drawing on his last reserves of energy to swim into the fray. The creature that was holding the Doctor's head beneath the surface glanced up as he splashed towards them, glaring at Galileo out of two small, red eyes that held a glint of madness within them. As Galileo moved to grab its arm it lowered its head toward him. The horn that extended amazingly from its head waved before Galileo's eyes like a fencing foil. He swam sideways for a few feet, but the creature followed him with its horn. It obviously wasn't going to let itself be interrupted.

The Doctor's struggles were growing weaker now, and his hands were fluttering against the surface of the water like drowning sparrows.

Something bumped against Galileo's arm. He jerked back, expecting another of the Doctor's Godless attackers to come lunging from the water at him, but it was only a hollow metal tube. It took Galileo a few seconds to recognize it as the Doctor's spyglass, and a few seconds longer to realize how useful it could be. Before the creature could register what he was doing he scooped it from the water and swung it like a club. The tube caught the creature just below its mighty horn, bending the metal and sending a jarring shock all the way up Galileo's arm. The creature bellowed in pain, and glared at Galileo with surprise and fury in its tiny mad eyes. Galileo swung the spyglass again, aiming at one of the eyes. The creature tried to duck but the Doctor's body bucked violently, jerking both of them out of the water a little further. The spyglass caught it at the almost imperceptible junction between its knob-like head and its skeletal body. The tube twisted even further, and green fluid sprayed from a gash in the creature's skin. Screaming shrilly, it let go of the Doctor. He bobbed to the surface, coughing and spluttering, as the creature fell back into the water.

It resurfaced briefly, its head at an angle, and scowled at Galileo. 'Later . . .' it hissed, then submerged again. Galileo waited, spyglass poised, for it to bob to the surface again, or grab at his legs and pull him under, but nothing happened.

'Thank you, my boy,' the Doctor said from behind him.

Galileo manoeuvred himself around in the water until he was facing the elderly man. 'What was that thing?' he asked. 'A demon from the nether regions of hell?'

'A creature from another globe, circling another sun,' the Doctor said, treading water. 'Perhaps you'll believe me now.' He paused, and closed his eyes for a moment.

'Are you alright?' Galileo asked.

111

'Perfectly fine, thank you very much,' the Doctor replied, opening his eyes again, 'although how much longer I would have remained in that state is a moot point. Thank you for your timely intervention.'

Galileo waved the buckled spyglass at the Doctor. 'You said it would come in useful,' he said, and smiled.

'Indeed,' the Doctor said. A scowl crossed his face. 'But did you have to damage it so badly? It *was* the only one I had.'

Cardinal Roberto Bellarmine was sitting on the edge of the sumptuously comfortable bed that he had woken up in, gazing around the plain but elegant room and amazed at the fact that people still slept in Heaven, when the door slid silently open. The creature that entered was thin to the point of starvation. Its skin was knobbly, like the bark of a tree, and a horn like a slender willow branch extended upward from a skull the size of a clenched fist. In fact, it looked like nothing so much as a man made out of sticks.

'Good morning,' it said, and bowed. 'Your presence honours us.'

Bellarmine fought down a moment of revulsion and crossed himself, hoping that the good Lord would forgive him. This . . . this *angel?* . . . was no less a servant of the Lord than he himself was. More so, in fact, as it was obviously in a position of some responsibility. Bellarmine sighed, and smiled slightly. He had spent his life talking about humility. The Lord was now giving him the chance to put his words into practice.

'Thank you,' he said, standing, 'but it is I who am honoured to be here. I . . .' He hesitated, unsure of himself for the first time in years. 'I am unfamiliar with what is required of me here. Do I . . . I mean, I am not worthy to, but will . . . *He* wish to meet with me?'

The angel, if that was what it was, nodded. 'He will talk with you soon, but there are more pressing matters to attend to in the mean time. They are waiting for you.'

'Ah,' Bellarmine said, 'of course.' The angel stood aside to let him leave the room. 'After you,' Bellarmine said, bowing his head. The angel nodded, and led the way.

They walked along a corridor whose ceiling was arched and whose walls and floor were made of what felt like blue marble veined with gold. There were no tapestries, no paintings, no decoration of any kind. Doors led off at regular intervals, indistinguishable from his own. Were all new arrivals to Heaven given rooms here, Bellarmine wondered. He opened his mouth to ask the angel, but restrained himself at the last moment. After all, he had eternity to find the answers to all his questions. There was no point in looking too eager.

A long balcony to his left distracted his attention. Outside he could see a blue sky and the tips of green trees. How like his native Italy. Even the air smelled the same. Perhaps Heaven was meant to feel like home to all new arrivals.

The corridor opened into a vast hall, still floored in the gold-veined marble. The ceiling was suspended so high above his head that clouds drifted across it. Winged forms circled in the distance. Seraphim, perhaps? Cherubim?

The angel led him across the empty plain of the hall towards a pair of large doors. They swung open as he reached them, revealing a room like an inverted cone, with a lectern in the middle of the small stage at its point and serried rows of seats receding into the distance towards its ceiling. The seats were occupied by angels of infinite variety: some winged and feathered like birds; some shelled like turtles with heads bobbing on the end of long, wizened necks; some with hard, glossy skins, bulging eyes and feelers extending from their foreheads; some short and squat with many legs; some furred and graceful like foals; some like metal boxes upon which tiny lamps winked on and off; some like men but with red skins, or green skins, or skins that glowed with pearly, shifting colours; some that were just blurs in the air with glowing red eyes – at least, he assumed they were

113

eyes. They were all watching Cardinal Bellarmine as he advanced uncertainly into the room. He turned to ask a question of the spindly angel that had guided him, but the doors were closing behind him. He was alone on the podium before the assembled multitude of Heaven. Taking a deep breath, he walked up to the lectern and rested his hands upon it. His eyes glanced around the room, meeting the gaze of as many of the angels as possible. What did they want of him? What was he there for? Was this some form of judgement upon him?

For a few moments there was an expectant, tense silence, then, without stopping to consider his words, Bellarmine said: 'I am unworthy to stand here before you. I am unworthy even to contemplate your faces, let alone dare to speak to you, and yet I am here. Let us begin.'

There was no change in the attitudes of the angels but somehow Bellarmine knew that he had said the right thing.

The canal was narrow, and the single bridge was empty. The walls of the houses rose like sheer cliff faces on either side, their paint faded and peeling and their windows shuttered blankly. The sun caught the tips of the roofs, glinting here and there off a gilded ridge or weather vane. A rat ran along a ledge just above the canal on secret business of its own. A cat lay sunning itself on a projecting windowsill.

Steven braced himself between a striped gondola post and a crumbling brick wall and pulled himself out of the canal. A ledge running beneath a wooden door provided a convenient seat, and he rested for a moment, trying to ignore the smell that was rising from his sodden clothes. Algae crusted his hair, and he daren't even think about some of the things that had brushed against him in the water. Didn't these people have any sort of sewage system apart from the canal itself?

Still, at least the Nicolottis had left. If he was lucky then they would assume he had drowned, and they would stop bothering him. If he was unlucky then they had merely assumed that he had surfaced somewhere out of their sight, and they would be waiting for him to turn up elsewhere in Venice. Either way, he had more important things to do. Vicki was his first priority now, and that spacecraft, or whatever it was, that had dragged him along the canal and around the corner was almost certainly connected with her disappearance. Either that or it was the biggest coincidence since he couldn't remember when.

He was fairly sure that the house he was sitting beside was the nearest one to the large opening from which the ship had emerged, and as he couldn't follow the ship, there was only one course left to pursue. Taking a deep breath, he slid back into the noisome water, letting it close above his head as his fingers explored the brickwork of its foundations. Little pieces broke off in his hands and drifted towards the bottom. He widened the area of his search, pulling himself along and quickly running his hands over the rough façade. Weed was slick beneath his fingers, and twined around them as if they were alive. His lungs were burning, and the cold water was numbing his skin, making it difficult to feel anything. Perhaps it was deeper. He laboriously pulled himself down further into the depths of the canal, jamming the toes of his boots into gaps in the brickwork to anchor himself, like mountain-climbing in reverse. His fingers scuttled across the building's hidden face, finding nothing but ever-more ancient layers of artifice.

And a hole.

Disbelievingly he ran his hands along the rim of what appeared to be a large, rectangular opening framed with metal. No time to think: his lungs were demanding air but he couldn't guarantee ever finding the right stretch of wall again. Pushing up against the metal rim he forced his legs down further into the water and then swung them into the opening. His body floated back up, buoyed by the air in his lungs, and he found himself flat against the smooth metal ceiling of a tunnel. Using his numbed hands, just lumps of dead flesh now, he pushed himself along the tunnel, scuttling crab-fashion until suddenly there was no metal above him and he bobbed back up to the surface.

When he had got his breath back, he looked around. He was floating in a pool of water in the middle of a white metal room. There was a ledge running around the edge of the room, on which a few small machines rested, and a door in one wall. Apart from that, and a control panel set into one wall, the room was featureless.

Paddling to stay afloat, Steven turned in the water to check the wall behind him: the wall above the entrance to the short tunnel.

'Swim no further, pretty sweeting,' said Giovanni Zarattino Chigi from his position crouching on the ledge, 'for journeys end in lovers meeting.' He wore the same scuffed leather jerkin that he had worn in the tavern when he saved Steven's life, and he was holding one of the knives that he had been juggling in that encounter loosely by the point. And the chances were, Steven thought sourly, that he could throw it just as well as he could juggle it.

116

Nine

Galileo and the Doctor trudged up the stairs to Galileo's door, trailing water behind them as they went. Galileo was still carrying the buckled remains of the Doctor's spyglass, while the Doctor had his amazing boat beneath his arm, folded into a bundle of fabric.

'When I was twenty-nine,' Galileo muttered, 'I went for a ride in the country with some friends. We ended up at Costozza which, if you've never been there, is well worth avoiding. Its only saving grace is the wine they make. Strong? It's enough to strip the varnish off a violin.' He glanced across at the Doctor, who was plodding on, weary and bedraggled, but there was no sign that the Doctor was listening.

'We stayed with a well-known member of the legal profession who had a villa there. It was the height of summer: the ground was baked harder than a biscuit and the air shimmered wherever you looked. Even the grass had turned brown. We drank enough wine to float a warship, and I passed out near to a crack in the ground.' He shook his head at the memory of his youthful foolishness. 'Not that I realized at the time, but there was a breeze coming out of that crack that had been cooled by an underwater spring. When I woke up, I'd contracted a chill. They had to carry me back to Padua in a litter. Soon after that I found I couldn't move my arm without it feeling like there was ground glass in the joint.'

Raising his hand, he looked at the swollen knuckles, turning the hand over and back as they climbed.

' "Arthritis", said Girolamo Fabricio. He was my doctor. One of my doctors, anyway. I could have told *him* I had arthritis. In fact, I *did* tell him. What I wanted to know was what I should do about it but, like all doctors, he knew all the answers except for the ones I wanted.' Galileo suddenly realized that they were standing in front of his door. He fumbled at the lock for a few moments, and they staggered into his rooms. 'If that one moment of stupidity cost me years of ill health,' he continued. 'I wonder what today will do.'

Without replying, the Doctor fell instantly into a chair. Galileo flung himself onto a couch, the Doctor's spyglass falling from his hand and bouncing on the floor. Reaching down blindly with his hand for it he found instead a bottle of wine standing where it had been left after the dinner party the night before. He pulled the cork out with his teeth and took a long swallow. Air and time had roughened the wine, but it was as sweet on his tongue as the most expensive liqueur.

The Doctor sighed. 'Not the most productive day I have ever had,' he murmured. 'I only hope that Steven has got closer to finding Vicki than we have. Poor child: she must be terrified.' He hit the table with his clenched fist. 'If *only* we hadn't had to destroy my telescope to drive that creature off! It might take days to get another one fabricated by the Venetian artisans, and that could be too late! Far too late! We need to know where those ships are heading for when they leave the moon, and to do that we need that telescope!'

'Telescope?' Galileo held the bottle out towards the Doctor. 'Tele-scope, from the Greek, a device for seeing far distances. Hmm, I like that. It has a ring to it.'

'Indeed,' the Doctor murmured, 'perhaps it will catch on.'

Galileo took another swig of wine and put the bottle down beside him. It clinked against something metallic. He rolled over to look, and saw the Doctor's spyglass — telescope — where he had dropped it. He picked it up and looked it over. The tube was bent and buckled, and in two places there were tears in the metal. It sloshed as he shook it, but it began to dawn on him through his tiredness that the lenses looked as if they had survived unbroken. 'Perhaps all is not lost,' he said thoughtfully. 'The lenses of my – telescope – were broken, but the tube survived unscathed. The tube of *your* telescope is useless, but the lenses are perfectly all right.'

The Doctor frowned slightly, and turned to gaze at Galileo. 'Do you mean that we could construct a working telescope from the remnants of the two we have?'

'The lenses may be too large or too small,' Galileo mused, 'but with judicious amounts of stuffing we should be able to make them fit.'

'Then you had better not make yourself too comfortable,' the Doctor said, standing from the chair. 'We have work to do!'

'You what?' Vicki exclaimed.

'Love you I,' Albrellian stammered. His wings furled and unfurled against the hard red shell of his body, and his eyestalks were retracted so far that they were just glints in the darkness.

Vicki wasn't sure whether to laugh or cry. 'But . . . but you hardly know me,' she said finally. 'I mean, we only talked twice. You can't suddenly decide you love me on the basis of two short conversations.'

'Why not?' Albrellian's eyes poked slightly out from their hideaways.

'Because there could be all sorts of things you don't like about me but haven't had a chance to find out yet. I mean, I might hate arthropods, for all you know. Or I might have a fearsome temper. Or –'

Albrellian held out a clawed hand to stop her. 'Kind and friendly are you,' he said, 'and so few friendly faces here on Laputa are there. Drawn to you found myself when first rowing towards Venice saw you I. Since then following you have been I.'

'You've been following me?' Vicki felt a surge of anger within her.

'Nothing sinister!' Albrellian protested. 'Face to see and voice to hear your wanted I. Stop thinking about you cannot I.'

Vicki folded her arms across her chest. This would have been disturbing if it hadn't been so funny. 'Albrellian, this is going to have to stop. I want you to take me back to Venice *now*.'

'A species thing it is?' he muttered, his shell dipping towards the floor.

'It is *not* a species thing. Some of my best friends were aliens, before I left Earth for Astra.'

Albrellian's eyestalks suddenly extended upwards. 'Someone else there is? That human male – Steven. Him it is?'

'No, no it's not him.'

'Then is it who?'

Vicki sighed deeply. 'Albrellian, this isn't funny. Stop it at once.'

Albrellian moved forward and reached out a claw. Vicki's first thought was to step backwards, but if Albrellian was doing something innocent then he might take offence. On the other hand –

Before he could touch her, the door to his room slid open. A man was standing in the doorway, silhouetted by the light from the corridor. 'Envoy Albrellian!' he snapped. 'I presume that you have some explanation for your actions?'

Albrellian whirled around to face the newcomer. 'Braxiatel, I –'

'He was just being friendly,' Vicki said, surprising herself. 'He hasn't hurt me.'

Braxiatel stepped into the room and glanced at her. He was tall, with finely chiselled features and straight brown hair that fell in a slight curl over his eyes, and he wore a pair of half-moon spectacles that struck Vicki as curiously anachronistic in the midst of this futuristic island city, and yet which wouldn't have attracted a second glance in Venice itself. He looked back at Albrellian. 'Envoy, you were made perfectly aware of the rules concerning the natives when you arrived. Fraternization is completely forbidden. They must not know that we are here. The only thing that is keeping this girl sane now is the fact that she doesn't understand what is going on.'

'Now wait a second –' Vicki began, but Braxiatel was still talking.

'The minute she does realize, she'll go mad. This *has* to stop now. We'll give her an amnesia pill and return her to Venice before anybody realizes she's gone. In the mean-time, you have a convention to attend. The Doctor has arrived.'

'The Doctor?' Vicki and Albrellian chorused.

Braxiatel looked from one to the other. 'You know of the Doctor?' he said to Vicki eventually.

'I travel with him,' she said. 'And *you* know him?'

'We are . . . acquainted,' Braxiatel said, frowning slightly. 'I invited him to come here to Laputa, in fact. He was here last night.'

'No he wasn't. The Doctor was with *me* last night.'

Braxiatel shook his head. 'Impossible. I was told that he was brought here. My people said that he was so tired he fell asleep when they picked him up, and slept all the way through to this morning.'

Albrellian clicked a claw to attract their attention. 'Story can confirm Vicki's I,' he said. 'In Venice in the early hours of this morning indeed was the Doctor. Saw him I. Talked to him I.'

'Oh no.' Braxiatel rubbed a hand across his forehead. 'The stupid . . . They've only gone and picked up the *real* Cardinal Bellarmine. It goes to show you should never employ Jamarians.'

Something occurred to Vicki. 'You said you invited the Doctor here,' she said. 'Was it a real invitation – a piece of card, about this big?' She held her fingers a few inches apart.

121

'Yes. Yes, it was.'

'But it didn't say anything apart from "Invitation". We only got here because the TARDIS brought us.'

'The card itself contained full flight details, compatible with the navigational equipment of any vessel up to and including a TARDIS,' Braxiatel explained, 'but it was really only a formality. When I gave the Doctor the card, I did explain what it was for.'

'But he forgot!' Vicki exclaimed. 'He suddenly appeared in the TARDIS holding the card, and he couldn't remember where he got it from.'

'They wiped his memory.' Braxiatel shook his head in exasperation. 'They didn't bother telling me, of course. No, that would have been too simple. They just let me witter on about how important it was that he come here, and then they wiped his memory of everything that had happened since they took him out of time.'

'Since who took him out of time?' Vicki asked.

'Our own people,' Braxiatel said simply.

There was an ugly feeling in Heaven. Cardinal Bellarmine could feel the tension in the chamber of angels. It must have felt like that before Lucifer and his minions rose up against the Lord and were exiled from His sight.

An angel leaped to its feet and waved a gloved fist at Bellarmine. It looked like a man wearing green armour, and its head was almost completely encased in a metal helmet, but what little could be seen of its lower mouth looked rough and scaly. One of the other angels had referred to it earlier as Ssarl during a heated exchange of threats. It and its larger, rougher, companion were aggressive and forceful angels, and were apparently reviled by most of the other angels present. The same applied to the gargoyle-faced angels in shiny black costumes, but there was particularly bad blood between them and the blobs of jelly that always referred to themselves in the plural. Bellarmine had also identified various other factions and alliances around the steeply

122

rising walls of the chamber. Truly he was present at the time that St John the Divine had written of. The words rose up unbidden in his mind: 'And there was war in Heaven: Michael and his angels fought against the dragon; and the dragon fought and his angels.'

'You have a question, Ssarl?' Bellarmine said mildly.

'If this Convention is to have any validity at all,' the armoured angel hissed, 'then it must address the issue of chemical and biological warfare. We all know,' and it gazed meaningfully around the assembled ranks of its brethren, 'that the Rutans have used plague bombs during their endless war with the Sontarans. The Daleks too have used disease to massacre entire populations. What remedy do you . . .' and it paused rhetorically, 'suggest? Can mere talking prevent the use of such devastating weapons?'

Bellarmine waited before answering. He'd been standing there for hours, listening to the angels discuss matters of theology that were so far beyond him as to prove almost impossible to grasp, and in that time he had come to realize what his task was. He was a peacemaker. The discussion, as far as he could tell, centred around war in Heaven, and what weapons would be allowed. It was his task to calm the angels down when violence threatened to erupt in the chamber, and to move the discussion on when it was deadlocked. For some reason, they deferred to him. They seemed to respect his words, although he couldn't see why. They listened. Every so often they would pose him a question – as Ssarl had just done – and he would do his best to answer. Perhaps they were just testing him. Surely they must already know the answers to their questions better than he did. All he could do was try.

Plague, Ssarl had said. Was it right to use plague as a weapon? His mind raced across the various books of the Bible, trying to recall whether the Lord had ever pronounced on the matter. Yes! Yes, he had! In the Revelation of St John the Divine it clearly said, 'And I heard a great voice out of the temple saying to the seven

123

angels, Go your ways and pour out the wrath of God upon the Earth. And the first went, and poured out his vial upon the earth; and there fell a noisome and grievous sore upon the men which had the mark of the beast, and upon them which worshipped his image.' That meant that plague was a suitable weapon for angels. There was no question about it.

'Plague is a suitable weapon,' he said. 'So it is written.'

Ssarl looked as if he was about to argue, but sat down rather heavily in his chair. An angel across the chamber from Ssarl stood up straight away. It had the head of a fish, and was wearing a glass bubble filled with water. 'And poison?' it asked. 'What about weapons that poison the seas? The Chelonians have used these against my people. Are these acceptable?'

Bellarmine sighed with relief. That one was easy. The verse from Revelations went on: 'And the second angel poured out his vial upon the sea; and it became as the blood of a dead man: and every living soul died in the sea.'

'Yes,' he said, 'poison too is allowed.'

The fish angel sat down again. A thick-set angel whose skin was covered in spikes stood in its place. 'Sun-blasters,' it yelled. 'Surely blowing up someone else's sun can't be allowed.'

Chapter sixteen, verse eight: 'And the fourth angel poured out his vial upon the sun; and power was given unto him to scorch men with fire.' 'Yes,' he replied, looking the angel in the eye, 'yes, it is right and proper.'

Instead of sitting down again, the angel began to argue. Five other angels sprang to their feet and began to debate the point with it. Bellarmine closed his eyes for a moment to gather his strength. He had a feeling he was going to be there for some time to come.

Eternity, perhaps.

The moon was almost full, and its pearly light illuminated the spires, domes, minarets and rooftops of Venice, making them all seem like paintings on a backcloth, close enough to touch.

Galileo stood, hands on hips, gazing out across the sea of architecture. The errant breeze caught a distant snatch of song and brought it to his ears. He turned, letting his glance rove across the entire city from Cannaregio to La Giudecca, from Dorsudo to Castello. He smiled as he realized something at once obvious and paradoxical: from where he stood he could see all of Venice, and yet there wasn't a single canal visible. How odd. How very odd.

'If you've quite finished sightseeing,' the Doctor said from the room below, 'then perhaps you could help me with this telescope.'

Galileo bent down and reached a hand through the trapdoor. The Doctor held the telescope up above his head and Galileo took its weight, pulling it through the hatch. He quickly checked it over. The Doctor had done an excellent job of work: his lenses were slightly smaller than Galileo's tube, and so he had packed the surrounding gaps with lead foil from Galileo's wine bottles and then melted wax over them to seal any gaps. The resulting conglomerate telescope wasn't pretty, but it would work.

As the Doctor scrambled up the ladder and onto the platform, Galileo set to work placing the telescope upon its stand and aiming it towards the moon's cratered surface. By the time the old man was standing beside him, he was gazing through the eyepiece.

'Well?' the Doctor queried. 'What do you see?'

Galileo didn't reply for a moment. The skull-like contours of the moon's surface filled his eyes, its shadows lengthening as he watched. As always, he felt humbled and elated seeing something that nobody else had ever seen. The resolution of the Doctor's lenses was incredible: far better than anything his glassmaker at Padua could fashion. Even the glassmakers of Venice – the very Empire of glass – would be hard-pressed to surpass them for clarity. He could make out features that he had never seen before – radial lines splaying out from the circular features and smaller pock marks all over the surface. There was so much to catalogue, so much to think about!

The Doctor tapped him on the shoulder. 'This is no time for dilly-dallying, young man. Kindly tell me what you can see.'

'Quiet!' Galileo muttered. 'I'm concentrating.' He shifted the telescope slightly, tracing across the harsh yet serene surface until he found a feature that he recognized: a tall, jagged range of mountains that put him in mind of the teeth of one of the lecturers at the University of Padua. Through the Doctor's lenses they seemed almost close enough to walk to. From the mountains he scanned downwards until a large elliptical area jumped into view. 'There,' he said. 'That's what I was looking at when I saw the moving object.'

The Doctor pushed him out of the way. 'Let me see,' he said. After a few moments, and a little nudge of the telescope tube, his tense shoulders relaxed. 'Yes . . .' he murmured, 'yes, it all becomes clear now.'

The Doctor stood to one side and let Galileo take another look. He had centred the telescope's field of view on a plain area of ground. Galileo had never bothered with it before – it was the features that interested him, not the stretches of ground between them. He had been wrong. Through the Doctor's lenses he could see large geometric shapes scattered across the surface: squares and rectangles, cones and cylinders, spheres and trapezoids. From the way their shadows were cast it seemed as though they stood proud of the surface, as if they were on legs. 'Are they houses?' he whispered. 'Houses for moon-men?'

'No,' the Doctor said darkly, 'they are ships that sail through space as a galleon sails through the oceans.'

'But they are all different in design.'

'I suspect that they belong to a number of different races.'

Galileo would have pursued the point further, but suddenly a smaller object detached itself from a diamond-shaped edifice and rose away from the surface of the moon. It was circular in shape, like a flattened egg. 'Doctor, there's something moving.'

The Doctor pushed Galileo out of the way and took a look himself. 'Excellent,' he said. 'As I suspected, it is some form of shuttle craft. Now if we can only keep it in sight, we should be able to determine where it comes to Earth.'

'And where it comes to Earth,' Galileo said, 'there we may find your companion Vicki.'

'I took you for a guard of the house,' Chigi confided to Steven. He took a long drink from the tankard in front of him. 'Or a demon.'

'A demon?' Steven glanced around the bar with the picturesque name of the Tavern of the Love of Friends, or of the Gypsies, wondering if anybody was close enough to overhear their conversation. As far as he knew, both he and Chigi had got out of the strange house without anybody noticing, but if there was one thing he had learned from the past twenty-four hours it was not to take anything in Venice at face value. The city was full of masks, obvious and subtle, and anything could be hiding behind them. Anything at all.

But the tavern was just a tavern – hot and noisy – and the patrons were just patrons.

'Have you not seen them?' Chigi gazed curiously at Steven, and the pilot was struck by how soft his grey eyes were in contrast to his rugged, scarred face and close-cropped hair. Another mask? 'They fly above us, walk amongst us and swim beneath us. Venice is full of them.'

'A riddle?' Steven asked.

'The truth. Oh, I am quite capable of turning the odd fanciful phrase – indeed I was once noted for it – but this time I am speaking God's honest truth. Or at least, I would be if I believed in God. But no matter – these demons are real enough. Some are as thin as sticks, with great horns growing from their heads, while others are shelled like crabs but have great wings which carry them aloft. I have seen them.'

Steven shivered. At first he had thought that Chigi was lying – that or hallucinating – but the latter description sounded uncomfortably close to the Doctor's description of the creature that had abducted Vicki. From the sound of it, Chigi had come across it as well, which raised the obvious question: what was Chigi's part in all this?

'So what were *you* doing in the house?'

Chigi smiled slightly. 'I suspect the same as you, my friend. Investigating.' He raised a hand and ran a finger along the scar that ran down one side of his face. 'A pastime that has been my downfall before, and no doubt will be again. "I see the better way and approve it: I follow the worse," as Ovid said.'

'Is that how you got that scar?' Steven asked.

Chigi nodded. 'A fight – a sordid affair in Holland, some five years ago now. My skull was split open. A sawbones had to piece it back together. I owe him my life – for whatever that is worth.' Chigi reached into his jerkin. When he pulled his hand out, he was holding a small, round metal object. 'The sawbones claims that he found this inside my skull,' he added. 'I've never been sure whether to believe him or not.'

Steven reached out for the object. Chigi shrugged, and handed it over.

'It's very light,' Steven said, hefting it in his hand. 'What is it – a musket ball or something?' Running his thumb over it, Steven thought he could detect striations in the sphere, indentations marking the outline of some hidden compartment perhaps, or symbols carved into the metal.

'If so, I know not how it came to be in my head, for I have never been shot.' Chigi laughed, and picked the ball from Steven's hand, managing as he did so to run his finger across Steven's palm. 'Or at least, I don't remember ever having been –'

He stopped abruptly, his gaze fixed on something

across the tavern. Steven glanced across. A man stood in the doorway. His clothes marked him as a foreigner, and he was carrying a bag. His forehead was high and balding, and his face was fine-featured. He was staring back at Chigi as if he had seen a ghost.

'God's hounds!' Chigi murmured. 'It can't be.'

The newcomer walked slowly across to their table. His eyes never left Chigi. He dropped the bag by Steven's feet.

'You bear an uncanny resemblance to a man who has been dead for fifteen years, sir,' he said. 'My name is Shakespeare. William Shakespeare. Might I make so bold as to enquire . . . ?'

Chigi made no move to answer. Instead he just shook his head again, nonplussed. 'I'm Steven Taylor,' Steven said finally, rising from his seat and extending a hand. 'And this is —'

'Marlowe,' Chigi said simply. 'My name is Christopher Marlowe.'

Steven watched, dumbfounded, as Chigi reached out, pulled Shakespeare to him and hugged him like a long-lost brother.

Ten

―――――

'It appears to be heading towards Venice again,' Galileo said, the brass of the telescope's eyepiece cold against his skin. He looked away from the spinning disc and refocused his eyes on the Venetian skyline: darker roofs and spires against the darkness of the sky. There was the beginning of a dull headache behind his forehead, and creaking pains in the small of his back. He'd spent too long bending over, looking through the telescope, straining too hard to make out details, and he was going to pay the price later. No amount of philosophy, no amount of science, could hold old age at bay.

When he turned back, the Doctor was at the telescope. 'Hmm, you're right, my boy,' he said, 'it does seem that the object in question is getting larger, and not diverging significantly from its flight path. Venice would appear to be its final destination.' He straightened up and frowned for a moment. 'I wonder,' he muttered, 'whether it is actually within sight yet.' He gazed upwards, along the line of the telescope, his eyes flicking back and forth as he scanned the heavens. Galileo joined him, and together the two men stood in silence, staring upward.

It was Galileo who saw it first – a tiny point of light moving on a steady course. For a moment he thought it was a falling star, but it was travelling too slowly for that. 'Look, Doctor,' he said, pointing. 'There it is!'

'My eyes are perfectly sharp and I can't make out a thing,' the Doctor snapped. 'Are you sure that your own eyes aren't deceiving you?'

Galileo glanced sideways at the Doctor and smiled

130

slightly. The old man didn't like to be upstaged. Too bad: neither did Galileo. 'Yes,' he said, 'I'm sure. Obviously your own gaze is too rheumy with age to make it out.'

'Nonsense.' The Doctor huffed and spluttered to himself. 'I can see it now. Yes, I can see it clearly.' He pointed to where it had been. Galileo pointed to where it was now, and the Doctor quickly shifted his arm downwards.

'It appears to be coming down in the lagoon somewhere,' Galileo said.

The Doctor reached into his pocket and brought out a compass. Galileo watched as he fussed around, taking a reading. 'We need a second reading,' he said finally. 'All we can tell from this is that its destination lies somewhere along this bearing. If we could only move half a mile or so and check again then we could determine at what point the two bearings cross, but by the time we get downstairs and across the city it will have landed.'

'Give the compass to me,' Galileo said. The Doctor frowned and made as if to argue, so Galileo snatched it from his hand and, without stopping to think through what he was doing, ran towards the edge of the roof platform and jumped into space. A sudden dizzying vision of the canyon between the houses flashed past, and then his feet were stumbling heavily upon the roof platform of the widow Carpaccio, who lived opposite. A short scramble up the eaves and down the other side left Galileo perched on a length of gutter. He launched himself across the gap to the next house, and laughed as he landed, feeling like a youth again. He had forgotten how exhilarating it was to jump, to run and not to care about dignity, decorum and pride.

For the next few minutes he forgot what he was doing and why: all he felt was fingers scrabbling at tiles, feet thumping against wood and the coldness of the air whipping past as he sprang from roof to roof. He lost count of the number of times he had jumped, the number of houses that he had crossed. Once or twice he had to go sideways to avoid particularly tall or short buildings, or to detour round churches or empty squares, but he did his best to keep going in the same general direction. Sometimes he could see upturned pink faces gawping from alleys as he crossed, like a thief in the night, and he wondered what the people actually saw. Was it a mysterious shape flying across the sky, or just a portly, middle-aged scholar acting the fool? A few times he heard the rattle of trapdoors or windows behind him as occupiers checked for nocturnal invasions. Once a cat squalled and shot out from beneath his feet, almost pitching him into an alley.

Every so often he glanced up to check the moving star. It was descending slowly but surely towards the horizon, and when it was a mere hand's breadth away from the rooftops he stopped and pulled the compass from his pocket. His body shook as he tried to draw enough air into his lungs to assuage the burning void within him, and he could hardly focus on the compass, but it only took him a few moments to make a reading. As the star vanished behind the rooftops, Galileo felt a wave of elation sweep over him. He could draw a line on a map from where he was to where he had seen the star vanish, and the Doctor could do the same from Galileo's house. Where the lines crossed, that was where they had to go.

Fatigue washed across him then, and his legs almost gave way beneath him. Carefully he picked his way across the roof, looking for a way down that didn't lead through someone's bedroom. His breath rasped in his throat, and he suddenly realized that his back was locked in a solid mass of pain. He was getting too old for this.

They were sitting in loungers out on a balcony, high up on the main central tower of the island of Laputa. Vicki was sipping at a drink that tasted of strawberries and had started off chilled but was now comfortably hot in her hands; Braxiatel was leaning back with his eyes closed, humming to himself. Below, Vicki could just hear the cries of birds and animals in the vibrant jungle.

'That jungle isn't natural, is it?' she asked sleepily.

'That depends on what you mean by natural,' Braxiatel said. 'If you mean "is it artificial?" then the answer is no. If, however, you mean "is it native to this area of the Earth?" then the answer is also no.'

Vicki frowned. 'Sorry?'

'I had it transplanted from South America. The vegetation around Venice consists primarily of small shrubs and scrubby olive trees. I felt that the envoys deserved something more picturesque.' He shook his head. 'No, that's not true. I felt that *I* deserved something a little more picturesque. That's why I have my living accommodation in Venice — it's much more attractive than here.'

Vicki nodded. 'It's very pretty.'

'Thank you.'

After taking a sip of her drink, Vicki said, 'Can I ask you another question?'

'Of course.'

'What are the envoys doing here? What are you doing here? And what are *we* doing here?'

Braxiatel opened his eyes and glanced towards her. 'That's three questions,' he said. 'Let me answer them by turning them back on you: what do you *think* is going on?'

Vicki considered for a moment. 'I think there's some sort of conference going on in Venice,' she said finally, 'and I think you're organizing it. I think you wanted the Doctor to go to it, and I think that Albrellian is supposed to be attending the conference but doesn't want to.'

'More or less spot on,' Braxiatel said, sliding upright in his lounger. 'It's called the Armageddon Convention, and I've spent the past twenty years trying to set it up.'

'The Armageddon Convention?' Vicki said, frowning. 'That sounds rather . . . warlike. You don't strike me as the sort of man who would go around arranging armageddons.'

'It's a peace conference.' Braxiatel placed his hands behind his head and shifted slightly in his lounger. 'It struck me some time ago that wherever I went in the universe, there were races who had spent millennia trying to kill each other for reasons that they had probably all forgotten. I thought that if I could get representatives from all of the major races in a room together then –'

'– then you could stop them fighting!' Vicki slapped her hands together. 'That's wonderful.'

Braxiatel looked downcast. 'I'm afraid that's not quite the case. I'm hoping for something much more pragmatic than that. I knew that if I told them it was a peace conference the only races who would turn up were the ones that were losing. There's no incentive for the winners to negotiate.'

'So what *are* you doing then?'

'Limiting the damage.' He stood up suddenly and walked over to the edge of the balcony. 'The one thing that most races could agree on was that some weapons were just too terrible to consider using – the doomsday devices, we tend to call them. Temporal disruptors, for instance, can rip apart the structure of the universe and set off a chain reaction that might unravel reality, while cobalt bombs are so unpredictable that nobody can tell what the resulting damage might be. The only races prepared to use doomsday devices are the losers – the races who will be completely wiped out otherwise and just don't *care* about long term effects.'

'So this is . . . what, an arms limitation conference?'

'That's right. The envoys all have the power to agree that their respective races will stop using certain weapons. The losers give up their doomsday devices in exchange for the winners giving up some of the dirtier weapons that don't discriminate between military and civilian targets. My hope is that by the time they've finished, there won't be very much left for them to fight *with*.' He sighed as he gazed down at the jungle. 'I sent out robot messengers twenty years ago with the invitations. The Daleks and the Cybermen refused even to respond, of course, and destroyed the messengers out of spite, but a lot of the other, second-rank races were interested. That was all I got for a while – interest. Nobody could agree on a location or a chairman that they trusted.'

'Until you chose the Earth for the location and the Doctor for the chairman,' Vicki prompted.

'Exactly,' Braxiatel nodded. 'The Earth is a developing world with a bright future ahead of it. Within a thousand years or so it will become a dominant force in this part of the galaxy, partly because of its unique strategic position but mostly because of the unique ability of its inhabitants.'

'I didn't know that we had any unique abilities,' Vicki said.

'You don't,' Braxiatel replied, 'that's your unique ability. Other races specialize in trade, or warmongering, or shapeshifting. You humans are generalists, and for that reason you can do everything reasonably well, rather than one thing very well and everything else badly. I thought that holding the conference on Earth would remind the various envoys that they were all young and powerless once.' He turned to face Vicki. 'It's also conveniently placed for everyone, of course, and at this point in its history it's on the verge of mass-producing cheap but effective weapons using a powder that was originally developed for fireworks – a reminder to all the envoys that even the most innocent of research programmes can be perverted to a military end.'

'And the spaceships of all the envoys are parked on the moon?'

He nodded. 'Less conspicuous that way. We shuttle them down here in spaceworthy skiffs. And, of course, all of the envoys' ships are heavily armed. Most of them brought examples of the weapons that they'll be discussing. It's safer to have them all out of temptation's way. The ships are all empty – the envoys and their crews have all been quartered down on Earth in whatever locations are most comfortable and, by and large, uninhabited. The Ice Warriors have a base near the North

135

Pole, the Krargs are in the Sahara, the Vilp are deep underground and so on. The Greld have been here longest. They agreed on the location almost straight away, twenty years ago, and I had them quartered out in what you would probably know as North America. They've used the time to teach themselves standard Galactispeak, but they can't quite come to grips with the fact that verbs and personal pronouns don't come at the end of sentences. That, incidentally, is why Albrellian is a little . . . flighty. He's been waiting so long for this convention to start that he's on edge all the time. I think they call it "stir crazy". We've had more problems with the Greld delegation going out formation flying than with anyone else.'

Vicki felt herself blushing slightly, and looked away. 'Is that why he said . . . that he loved me?'

Braxiatel was equally embarrassed, judging by his tone of voice. 'The Greld are a very . . . sensuous . . . race. They take their physical pleasures very seriously, and they're enlightened enough not to restrict themselves to members of their own race.' Vicki glanced over to find Braxiatel furiously polishing his bifocals. 'There are no female Greld in the delegation, and I've been trying to discourage Albrellian from . . . from accosting . . . women of this era, because the women would see it as a visitation from their devil. He's tried it on with several of the other envoys, but they all turned him down. I think having an attractive human female nearby who is intelligent enough not to be scared by him is . . . er . . .'

'A turn on.'

'Indeed.' He looked away. 'Not that I'm trying to denigrate your own unique physical attributes, of course. Don't take Albrellian seriously – apart from the way he mangles grammar, he's harmless.'

'Thanks for reassuring me,' Vicki said. 'Can I ask where the Doctor fits into all this?'

'The Doctor was the only person that the major races could agree on as the chairman of the conference.'

'You mean they all respect him as a fair and wise person?'

'No, they all hate him equally.' Braxiatel smiled. 'Actually, that's not quite fair. The Doctor has a growing reputation, but it was what he did with the miniscopes that impressed everyone.'

'What *did* he do to the miniscopes?'

'He persuaded our people to ban their use across the nine galaxies. Miniscopes were a barbaric invention – zoos of intelligent creatures, miniaturized and kept in time loops for the pleasure of other, more "developed" races. The Doctor petitioned for their abolition and our people – for once in their long lives – acted.' Braxiatel shrugged. 'The Doctor always was one for causing trouble. I, for my part, preferred to keep a lower profile.'

'Great.' Vicki cocked her head to one side and gazed at Braxiatel. 'So you're one of the Doctor's people, then?'

He nodded. 'You don't seem surprised.'

'There seem to be a lot of you about,' she said. 'We met another one recently. He was pretending to be a monk in the time of the Vikings. He was planning to give atomic bazookas to some king named Harold. The Doctor stopped him.'

Braxiatel nodded. 'Mortimus. I heard he headed this way when he left ... when he left our planet. What happened to him?'

'The Doctor sabotaged his TARDIS. Do you all meddle this much?'

'Far from it.' Braxiatel laughed. 'We're the exceptions that prove the rule.'

Something suddenly occurred to Vicki. 'But if the Doctor's back in Venice and this Cardinal Bellarmine is chairing the Armageddon Convention, shouldn't you be doing something? I mean, like finding the Doctor, or stopping the Cardinal?'

'What's the point? I can't suddenly push another Doctor in there and pretend nothing's changed. Even if I

137

give the real Doctor a hologuise and make him look like the Cardinal, the envoys will realize that something about him has changed – his body language, or the way he phrases things. And besides, when I popped into the conference hall earlier on the Cardinal was handling himself very well. The envoys seem to be listening to him. I don't know what he thinks has happened but the envoys' automatic translators seem to be ironing out anything strange he says, and interpreting his religious pronouncements as best they can. I think . . .' and he paused cautiously, 'that it's working as well as can be expected. The last thing I want to do is to start changing things now.' He shrugged. 'Of course, this is all *their* fault. If they had told me that I was talking to a Doctor from a different time stream and that they were going to wipe his mind of everything that had happened during the Omega crisis then I would have chosen a later incarnation.'

'A later what?'

'Don't worry about it. The convention is progressing nicely, everyone is happy, and I'm not going to rock the boat. My job finished when the convention started. So, perhaps I can buy you lunch in the refectory, and then I'll take you on a quick tour.'

Vicki laughed. '*Buy* me lunch? I thought you built and ran this entire place?'

He shrugged. 'No privileges for the boss. The Jamarians would never forgive me.'

'I meant to ask,' Vicki said, 'who are the Jamarians?'

'I couldn't organize all this without help,' Braxiatel said, nodding toward the buildings and jungle of Laputa on the viewscreen. 'I needed assistance, and my own race wouldn't cooperate. They gave me their blessing, of course, and they helped me find the Doctor – not that they did any more than they had to on that front of course, like telling me that they were going to wipe his memory just after I handed him the invitation. Oh yes, and they declared this area of space and time closed for the duration of the convention, but apart from that, I was

138

on my own. It was obvious that if I asked any of the galactic powers for help, the rest of them would accuse me of favouritism, so I chose a minor race with no power base, no weapons to speak of and no strategic position in the galaxy. Apart from a tendency towards paranoia and stupidity, the Jamarians are a perfect workforce. Great organizers. They'll make someone a lovely civil service one day.' He smiled. 'Come on, let's get some food.'

William Shakespeare reached out a trembling hand and touched Christopher Marlowe's shoulder. 'I can't believe it,' he said for the fifth time that night. 'You were stabbed by Ingram Frizer in the house of Eleanor Bull: Walsingham himself told me that Nicholas Skeres and Robert Poley were there and saw the whole thing. It was an argument over a bill of reckoning for the fare that you all had consumed. For sixteen years I've believed you dead.'

'Marlowe?' The man with Marlowe looked puzzled. 'I thought your name was Chigi?'

Christopher Marlowe swigged back a draught of wine and wiped his hand across his mouth. 'It is,' he said. 'A man can have many names during his life, as he has many natures. Once, long ago, I was known as Kit Marlowe to my friends, and as a fiend in human form to my enemies, of which there were many.' He glanced at Shakespeare. 'Will, this is Steven Taylor, a beautiful lad who has as able a facility at making enemies as I do. Steven, this is William Shakespeare, a playwright of some small repute in London.'

'Pleased to meet you,' Steven said, shaking hands with Shakespeare.

'We were at Eleanor's house, true, 'tis true,' Marlowe said to Shakespeare, 'but it was a meeting, not a meal. You know that Skeres and Poley were in the pay of Walsingham?'

Shakespeare nodded. They had all been working for Walsingham: Shakespeare, Marlowe, Ben Jonson, Skeres, Poley, Frizer and others. Sometimes he had felt that it was difficult to move in London without tripping over an agent of the Government on the lookout for seditious activity or evidence of blasphemy.

'You remember when Thomas Kyd was arrested in April of the same year,' Marlowe continued, 'he was brought before the Privy Council and accused of writing atheistic and seditious literature?'

'I remember.' Indeed he did. Once one playwright was arrested for sedition, the rest immediately reread everything they had ever written, wondering if they would be next to hear the knock on the door.

'Kyd told them that *I* had written those papers, not he. The Privy Council sought other witnesses: aye, and found them.'

'You made enemies, Kit,' Shakespeare said. 'You had that way about you. After all, you committed –'

'Fornication? Aye, but that was in another country, and besides, the lad is dead.' Marlowe smiled. 'Not that it mattered. The Queen herself was sent a document part entitled "The Most Horrible Blasphemies Uttered By Christopher Marlowe", in which people were prepared to swear that I had called Christ a bastard, Mary Magdalene dishonest and all Protestants hypocritical asses. They also imputed to me the words "if there be a God or any religion it is the papists." Now you know me, Will.' He spread his hands imploringly. 'I count religion but a childish toy, and hold there is no sin but ignorance. Would I, who believed in no God at all, claim that the Pope was God's only messenger?' As Shakespeare shook his head, Marlowe continued: 'They were to call me before them to answer for my sins. I would have been tortured and killed. Walsingham was my . . . my friend, as well as a generous employer. He knew what fate lay ahead of me.'

'A fate he might have shared,' Shakespeare said, 'if he also fell under suspicion.'

'Indeed.' Marlowe frowned. 'He contacted Skeres, Poley and Frizer, and together they concocted the tale of my death. The Coroner of the Household of our Lady the Queen was bribed to pass a verdict of death in self defence. Frizer was not punished in any way — indeed, the Privy Council were very pleased with him for removing me.'

Shakespeare's head was awhirl with fragments of thought. He could hardly reconcile sixteen years of belief with what he had just been told. The two contradictory stories sat together in his mind, indigestible and uncomfortable. 'I tried to find your grave at Deptford,' he said finally, 'but it was not marked.'

'As befits a man who has no truck with God or with churches,' Marlowe laughed. 'I am alive, Will. Believe the evidence of your own senses.'

'I'm confused,' Steven Taylor sighed from the other side of the table.

'But . . . sixteen years!' Shakespeare breathed. 'Where did you go? What did you do? Why didn't you communicate with any of us?'

Marlowe looked away from Shakespeare's accusing, wounded gaze. 'Do you remember,' he said, 'three years before my purported death, I disappeared from London for a year. Nobody could find me.'

Shakespeare nodded. It had been a minor scandal of the time. There were many who had believed that Marlowe was on the run from his debtors, or from justice, or both.

'During that time,' Marlowe continued, 'I travelled to the New World, to the Roanoake colony that had been set up in the land of Virginia by Walter Ralegh.'

'Ralegh?' Shakespeare cried. Heads turned around the tavern.

Marlowe smiled at Shakespeare's expression. 'Her Majesty was suspicious of Ralegh, believing that he was not loyal to her. You must have known that Ralegh too was an atheist, Will. A group of us used to meet at his house and debate theology. The School of Night, we called ourselves. Not knowing then that I shared his beliefs, Her Majesty instructed me through Walsingham to obtain statements from the Roanoake colonists as to Ralegh's demeanour, and his statements about Her Majesty to them. I had to be seen to go, otherwise I would have been tarred with the same brush as Ralegh. I shall not dwell on the journey, which was long and tedious, but while I was there, the colony was wiped out – attacked by animals the like of which I pray that I will never see again.' Marlowe winced, and raised a hand to his head. 'Strange creatures of this New World with hard skin, wings and many arms. I was knocked unconscious, and the animals left me for dead. When I awoke the next day, the bodies had gone: eaten, I presumed, or taken for strange, unnatural rites. The colony was deserted. I returned to England on the next supply ship, having survived until then on the dead colonists' supplies and local food, and I reported the matter directly back to the Queen, and to John Dee.'

'Who's Dee?' Steven Taylor asked.

'Doctor John Dee,' Marlowe replied, 'the Queen's personal astrologer. Some of us believed that he had more influence upon her than was entirely healthy. Shortly after that, while wandering around London, I *saw* one of the colonists from Roanoake! I recognized her, as clear as day, but when I approached her she ran! I swear she fell beneath a brewer's dray and was greviously injured, and yet she climbed to her feet and ran off as if her leg were not bent almost in half.'

'Are you –?' Shakespeare began.

'Sure?' Marlowe nodded. 'As sure as I am that you are sitting here before me. I told Walsingham the news, and he suggested that I should investigate what had happened to the colony. Shortly after that, I "died".' He laughed. 'But I hear you took on my mantle, Will, and discovered Ralegh to be a traitor.'

Shakespeare nodded weakly. 'Walsingham put me to spy on him. As William Hall I infiltrated his circles and passed reports back. When Elizabeth died and James was made King, ten years after you . . . after you vanished . . .

Ralegh plotted with various Catholics to kill the King and enthrone his daughter. His plot was discovered, and –'

'Discovered?' Marlowe clapped Shakespeare on the shoulder. 'You do yourself a disservice, Will.'

Shakespeare shrugged. 'No matter. Ralegh was imprisoned in the Tower, and rots there still. But you – where did you go when I thought *your* bones were rotting in Deptford, done to death by slanderous tongues?'

'In my strange afterlife, the only kind that I am expecting, I have trailed these vanished colonists around the globe – from England to Spain, from Spain to France, from France to Germany, from Germany to Austria and from Austria to Italy, gaining in numbers all the way – until they have all come together here.'

'Here?' Shakespeare repeated.

'Venice,' Marlowe confirmed. 'I have listened to their conversation in taverns and in alleys, and they talk of a conference which is to occur here, one that will concern great wealth and weapons whose like has not been seen before. I know not what is to happen at that conference, and I know not how these colonists from Roanoake are connected to it, but I like it not.' A scowl crossed his face, and his fingers trailed through the puddles of spilled wine on the table, drawing patterns. 'And I swear that late at night, I have seen a creature akin to the ones that attacked the Roanoake colonists flying above the spires of this fair city. Walsingham having died during my travels, I sent a message back to his cousin telling him of my discoveries. He knew that I was still alive, and he contacted the King. His Majesty, trusting in you, Will, sent you to investigate my claims.'

Shakespeare shook his head. He felt as if he had fallen into a fast-flowing torrent of words, and was being dragged along by the current. 'Kit, if your story were played out on a stage now I should condemn it as improbable fiction, but as it is you telling the tale, I must perforce accept it as it is. And now I am in Venice, the

143

more fool I: when I was at home I was in a better place, but I suppose travellers must be content.'

'What I still want to know,' Steven asked, 'is what you were doing in that house: the one with the basement and the pool?'

'The lost colonists have been congregating near it,' Marlowe replied. 'They drink in taverns around it, they lodge in hostels near it and they stand outside it, watching its doors. It has some connection to their presence, and this conference.'

Steven looked from Marlowe to Shakespeare and back again. 'There's a man I think you both should meet. He's called the Doctor, and I think that he has some pieces of the puzzle that you need.'

'And that,' the Doctor proclaimed, pointing at an expanse of ocean on the map where two hand-drawn lines crossed, 'is where we will find Laputa.' He leaned back in his seat and, hands folded on top of his cane, nodded firmly.

Around Galileo and the Doctor, the hurly-burly of the Tavern of Fists carried on as if nobody had been kidnapped, pieces of the moon had not fallen to the Earth and creatures like demons did not stalk the streets and swim in the oceans.

'Let us not extend logic into areas in which it is not comfortable,' Galileo muttered. He took hold of the bottle of wine and poured a generous measure into his tankard: then, for good measure, he swallowed the rest directly from the bottle. 'We know,' he continued after he had wiped his hand across his wine-sodden beard, 'that this astral coach has fallen to Earth. We know —' and he indicated the map, '— as best we can ascertain, where the coach came to rest. We *assume* that at that point is this island of which you speak. We cannot prove it.'

'We can prove it,' the Doctor snapped, 'by going there with as much haste as we can. You forget, sir — my companion is in danger.'

Galileo smiled despite himself and shook his head. 'You have gall, I'll say that for you. Old men should be timid and cautious, but you ... By God's breath, I like you, Doctor.'

The Doctor smiled. 'Thank you, Mr Galilei. I shall take that compliment in the spirit in which it was –'

'Galileo Galilei?' a voice said from beside them.

'Not *again*,' Galileo sighed, and turned to see a man of medium height and build standing next to him. The man was unremarkable both in terms of looks and the expression upon his face. 'Yes,' Galileo said, 'I am he. And you are –'

'Your assassin,' the man replied. His hand appeared from behind his back, holding a knife, which he thrust toward Galileo's eyes.

Eleven

The curious noises of the various envoys eating reverberated through the marble hall, making thought difficult and conversation nearly impossible. Near where Vicki was sitting waiting for Braxiatel, an eight-foot tall ferret was pulling live rodents from small plastic boxes and letting them run, squealing, across the table before snatching them up and swallowing them whole. Compared to them, Albrellian and his group of Greld at the next table were the models of decorum, although the slurping sound of their extendible mouthparts as they sucked the juices from small, anemone-like objects was a trifle obtrusive.

'And when did you die, my child?'

Vicki looked up from her food to find an elderly man smiling down at her. For a moment she thought it was the Doctor come to rescue her, and she smiled in relief. It took her a few seconds to realize that, apart from the long white hair and the angular features, the man looked nothing like her mentor and protector.

'You must be Cardinal Bellarmine,' she ventured, the smile fading from her face. Glancing around, she spotted numerous empty places at the tables in the refectory. Of all the places he could have chosen to sit . . . and there was no sign of Irving Braxiatel with their food.

'Indeed I am,' Bellarmine confirmed, carefully placing his tray on the table and sitting down opposite her. 'And I am relieved to find another person here who isn't an angel.' His gaze flickered across to the group of Greld,

146

whose voices were beginning to raise in argument. He frowned slightly. 'You're not an angel, are you?'

Vicki shook her head. 'I'm as human as you are.'

He pursed his lips. 'No my dear, we *were* human. Now our souls are with God. When *did* you die?'

'I'm not –' Gazing into Bellarmine's eyes, Vicki suddenly noticed the wild gleam of barely suppressed hysteria. The Cardinal had built himself an entire edifice of fantasy and was doing his best to cram the facts into it. He must have known by now that he wasn't in Heaven, but any other explanation would have driven him mad. 'I'm not sure,' she continued. 'It's all very hazy.'

'Indeed.' He picked up an implement that looked something like a half-melted fork. 'As it is with me. Heaven is so –' he shrugged helplessly '– confusing. I confess, some of the discussions I have been mediating today have been completely beyond my understanding.'

'You seem to be doing okay,' Vicki said. 'I hear the talks are going well.'

Bellarmine took a mouthful of food, and chewed it cautiously. 'It had never occurred to me,' he said, 'that we would eat food in Heaven.'

Vicki was about to make some anodyne reply when she suddenly caught a snatch of the conversation from the table of Greld nearby. '– All promised to die, have we Albrellian,' one of the Greld was saying, 'all of us. And now trying out of your word to wriggle are you –' The rest of the arthropod's words were obscured by a particularly loud squeal from the eight-foot ferret-like envoy nearby. Albrellian was replying, but all Vicki could hear was, '– have changed! About the Doctor and his companions did not know we –' The rest of the group obviously disagreed with him, because they were shaking their bamboo-like limbs violently. 'For the sacrifice should be prepared you!' one of them shouted, its voice cutting through the din. 'To die with the rest of us should be prepared you, but too scared are you. Cannot now run out on us, just when together are coming carriers!'

Albrellian tried to quieten down the argument while two of his eyestalks rotated to see whether anybody was listening. Vicki quickly stared down at her plate, but she was sure that Albrellian had seen her. After a few moments, she looked up. Albrellian was still staring at her. She smiled hesitantly, and he finally looked away.

'Is something wrong, my child?' Bellarmine asked, concerned.

'I don't know,' she replied. 'I really don't know.'

'Let's go through this one more time,' Sperone Speroni said wearily. 'Starting from when the coach stopped.'

The flickering torchlight emphasized the haggard face of the soldier sitting opposite him. The man's eyes were wide, as if he had been drugged, and a muscle in his cheek was twitching. He was gazing at a point somewhere over Speroni's shoulder. 'Angels of the Lord descended from on high and took Cardinal Bellarmine from us,' he whispered. 'They were beautiful, and the sound of their voices was like honey in my ears.'

Speroni ran a hand across the stubble of his scalp, wishing he was back in the Arsenale, hammering planks of wood together and watching a ship's hull take form in front of him. Not sitting in a stuffy, torch-lit room, listening to the ravings of a madman. 'Now how many of these angels did you say there were?'

The soldier's eyes flickered suspiciously toward him. 'You don't believe me,' he said. 'You think I'm touched by the sun, or drunk!'

Speroni shrugged. 'You say this happened last night? On your way to Venice?' The soldier nodded, and Speroni continued: 'Well, I don't know who you had in the coach, but Cardinal Bellarmine has been a guest of the Doge here in Venice for the past few days, and the only incident that he has been involved in to my knowledge has been an attempted abduction by Turkish spies.'

The soldier's gaze had strayed to a point above Speroni's head, but from the vacant look in his eye

Speroni guessed that he wasn't seeing the wall, but something else entirely.

'They were beautiful,' the soldier said.

'Then they can't have been Turkish spies,' Speroni said. 'And, as far as I am aware, no heathen Turk has ever been described as having a voice like honey.' He shook his head, and wished to God that he might wake up and find that the past ten years had been a dream, and he was making warships in the Arsenale again. Anything but this. *Anything* but this.

As the knife plunged toward Galileo's eyes, everything seemed to be happening slowly, as if he, the assassin, the Doctor and everybody else in the Tavern of Fists were moving through water, caught in weeds. He could see the way the light gleamed off the blade – the curiously pristine blade – and reflected on to the wine bottle, casting a red glow across the Doctor's face. He could see the way the assassin's face remained calm, and the way the shadows on his face didn't seem to match with the way the sunlight was streaming through the windows. Motes of dust spun slowly through the beams of sunlight, which themselves seemed almost solid enough to support the weight of the wall. Nothing mattered – time was as massive and as immobile as a cathedral.

And then time speeded up, and the knife was hurtling towards him, and there was nothing he could do but die.

The Doctor's arm suddenly lashed out. His cane thudded home into the assassin's stomach – deep into the assassin's stomach – and the man bent double with a curiously high-pitched retching noise. Without conscious thought Galileo leaped to his feet, grabbed the wine bottle and brought it crashing down on the man's head. Shards of glass exploded across the table and surrounding floor and the assassin fell heavily along with them. The impact shook the boards of the floor. The patrons of the tavern moved back a few feet and, for a moment, the normal hubbub was stilled. But only for a moment.

'Let's get out,' Galileo said, 'lest the Nicolottis send another of their paid men after me. They will never believe that I didn't poison that young cur. My life in Venice is not worth a holed florin now. The Doge will never —'

'I think,' the Doctor said, kneeling down beside the figure, 'that this . . . man . . . was not sent by any human agency.'

'What do you mean?' Galileo gazed wildly around. 'Of course he was. The Nicolottis want revenge. It's as plain as the nose on your face.'

The Doctor reached out to touch the stunned assassin's back, and Galileo gaped as the Doctor's hand seemed to plunge *through* the man's clothes and skin up to the wrist.

'I . . . I don't . . .'

'No,' murmured the Doctor, 'you probably don't.' He twisted his invisible hand, and with a sound that reminded Galileo of the cheep of a bird, the assassin's body shimmered and vanished. In its place was a figure so thin that it could have been built out of the branches of a tree. Its skin was blue and glossy, covered in wart-like bumps, and from its head there sprouted a horn fully a foot long that had been broken in two by the wine bottle. It moved weakly, trying to rise, but its twig-like fingers kept slipping on the wine-soaked floor.

The Doctor's hand was resting on a small device of bright metal that was attached to the creature's belt. 'As I suspected,' he said, 'a hologram generator. Did you notice the way the shadows on its face didn't accord with the direction of the sunlight? I do believe that this attempt upon your life was something to do with Envoy Albrellian, and the island of Laputa. And there, of course, we will find all the answers we seek.' His nimble fingers undid the buckles that held the metal device. Pocketing it, he stood up. 'I think we should follow your most excellent advice, and make ourselves scarce.'

'But what about . . .?' Galileo pointed to the creature, unable to finish his sentence.

'Oh, there will no doubt be some consternation when it is noticed, hmm?' the Doctor said, 'but I'm sure it will manage to make its escape.' He walked quickly towards the tavern door. Galileo followed, pausing only to take a half-empty bottle of wine from a table as he passed. A commotion arose behind him as he emerged from the tavern into the bright sunlight by the side of a canal, but he couldn't tell whether it was because the creature had been noticed or because he had taken the wine.

As he stood squinting beside the canal, a man in fine velvet clothes walked up to him. 'Galileo Galilei?' he said.

Galileo tensed. The Doctor turned, his cane half-raised.

'Doge Leonardo Donà sends his apologies for the delay. He will see the most excellent device of which you spoke tomorrow morning at ten o'clock.'

The man turned on his heel and was gone. Galileo turned to gaze at the Doctor.

'It never rains,' he said, 'but it pours.'

'Doctor?' Steven pushed the doors wide open and glanced around the rooms in the Doge's palace that had been assigned to the three travellers. 'Doctor, are you there?'

Nobody answered. A stray breeze from the window fluttered the corners of the tapestries and, outside the window, the voices of the crowd melded together into an incessant buzz. There was no sound from anywhere in the suite of rooms. The Doctor wasn't there.

Steven hadn't been with the Doctor long, but he knew that his mysterious companion was very rarely silent. Whatever he did was accompanied by a constant stream of 'hmm?'s, 'hah!'s and subvocalized murmurs. The Doctor seemed incapable of doing anything in silence.

151

Behind Steven, Marlowe and Shakespeare entered the room.

'Very impressive,' Marlowe said appreciatively. 'I would swear that even the palace of Good King James himself could not rival this for splendour, eh Will?'

Steven glanced back to see Shakespeare looking around the room. 'Indeed not,' the playwright said morosely. 'Mostly the palace's walls are bare, these days, and we perform in draughty halls to an audience so muffled in robes and coats that they can barely make out what we are saying.'

'Times are harsh then?' Marlowe clapped a hand on Shakespeare's shoulder. 'Word reached me that purse strings were being tightened and bellies were rumbling, but I put it down to jealousy and the tendency of all foreigners to malign our fair country.'

Shakespeare shrugged. 'The web of our life is of mingled yarn: good and ill together. I shall not complain. Good King James is a fair patron and a bonny monarch, but his largesse might lead one to believe that he had access to a dragon's hoard. In his first year as monarch he made nine hundred knights of his friends and would-be friends. He gives them money, and favours, and all manner of privileges. A while ago one of his advisers, distressed at the flow of money from the King's coffers to the pockets of his favourites, ordered the latest round of "gifts" to be counted out before the throne, coin by golden coin. It took three hours.' As Marlowe chuckled, Shakespeare continued: 'It helped, but not for long. Money is flowing from the Treasury as blood flows from a man with a cut throat.'

'Can we cut the reminiscences?' Steven snarled. 'I know you two guys have got a lot to catch up on, but we need to find the Doctor. He has to know what you've both told me.'

'And what is that, hmm?' a voice said from behind them all. Steven blinked, surprised, as the Doctor swept into the room. Reaching the centre of the room he turned to face the group. His face was imperious, and the light from the window back-lit his head, turning his long white hair into a glowing halo. 'Now, before you say anything, I have something to tell you all, and it concerns –' He paused, and glanced from Marlowe to Shakespeare and back again. 'Steven, who are these companions of yours? I hope you haven't been wasting time while Vicki is undergoing heaven knows what ordeals in drinking and carousing with disreputable companions?'

'Sorry?' Steven asked.

'I asked you –' He stopped and glanced to Steven's side. 'Surely you are William Shakespeare, are you not?' he enquired.

Shakespeare bowed low. 'Honoured to make your acquaintance, sir,' he murmured. 'And doubly honoured that you know my face, when I do not recall ever having met you. Although –'

'Yes?' the Doctor said.

Shakespeare frowned slightly. 'You do not have a younger brother, do you? Tall, with curled brown hair and as strange a taste in clothes as your own?'

'I do not,' the Doctor replied. 'Why do you ask?'

'You put me in mind of him. I never knew his name, but he gave me some small assistance with writing out *Hamlet* when my wrist was sprained. I thought perchance he had described me to you.'

'No, no,' the Doctor said. 'I saw your face on the Space-Time Vis – ah –' he caught himself '– drawn in a pamphlet which came my way describing the great playwrights of London.' As Shakespeare bowed again, the Doctor quickly turned to Steven's other companion. 'And you, sir? Whom do I have the pleasure of addressing?'

'This is Giovanni Zarattino –' Steven closed his eyes and sighed. 'No, it isn't. This is actually Christopher Marlowe, who apparently should be dead but isn't, and used to write plays but is now a spy.'

'Well,' the Doctor said, clapping his hands together,

'thank you for making it all perfectly clear. I am the Doctor, of course, and this,' he gestured towards the door, 'is Galileo Galilei.'

Steven turned again towards the door, and couldn't help smiling as he saw Galileo standing there, a half-empty bottle of wine in his hand. Galileo waved it at Shakespeare and Marlowe, and nodded at Steven.

'Now, Steven,' the Doctor snapped before anybody could interrupt, 'Galileo and I have traced the spacecraft from the moon to a point out in the lagoon. We intend rowing out there tonight to determine precisely what is at that point. I anticipate that we will find this Laputa of which Albrellian spoke, and I believe that Vicki will be held prisoner there. We fully intend to rescue her.'

'Wait, Doctor,' Galileo cried, and took another swig of wine. Tiny rills of red-hued liquid ran down either side of his mouth. Judging by the matted state of his beard, a lot of what he had already drunk had gone the same way. 'I have an appointment with the Doge. I have a . . . a spyglass to demonstrate. Can't afford to miss it. Doesn't do to make the Doge angry, you know.'

'I need you with me, Mr Galileo,' the Doctor said in a tone that brooked no argument. 'Your incisive mind could prove to be invaluable. Steven can use the hologuise generator and pretend to be you while we are –'

'Doctor,' Steven interrupted, 'Marlowe and I saw a space shuttle come out of a house here in Venice. There's a sort of basement thing beneath the water level, and there's a gate that leads out into the canal.'

The Doctor's bird-like gaze fastened on Steven. 'Are you sure?' he asked.

'He speaks the truth,' Marlowe agreed, stepping forward. 'I saw it too. The house is owned by a man named Irving Braxiatel.'

The expression on the Doctor's face didn't flicker, but the atmosphere of the room suddenly changed. The shadows were deeper all of a sudden, the breeze cooler, the silence more intense. 'Braxiatel, you say?' He half-turned towards the window. 'Braxiatel, *here*?'

'You know this man?' Marlowe said, stepping forward.

'Yes, yes,' the Doctor fussed, waving his hand at the man. 'Yes, Braxiatel is my . . . Well, well, well. Things are suddenly becoming a little clearer.' He smiled, and it was not an expression that Steven liked. 'Perhaps you should tell me everything.'

Steven sighed. 'That's what we were trying to − oh never mind.'

As Braxiatel's skiff rose steadily into the air, Vicki watched the emerald foliage of Laputa fall away on the viewscreen with a shiver of recognition. The last time she had seen a sight like that, her father had been with her. They had been leaving Earth together, hoping to make a new life on one of the Outer Rim colony worlds after her mother died. He had joked about her eagerness as she pressed her nose against the viewing window. She could remember his laugh and the warmth of his hand on her shoulder. All gone now.

They had taught her in school that matter and energy were neither created nor destroyed, but they were wrong. Mothers died. Fathers died.

Hope died.

Around the edge of Laputa a fringe of golden beach appeared and, around that, a line of pellucid blue water. The skiff rose farther and faster, and she could see layers of structure within the lagoon that sailors never saw: the sandbanks that came within inches of the surface but were invisible if you were floating on it, the blackened ribs of wrecked ships and the small specks of fish swimming between them, the gently waving strands of weed that bent over like a forest in a high wind. And then they were too high to make out the detail, and the sea was as it appeared from a few feet away: opaque and mysterious. Other islands crept in around the edge of the screen, but then they passed through the first layer of cloud and the glorious sight of the unspoiled Earth was hidden.

'How long does the journey take?' she asked Braxiatel.

'A few minutes,' he answered without taking his eyes off the controls. 'We don't normally travel through the atmosphere very fast because we don't want to cause any sonic booms – might alert the natives, you see. Once we're above the troposphere we can speed up a bit. Are you enjoying the flight?'

'I am. Thanks for offering to take me out.'

He smiled. 'I was afraid that you might be feeling a little cooped up. I'll show you where the spaceships are all parked, then we'll head back to Earth and tell the Doctor you're all right. I assume that he'll be worried.'

'I hope so,' Vicki said. 'I'll be annoyed if he's not.'

Outside the viewscreen the sky had turned the purple of a fresh bruise, and the line of the horizon was visible right at the edge.

'Mind if I reorient the sensors?' Braxiatel asked. 'You might want to see where we're going.'

'Go ahead.'

Braxiatel caressed a control, and the screen blurred and re-formed to show the battered surface of the moon ahead of them, sailing quietly through the black void. Vicki jumped as a sudden *ping* echoed through the cabin and a red light flashed on the control panel.

'What's that?' she asked.

'Not to worry – we're just being scanned,' Braxiatel said reassuringly.

'Scanned by what?'

He pointed to a small speck, dark against the brightness of the moon's surface. It looked to Vicki like the fish that had been swimming in and out of the wrecks in the lagoon. 'Scanned by that. It's one of my automatic sentry satellites. Everywhere within a light year of Earth has been declared a no-go area by my people for the duration of the Armageddon Convention. With anything this big, there's always the risk that a race like the Daleks or the

156

Cybermen will attempt to disrupt it. Intelligence reports have already indicated an increase in activity around the Seventh Galaxy. Any ship coming within range of one of these satellites – and I have them scattered around the entire solar system – will be destroyed if it isn't expected or recognized.'

'Very reassuring,' Vicki said quietly. 'I presume it recognizes us?'

'I hope so,' Braxiatel said, smiling quietly. 'I'll be annoyed if it doesn't.'

As they grew closer to the satellite, Vicki could make out more of its shape, and the more she saw the more she was reminded of a fish. The satellite was long and sleek, optimized for pursuit in space or in an atmosphere, with a viciously pointed front end and a tail that fanned out into a broad, flat warp blade. Fins along its length held a variety of missiles and gun turrets.

'Nasty,' she murmured.

'Very,' Braxiatel agreed. 'I couldn't use sentry satellites manufactured by any races at the conference or with a vested interest in seeing it disrupted, just in case they had been programmed with other instructions. Trojan horses, if you like. So I went back in time and obtained these from a race known as the Aaev. They were glad to sell the satellites to me – apparently the things had been sitting around for ages and never been used.'

'And the Aaev aren't around any longer?' Vicki asked.

'No,' Braxiatel replied, and coughed slightly. 'I later found out that they were invaded and destroyed shortly after I left. No defences, you see.'

Vicki glanced at his face, which was studiously directed towards the controls. 'You're very much like the Doctor, you know?' she said.

'I should hope so,' Braxiatel said, affronted, 'after all, we *are* –' He suddenly pointed toward the screen. 'Ah, here we are – close enough to make out the landing field now.'

Vicki gazed towards the crater that Braxiatel was

indicating. What initially looked like a collection of large rocks suddenly resolved itself into a group of spacecraft of wildly different design parked haphazardly together in a crater. Some were rectangles, some cubes, some spheres, some tetrahedrons, some just collections of geometric shapes stuck together. All of them bristled with short-range weapons, and none of them looked as if they were designed to enter an atmosphere. Scattered around the perimeter of the crater were a number of small skiffs like the one that Vicki and Braxiatel were travelling in. As Vicki watched, one of the skiffs rose from the ground, sending great clouds of lunar dust puffing out in slow-motion around it.

'Aren't you worried that these ships might be seen from the Earth?' Vicki asked.

'Not particularly,' Braxiatel replied. 'One of the reasons that I wanted to hold the Armageddon Convention here on Earth at this precise moment in its history was that the human race is on the brink of great scientific discoveries which can be, or will be, perverted to military ends. The telescope is one of them. Galileo will persuade the Doge of its worth by stressing the advantage it will give Venice over its Turkish enemies – any invasion fleet can be seen much further away than before. That gave me a problem of course – anybody with a telescope was a potential threat because the ships on the moon are too far away to be seen by the naked eye. Fortunately there are only a handful of people on Earth with a telescope, and only one of those is interested in what's happening on the moon rather than the Earth.'

'Galileo, of course,' Vicki exclaimed. 'So it was you that broke his lenses!'

Braxiatel nodded. 'That's right – or rather, it was one of the Jamarians that work for me. I had to ensure that, for the duration of the conference, he posed no threat either to our security or to the blithe disregard that humans have for the existence of other races.'

The edges of the crater had expanded beyond the

confines of the viewscreen now, and Vicki could make out markings on the sides of the ships: ornate crests, thorn–like writing, portraits of the envoys being carried, lists of battles won and lost. The ships themselves were looking less and less like simple geometric shapes as their details became clearer, and Vicki could make out the fine traceries of pipes and spars that connected their various parts.

'And does that include killing him?' she murmured.

Braxiatel glanced across to where Vicki was sitting, and frowned. 'Killing him?'

'Someone tried to poison Galileo in a tavern. He told us.'

'I didn't leave any orders that he be killed.' His voice rose. 'That would have meant a completely unwarranted interference in the affairs of this planet. My people tend to frown on that sort of thing.'

'Well if you didn't try to kill him,' Vicki mused as the crater walls rose above them, hiding the horizon, and clouds of lunar dust rose in their turn to hide the walls of the crater, 'then who did?'

'A boat?' The old fisherman smiled and shook his head. 'What do you want a boat for?'

Galileo glanced across at Shakespeare. The Englishman was gazing morosely along the broad quayside of the Riva Degli Schiavoni towards where a crowd of his fellow countrymen were standing beside another small fishing boat – one of the many that lined the quayside at this time in the afternoon. Galileo watched them too for a few minutes but, in their heavy black clothes, they looked too much like dowdy birds for his liking. He found his gaze wandering away from them and towards the golden domes of the Church of St Mary of Health that lay in the Dorsoduro district, just across the mouth of the Grand Canal. Beyond the corner of the island of La Giudecca the lagoon stretched away, and he winced at the bright shards of sunlight that were glancing off the water and into his eyes. His head ached with old wine, and he was beginning to bitterly regret being talked into letting Steven represent him to the Doge. He should have been there himself! His golden tongue would have charmed the Doge's purse into disgorging a huge amount of gold for the secret of the spyglass.

Then again, he had to admit to a burning curiosity over what lay on this fabled island. If its inhabitants could construct devices that could carry them through the air as a coach could carry men along a road, then Galileo wished very much to talk to them. Perhaps it *was* for the best after all. Steven was an adequate pupil – Galileo had tutored him in exactly what to say. It was no different from a master painter – Titian, for instance – employing an assistant to fill in the colours while the master concentrated on the details.

'I do not intend entering into a debate with you about my requirement for transport,' the Doctor snapped. 'I merely wish to hire a boat. Are you in the market for such services or not?'

'Well,' the fisherman replied, 'that would depend upon what terms.' His face was as creased and worn as an old leather jerkin, and his eyes were screwed up against the sunlight. He reached down and picked up a small squid from the pile at his feet.

'On what terms?' the Doctor repeated. 'My good man, we will pay whatever the current market price is for the hire of a boat, and not a penny more.'

Galileo caught Shakespeare's eye and shrugged. The Doctor was forceful, that much was undeniable, but the Venetians couldn't be hurried or badgered or argued with. They did things in their own time and in their own way, and their way was always the best way.

'Ah,' the fisherman sighed, turning the squid over in his hands and examining it, 'but the market price depends on so many factors – what you want to do, where you are going, what religious festivals are occurring . . .'

'What do religious festivals have to do with it?' the Doctor snapped.

The fisherman smiled, revealing a mouth devoid of all but a single tooth. 'For instance, today is the festival of St Martin the Lame, and by time-honoured custom the prices for the hire of a boat are doubled after noon on this day.'

The Doctor seemed about to explode with indignation, so Galileo caught hold of his elbow and moved him a few steps away. 'Doctor, let me negotiate – I am used to dealing with Venetians.'

'Nonsense,' the Doctor expostulated, 'I am quite able to fix an adequate price, and I'll have you know that I am used to dealing with *Venusians*. I'm not senile, you know.'

'Indeed, Doctor, but . . .' Galileo paused and took a deep breath. 'Can I ask why we are not using the boat in which you and I sailed to fetch your telescope?'

'Oh, completely unsuitable,' the Doctor said. 'You remember how unstable it was when we were attacked. Why, one good heave and the whole thing might turn over. No, if the three of us are going in search of Laputa then we need something a lot safer than my dinghy.'

'Your what?'

'My – never mind, young man. If you're going to fix a price with this ruffian, hadn't you better get on with it, hmm?'

Galileo opened his mouth to say something, but closed it again. He'd argued with some of the greatest debaters in Europe in his time, but there was something about the Doctor's peremptory manner that brooked no argument.

He was about to turn back to the fisherman when he noticed that Shakespeare was staring rather fixedly at the group of Englishmen who were now moving towards them.

'Friends of yours?' he asked.

'I travelled with them on the boat that brought us here,' Shakespeare said quietly. 'They seemed healthy enough then, although they kept themselves to themselves. But look at them now.'

161

The fear in Shakespeare's voice brought Galileo up short, as if he had just been caught in a sudden shower of cold rain. The Doctor too picked up on Shakespeare's tone and peered at the dowdy Englishmen as they passed by, talking animatedly amongst themselves. For a moment Galileo saw nothing untoward – their clothes were unfashionable and much patched, true, and their faces were pale and lined, but apart from –

No. Those faces. Pale they might be, but there were patches of red on them. He had thought for a moment that they were wearing rouge on their cheeks, but the patches were too irregular for that, and some of them had blisters in their centres. One of the women raised a hand to scratch at one of the blisters, and a shiver ran through Galileo as he saw a weeping red sore upon the back of her hand.

'God's truth!' he whispered, aghast, as the Englishmen passed by. 'They have the plague!'

'No,' the Doctor said quietly, but with firm authority. 'Those wounds have nothing to do with the plague. Those are radiation sores.'

Twelve

'Well,' Steven muttered to himself as he stood in a small niche on the stairs that led up to the Doge's chambers, 'here goes nothing.' His voice was lost amid the muted roar of conversation from the crowd bustling up and down the great marble steps and along the wooden corridors. The huge portraits around the wall gazed down on him with unreadable expressions. His palms were moist, his stomach was fluttering, and his muscles felt so weak that he kept expecting the telescope tucked beneath his arm to fall and smash on the steps. He hadn't felt this nervous since he had ridden his ship down in flames, surrounded by Krayt fighters, watching the indicator lights on the control board explode one by one, hearing the grinding noise as the rocket engines tore loose from their mountings.

Glancing around to ensure that none of the courtiers, petitioners and general hangers-on were paying him any attention, he casually slid his fingers down his tunic to his belt. For a moment he couldn't locate the small metal device that the Doctor had given him. His fingers scrabbled around the leather strap, frantically searching for the damned thing. If it had fallen off he might just as well find a nice little set of rooms overlooking a canal and settle down, because the Doctor would never let him back on the TARDIS again. Not if he screwed up Galileo's big presentation.

His little finger touched cold metal. Sighing with relief, he closed his hand over the device, feeling the raised stud beneath his palm. The thing must have slid around the belt when he brushed against someone in the crowd.

Well, he'd have to go through with it now.

Before he could change his mind, he closed his eyes and pressed the stud. When he opened them again, nothing had changed. The corridor still looked the same. The people still looked the same.

He raised his right hand and looked at it. Well, *that* didn't look the same. It was thicker, the fingers longer, and the veins that snaked across its back were more knotted and purple. It was Galileo's hand, projected from the image that the Doctor had scanned into the device earlier on. Steven raised his left hand and touched his right hand with his left forefinger. It felt the same as it always had, but then, he supposed that it would. After all, it was just a hologram. His hand was still underneath the image, like a face beneath a mask. The only giveaway was the fact that the image of his forefinger disappeared into the image of his right hand by a few millimetres before he could actually feel them touch, because his fingers were shorter than Galileo's.

He was wasting time. Taking a deep breath, Steven tucked the telescope tighter under his arm and walked firmly up the stairs. The quicker he did this, the sooner he'd be out.

The vibrant green of the island stood out against the blue sea like an emerald against velvet. Vicki watched its approach wide-eyed, her breath held.

'This is a beautiful place,' she whispered.

'I know,' Braxiatel murmured, glancing up from the controls. 'I can see why the Doctor prefers Earth to anywhere else.'

It had never occurred to Vicki before, but Braxiatel was right. The Doctor did seem to spend an awful lot of time on or near Earth. 'I suppose you're right, but with all of time and all of space to wander through, why choose Earth?'

Braxiatel shrugged. 'There are lots of reasons why your

164

race are of interest to our race. Your curiosity, your ability to apply yourself to any problem or situation, your sheer persistence and adaptability, your –' He paused, and smiled slightly. 'Well, there are things that I'm afraid I can't actually tell you about your past, and your future. Suffice it to say that we feel for humanity as a father might feel towards a rather wayward daughter.'

Vicki felt her heart thud slightly harder in her chest. No matter how often she thought she would get used to it, the pain attached to the memories surprised her. She watched the approaching landing pad, trying to wipe her mind clean of the grief, but the prickle of approaching tears in her eyes made her turn her head away from Braxiatel.

'I've hurt your feelings,' Braxiatel said softly. 'I'm sorry.' He removed his half-moon glasses and began to polish them with a small cloth that he took from his pocket. 'Please accept my apologies,' he said, not looking at her. 'I have an unfortunate habit of saying the wrong thing at the wrong time.'

'No,' Vicki protested, and stifled a sob, 'please – it's not your fault. It's just . . .' She took a deep breath and tried to calm her churning stomach. 'My father died. He was killed in an explosion on the planet Dido. That's where the Doctor found me. I still dream about him sometimes, but you weren't to know.'

As the skiff settled gently upon the landing pad, Braxiatel reached out to pat her hand. 'I apologize anyway,' he said. 'Now, let's try and find the Doctor and tell him you're all right, shall we?'

Vicki nodded. 'Can you – do you mind if I follow on in a moment? I want to collect my thoughts.'

Braxiatel nodded. 'Of course,' he said quietly. 'I'll be in the main hall when you're ready, and we can go and find the Doctor.'

'Your explanation is as subtle and as illuminating as ever, Signor Galileo,' the Doge said in his dry, quiet voice.

165

Behind him loomed a vast painting of scantily dressed ladies and plump lions. 'To think, that such a simple device, so cheap and so easy to construct, could do all that you claim. It is truly a marvel.'

Around him, the Doge's advisers nodded wisely. They were wearing black and, in the shadows of the Hall of the Ante-College, their heads seemed to float in mid-air. The nods of agreement rippled outward to the Council of Ten, then to the Sages of the Order who commanded the great Venetian navy. At least, that was who Steven thought they were. Galileo had been a little the worse for wear when he explained the set-up to Steven, and some of the details had been a little confused.

One of the men that surrounded the Doge – a tall man with a thin face and a great beak of a nose – glared down at Steven. Beneath the hologram, Steven felt patches of sweat-sodden cloth shift clammily against his skin. Had the man penetrated the disguise?

'Your . . . your Serenity is most gracious,' Steven said, bowing so low that the telescope under his arm poked up above his head. Although the Doge's tone had been calm and measured, there was something about his words that Steven didn't like. What had he said? 'So cheap and so easy to make.' Galileo had warned Steven not to underestimate the Doge's business acumen. He was implying that Galileo's telescope was hardly a discovery at all – just a tool like a screwdriver that could be built by anybody at all. And if he continued along that route, Galileo wouldn't get any money at all. 'This spyglass is, as you say, simple and easy to construct from materials which are easily available,' Steven blurted, 'but so are the works of . . . of any writer of antiquity that you care to name. Words are available to anyone, and paper is common, but it takes genius to create a work of literature. In the same way, it takes genius to *think* of a spyglass, even though a fool may buy all the parts.'

The Doge nodded, and another ripple of agreement spread through the crowd around his throne. 'Of course,'

166

he continued, 'you will be aware from your friend, Friar Sarpi, that a Flemish gentleman has lately been importuning this Senate to buy an instrument similar to the one that you possess. He has asked one thousand florins for it. We are intrigued by the idea, but with the device itself I was barely able to make out the details of the paintings at the far end of this room.'

One of his advisers immediately pointed over Steven's shoulder. Turning, Steven could make out a large canvas that seemed to consist of blue sky, white clouds and pink cherubs with trumpets. Another trap. The Doge was simultaneously warning Steven that Galileo was not the only man with a telescope, that he wasn't terribly impressed with the telescope that he *had* seen and that price was a definite issue. Galileo had warned Steven about this.

'Your Serene Highness,' Steven began, 'this *adventurer* —' which was the description that Galileo had spat out earlier '— possesses an inferior model which can make objects appear to be only one third of their actual distance away, and as such is little more than a toy. *My* spyglass, by contrast, makes things appear to be one *tenth* of their actual distance away, and is fit for a range of . . . er . . . military applications, for instance.'

'Military applications?' The Doge leaned forward, suddenly interested. His advisers, the Council of Ten and the Sages of the Order all leaned forward as well.

'Indeed.' Steven's mouth was dry, and he had to suck hard on his cheeks to provide enough saliva to continue. 'With this spyglass, a watcher in the tower in the square outside —' whatever it was called, he thought desperately '— could see an invading fleet as it came over the horizon, rather than when it was almost on top of you.'

The Doge nodded. 'Indeed, an invention to rival the military compass that you designed. I would see this spyglass demonstrated on ships rather than paintings. Let us remove ourselves to —' he smiled slightly '— the tower in the square outside, which we Venetians refer to as the bell-tower of St Mark's. There we will test your claims against the fishing boats as they return for the night.'

Steven breathed a sigh of relief. It seemed to be working.

And then he caught sight of the hawk-nosed Councillor glaring down at him, and his mouth went dry again.

The mist had closed in around them like the gauze backcloths of the Globe Theatre, and Shakespeare found himself thinking that he would have to have words with Burbage about the way he portrayed stormy seas on stage. Those billowing sheets, streaked with green and blue, that Burbage thought looked like waves were too dramatic. Far too dramatic. The waves here in the lagoon were more like the gently rolling hills of Stratford-upon-Avon, but the way they made the tiny boat pitch and toss was almost beyond credibility. Waves the size of Burbage's would have overturned the boat before they'd even got out of sight of land.

He glanced along the deck of the boat, and was annoyed to see the Doctor standing by the mast, his white hair billowing in the wind like a miniature of the billowing sail above his head, looking for all the world as if he were enjoying himself. Shakespeare was sick to his stomach. After all, he'd only just stepped off the boat from England, and he had been looking forward to a few days standing on dry land. Venice wasn't exactly dry land, of course, but it was an acceptable substitute.

A gull flew close overhead, and Shakespeare cursed at it.

'What was that?' Galileo shouted from his position by the tiller.

'Nothing of import,' Shakespeare shouted back.

'Coming into port? But we've barely been out half an hour.' Galileo's beard bristled angrily. 'If that's a slur on my navigation, I'll have your liver and lights Master Shake-Shaft!'

'What I said was –' Shakespeare sighed. 'Oh, never

mind. It's not worth going to war over.'

'Having a bit of trouble making yourself understood?' the Doctor asked, glancing over his shoulder with a superior smile on his face.

'I confess, Doctor, that I do not understand why I am here.' Shakespeare scowled as best he could, but it turned into a clownish grimace as a spray of sea water hit him in the face.

'I thought I had made it all perfectly clear,' the Doctor said. 'We are seeking the island of Laputa, where I believe my companion to be held.'

'That's all very well,' Shakespeare snapped, 'but it doesn't explain what *I* am doing here, especially while Kit Marlowe is wandering around Venice. I have a mission to fulfil for my Monarch.'

The Doctor ran his thumbs under his lapels and cocked his head to one side. 'If, as you explained, you have been instructed to seek the representatives of some foreign empire and do business with them, then I suspect that you may find them on Laputa. Although –' and he chuckled '– you may discover that they are from an empire that does not lie on any of the standard trade routes.'

Shakespeare was about to reply when something loomed up out of the mist ahead: a sketchy shape, a darker shadow against the grey veils, like a piece of scenery forgotten and unlit behind a backcloth. 'What is that?' he cried as it became clearer – a fabulous, fantastic city of cloud-capped towers, gorgeous palaces, solemn temples, great globes and slender spires, paths that hung in mid-air and stairways that moved by themselves, like Jacob's ladder. 'Is it . . . is it heaven?'

'No, it's Laputa,' the Doctor said with satisfaction. 'Mister Galileo, prepare to make land.'

'Aye, Doctor,' Galileo shouted from the stern of the boat. 'But I warn you, we have company.'

Shakespeare and the Doctor both turned to face Galileo. The bearded Venetian was pointing off to one side, to where a patch of mist had been cleaved by the bows of another boat. And beside it, another. And beyond that, a third. Figures moved on their decks, clad in stark black cloth. Shakespeare strained his eyes. Perhaps it was the mist, but they looked like corpses, freshly animated, staring blindly ahead. The wind whipped the sea-spray into their faces, but they didn't blink, or wipe their eyes. And as the wind carried their boats closer, Shakespeare was unsurprised to see the weeping sores that covered their exposed skin.

The bell tower was set on the edge of the crowded market-place that was St Mark's Square, a few hundred yards from the edge of the lagoon. Stalls selling foods, sweets, trinkets and pets were gathered around its base like ducklings around their mother. As he emerged from the Doge's palace, Steven breathed in the scented air, and the mingled scents of wood smoke, incense, cooked meat made him dizzy for a moment. Past the edge of the quay, the surface of the water was bright with momentary flickers of light as the sun caught the tops of the waves. The ornate prows of the gondolas that were tied to the wooden piers nodded one by one as the waves lifted them, like a row of penitent priests.

Steven sighed as he remembered arriving at one of those piers. How long ago had it been? One day? Two? It seemed that when you were a time traveller, time lost all meaning to you. Events seemed to crowd together until your life was a succession of freeze-frames: run, hide, fight, run, hide, fight. He was tired. He wanted to stop, just for a while. Just for a rest.

The Doge's guards pushed past him and began clearing a path through the crowds of Venetians and foreign travellers. Two of them appeared to have acquired a horse from somewhere, and were leading it over. Steven gazed up the crumbling red brick of the bell tower. This was it. Make or break.

'Please, lead the way,' the Doge's dry voice murmured behind him. Steven took a deep breath, and walked across the flagstones towards the portico. He could feel the eyes of the crowd on him as he walked. No doubt they were wondering what he was doing there. He was beginning to wonder the same thing himself.

At the portico he turned to see the Doge and his advisers following like a row of chicks. The black-clad advisers were bent over as they walked, and their little nodding heads reminded him of the gondolas. He sniggered, and the Doge shot him a dark glance.

'My apologies,' Steven muttered, coughing into his handkerchief.

'The belfry is small,' the Doge said. 'You will demonstrate your spyglass to us one at a time.' He gestured to one of the guards. 'Starting with me.'

After an uncomfortable moment while Steven waited for someone to go first, he realized that he should be leading the way. The shadowed portico led immediately onto a narrow ramp that spiralled around the inside of the tower. Bell ropes hung down its centre. Steven began to climb. Within ten steps his calf muscles were beginning to ache and within twenty his breath was hissing in his ears. By the time he got to thirty steps he could feel the thudding of his pulse in his ears and he had lost track of how many revolutions around the tower he had made.

By the time he got to the top of the bell tower, sweat was running down his face. He stood in the cold breeze for a moment, his eyes closed, the sound of the crowd far below just a murmur in his ears. When he opened his eyes, he found himself on a square wooden platform surrounded by stone pillars and topped with a pointed roof in which bells gleamed. Through the pillars Steven could see all the way across Venice. Gilded domes and roofs glowed in the sunlight while whitewashed walls were tinted a rosy pink. Flocks of pigeons wheeled and swooped in a pattern too large to appreciate from any aspect except above. Beyond the city, beyond the island, the view reached to the distant white-capped mountains in one direction and the mist that hid the far reaches of the lagoon in the other.

Steven's heart was still thudding in his ears, and he took a deep breath to calm it down. It didn't help: the pounding just got louder. For a moment he started to panic, until he realized that the wooden platform of the bell tower was vibrating in time to the thudding. He turned towards the source of the noise when, from the dark hole in the floor that led to the ramp, the Doge appeared. On a horse, led by one of his guards.

'Have you been up here before?' he murmured, not making any effort to dismount.

'Er . . . no, your most Serene Highness,' Steven stammered.

The Doge raised his eyes and gazed upward, into the pointed roof. 'But you must have heard these bells ring out across Venice, tolling sunrise, noon and sundown, calling councillors to Council and senators to Senate?'

'Of course, your most Sere-'

'That one, over there,' he continued, cutting across Steven's words and indicating the smallest bell, 'is called the Maleficent. It's the one we use to signal executions.' He smiled. 'Please – your demonstration.'

Steven's hands shook as he took the telescope from inside his jacket. 'If you place the spyglass against your eye, your most Serene Excellency, and look out across the lagoon . . .'

The Doge took the telescope from Steven's outstretched hand and raised it to his eye. For a moment he gazed out of the bell tower and across the water. Steven turned to follow the line of the telescope. Far, far away, mere specks against the background of the sea mist, he could just make out the sail of a small ship. With Galileo's telescope, the Doge should have been able to recognize the faces of the crew, and Steven's heart missed a beat as he suddenly realized that the ship might be the one that the Doctor was sailing on, and the Doge might be staring straight into the unmistakable features of Galileo Galilei. That would sink his plans for good.

The Doge lowered the spyglass from his eye. His face was thunderous.

Steven prepared to sprint down the ramp as fast as he could, and hoped to God that he could outpace the Doge's guard.

'This device is worse than the one demonstrated to us by the Flemish merchant,' the Doge said. 'It is a toy fit only for children. Friar Sarpi has misled us, and both you, and he, will pay for wasting my time.'

The guard rested a hand on his sword. Through his helmet, Steven could see a smile of anticipation on his face. 'Ah – your most Serene and ... and Munificent Highness ...' he stammered, dredging up all of the flattery and flannel that he had ever heard, 'I beg you to –'

Something about the telescope that the Doge was holding caught his eye. Something about its shape. Surely ... surely when Galileo had demonstrated it to Steven, he had held the narrower lens against his eye and pointed the wider lens at the sky. The Doge appeared to have been holding it the other way around.

'Perhaps,' he said hesitantly, 'we could try it one more time ...?'

When Braxiatel had gone, and Vicki could see him on the viewscreen, walking across the white surface of the Laputan landing pad towards the nearest tower, Vicki wiped a hand across her eyes. It came away wet, and her cheeks were suddenly cool as the thin film of tears began to evaporate. Memories were like minefields, she decided – you had to pick your way carefully across them, and sometimes you stepped on something unexpected and it exploded beneath you. She took a deep breath and closed her eyes.

And opened them again as something scrabbled in the hatchway. She twisted in her seat. The headrest was in the way, and she had to slide sideways before she could see round it.

173

Into a pair of eyes on stalks.

'Albrellian!' she squealed. 'You startled me!'

'Vicki.' Albrellian's voice was neutral. 'Better your safety belt fasten had you: for a bumpy ride in are we.'

'What do you mean?'

Instead of answering, Albrellian swung his crab-like body into the seat that Braxiatel had vacated only a few moments before. The seat automatically adjusted itself to the odd contours of his body and wing-casings, and he ran his multiple claws across the controls.

'Albrellian, what's going on?' Anger sharpened Vicki's voice. 'If this is another attempt at kidnapping me, Braxiatel won't be pleased.'

The skiff shot straight up into the air, so fast that the ripple of turbulence was replaced within moments by a sudden explosive *bang!* as they broke the sound barrier. Vicki watched the screen disbelievingly as Laputa dwindled and vanished beneath them.

'Even less pleased will be Braxiatel,' Albrellian announced grimly, 'when precious little island sanctuary in one great explosion disappears his!'

'An explosion?' Vicki couldn't assimilate the word. 'What do you – I mean – an *explosion*? When?'

One of Albrellian's eyestalks rotated to glance at her. 'In a few minutes' time,' he said. 'That's why leaving we are.'

Steven gazed out across the roofs of Venice, watching pigeons wheel against the deep blue of the sky. The breeze off the sea was cool, and the crowds far below were just multi-coloured dots that surged randomly to and fro, like bacteria under a microscope.

He leaned against one of the columns and relished the cold stone against his forehead. The last little knots of tension were finally untangling inside his stomach. The Doge had finally accepted that the telescope worked. More than that, he had instantly grasped the military applications and had promised Galileo an increase in

174

salary, a bonus and an extension of his tenure at the University of Padua. Hopefully it would be enough to satisfy both the Doctor and the real Galileo.

It was all plain sailing from here. All Steven had to do was to demonstrate the telescope to the Doge's advisers and the Council and Senate members, one by one, until either they were all satisfied or darkness had fallen. He had talked five of them through it so far, and he could hear the horse that was bearing the sixth heading up the spiral ramp now.

Steven turned as the horse placidly entered the belfry, being led by the guard. As the man on it dismounted, Steven held out the telescope to him.

'This, esteemed Sir, is my —'

'I care not about your baubles,' the man snapped. For the first time Steven actually looked at his face, and he felt his heart give two quick beats. It was the hawk-nosed man who had been glaring at him in the Hall of the Ante-College.

'I — Sir, I do not —'

'Save your stammering apologies,' the man said, sneering. He stepped towards Steven, who backed away until he could feel the stone balustrade against the back of his thighs. The guard and the horse looked on from across the belfry without showing any signs of wanting to interfere.

'I am Tomasso Nicolotti,' the man said. 'You killed my son by poison. I am persuaded that you have the trappings of a gentleman, even though you are scum in the pay of the Castellanis, and so I challenge you to a duel. Be at the Church of St Trovaso when the bells in this tower strike the end of the day.' He smiled. 'Or I shall hunt you down and kill you like the dog that you are.'

Thirteen

They were in a race, and something told Galileo that it was one they had to win.

From his position in the stern of the boat he had a panoramic view of the boat itself and of the water around them. To their left and right, other ships paralleled their course, cleaving the waves apart as they all headed for the island of Laputa. Some were small, barely large enough to hold two drab Englishmen and a mast, while others were thrice their size and supported a crew of Venetian fisher-men presumably hired along with their boat. Others, hidden in the mist, could be heard as they splashed through the water and as their crews shouted instructions to each other. The Englishmen were clustered in the bows of all the ships in sight, all staring fixedly towards the island, ignoring the salt sea-spray that drenched them. The closest boat was only a score of yards away, and slightly ahead, and Galileo could easily make out the unnatural whiteness of the Englishmen's faces, and the rouge-redness of the sores on their skin.

The Doctor was standing by the mast, occasionally tightening or slackening the ropes that led up to the sail. Although he was old, his movements were assured and strong, and he seemed to know what he was doing. Shakespeare, by contrast, was huddled in the bows of the ship and looked as if he might throw his guts up over the side at any moment. Englishmen – effete and unworldly, the lot of them – except for that Marlowe fellow, who seemed to have a practical head on his shoulders despite the lascivious way he eyed young Steven Taylor. A shame

176

that he was not with them now, but had elected to follow his own path in the city itself. He would have been worth ten of Shakespeare in their current situation.

The island of Laputa loomed against the misty backdrop ahead of them, an island paradise of slender trees crowned with spreading foliage, and white towers that reached up, like Babel, to Heaven. Galileo wasn't sure whether to believe the evidence of his own eyes or not, but he was positive that an island such as that would have been spotted by the local fishermen long ago and colonized: or used, like the island of Sant' Ariano, as a reliquary for the bones of dead Venetians. Was it, therefore, new to these seas? Had it been constructed by these travellers from a foreign star that the Doctor talked about, and whose stellar chariots he had seen through his spyglass?

Galileo let his breath whistle out through his teeth. To build an entire island – what a massive feat of engineering that would be. He would like to meet the people who could achieve that.

As he watched, entranced, a small shape like a flattened egg that glinted like metal rose up rapidly from the far side of the island, moving upward as smoothly and inexorably as the ebony balls that he had dropped from the tower of Pisa to test Aristotle's theory had fallen. The object was twin to the ones that Galileo had seen through his telescope. A method of getting to and from the island, perhaps? Truly he would like to ask these people how they achieved these marvels, but was he capable of understanding their explanations?

Of course he could understand. He was Galileo Galilei, foremost natural philosopher in Christendom.

'Hard a port!' the Doctor yelled back from his position by the mast, just as the egg-shape vanished into the clouds.

'Hard to where?' Galileo yelled back.

'Hard a *port*!' The Doctor's eyes gazed Heavenwards in exasperation. 'To the left, Mr Galileo, to the left.'

'Why?'

The Doctor took a few steps towards Galileo, as if to remonstrate with him, but one of the guy ropes pulled taut with a twang like a lute string, and he quickly stepped back to loosen it. 'Because there is a suitable spot at which we can disembark to the left!' he cried. 'Now please stop asking stupid questions and do what I tell you, hmm?'

Galileo grimaced, and pushed the rudder slowly to the right, feeling as he did so the shift in motion as the ship's path altered to favour the left.

'If you have nothing better to do,' the Doctor called to Shakespeare in the bows of the ship, 'perhaps you would lend a hand, Mr Shakespeare.'

Shakespeare's fine clothes were drenched with water, and his sparse hair was plastered across his great bald forehead. 'What would you —' He sucked his cheeks in suddenly and held a hand to his stomach. Galileo grinned. The spasm passed, and the man continued, '— have me do, Doctor?'

'Hold this line tight,' the Doctor snapped, and threw a guy rope to Shakespeare, who took it gingerly. To Galileo's amazement, the Doctor scrambled like a monkey up the mast and set about loosening and retying the ropes that kept the sail attached to the mast. Moments later he returned to the deck, and Galileo was astonished to feel his body forced back slightly against the wooden stern as their speed increased. The ships hired by the Englishmen began to drop back as their boat surged ahead.

'A little trick I learned some years ago when I sailed with Edward Teach,' the Doctor yelled back, the wind of their passage snatching the words from his mouth. 'The material of the sail tightens if it's damp and there's a strong wind, and you can get a few more knots of speed by loosening it again.'

Their boat was five lengths ahead of their leading pursuer now, and the gap kept increasing. The island filled the horizon ahead of them, growing larger by the

178

moment. A spot of yellow close to the water resolved itself into a beach, and Galileo tacked slightly to make sure that they headed for it at a slight angle. Glancing back, over his shoulder, he could see the boats behind them as grey shadows in the mist, like charcoal marks on paper. They were well ahead now: the Doctor's trick had gained them a few precious minutes. The island was growing ever larger, and Galileo could make out details on the towers: windows, ledges and what looked like misshapen people gazing back at him.

And then their keel scraped over sand, and the ship lurched to one side.

'Quickly,' the Doctor called, 'we must get to Braxiatel before those other ships arrive.' He scuttled over the side of the boat, and Galileo heard the splash seconds later as he hit the water. Shakespeare was standing uncertainly in the bows. Abandoning the tiller, Galileo ran to the side and dived over without a moment's thought. He caught a confused glimpse of a stretch of smooth sand and a knot of etiolated figures who were already hauling the Doctor out of the water before the surface rose up to embrace him. For a few confused moments everything was grey and bubbly, and there was a rushing noise in his ears, and then what felt like twigs fastened on his arms and tugged him out of the water.

The Doctor was standing, bedraggled, on the sand. Two thin, horned figures were holding him, and a third was pointing its horn at his chest. They were identical to the creature that had overturned the Doctor's boat when he and Galileo had gone to fetch the Doctor's telescope. Two more of the creatures were hauling Galileo up the beach to join the Doctor.

'Take me to your leader,' the Doctor said imperiously, drawing himself up and brushing sand from his lapels. 'I have to see Braxiatel.'

One of the stick-creatures leaned close to Galileo's ear. 'I promised we'd meet later,' it hissed.

For some reason, the first thought to cross his mind was

the hope that Steven Taylor was having better luck as Galileo than he was.

'What do you mean, an explosion?' Vicki said. 'Take me back to the island, Albrellian. This is going too far.' She leaned forward to the controls, but Albrellian reached across with a claw and nipped her gently on the back of her hand. Blood welled up in the crescent-shaped cut, and she jerked her hand away. A tingling feeling spread up her arm and through her chest and she fell backward into the chair. Waves of tiredness lapped at the edges of her mind, and she had to use all her force of will to keep her eyes open and not slip into sleep.

'Sorry about that am I,' Albrellian said. 'A genetically engineered toxin, afraid am I – the only thing past Braxiatel's scanners could get I. Afford to have interfere with plans my you cannot I.' His eyestalks dipped slightly, as if even he was confused by his tortured syntax.

Vicki's thoughts had to force their way through a thick, treacly miasma. 'What . . . Are . . . You . . . Doing?' she said, articulating the words separately and forcing them past her uncooperative lips.

Albrellian's foreclaws moved across the skiff's controls. One set of eyestalks was directed at the darkening viewscreen while the other was pointed at Vicki. 'Afraid guilty of a little deceit have been I,' he said. 'Of you, of Braxiatel and of the envoys.'

Vicki opened her mouth to ask what sort of deception, but Albrellian raised a claw to her mouth.

'Speak try not to,' he said. 'The effects of the toxin for a while will last. An explanation for all the things put you through have I owe you I.' His eyestalks dipped slightly, as if he was ashamed of himself. 'Explain that my race – the Greld – are represented at the Armageddon Convention not because at war with anyone are we, and not because ever likely to be are we, but because supply weapons to races that are do we, should I. Arms dealers are we, and much of economy towards research and

180

development of bigger and better devices of destruction is dedicated our. Speciality that is our. If plans to fruition of Braxiatel's come, and agreements about what can and can't be used there are, then redundant will become we. Best weapons, most expensive technologies, will not be required our. Cannot happen let that, can we?'

'Sab . . . otage,' Vicki stammered.

'Exactly,' Albrellian said. 'Intelligent as well as beautiful – knew the right choice had made did I.' His eyestalks perked up. 'The biggest obstacle security precautions was Braxiatel's – the sensor systems that from the legendary lost Aaev race purchased did he any weapon, no matter how small, can detect, and whatever ship or person is carrying it destroy can they. Never a weapon close enough to this planet get could we. So, when on this planet first arrived the Greld delegation – some twenty years ago, the components of a meta-cobalt bomb out of locally mined material built we and a group of humans from the local area kidnapped we. A hypnocontroller and a fragment of radioactive meta-cobalt in each of them implanted we, and into forgetting the operation them hypnotized we. Then scattered around the planet them left we, knowing that when all of the races had agreed to come and the envoys were on their way, the carriers together call using the hypnocontrollers could we. As soon as the envoys had all arrived the final command gave we, and for Laputa headed all the carriers. Destroy them the security systems won't because the weapon exist won't until in a small enough space gather together the carriers. As soon as they do that the meta-cobalt critical mass achieves and a huge explosion there will be – big enough the island to destroy and kill all the envoys. The Armageddon Convention a byword for disastrous med-dling in other people's wars will become, and in profit again will be the Greld.'

'What . . . If . . . Some . . . Of . . . Them . . . Die . . . Too . . . Early?' Vicki struggled to force the words past her numb lips, but she knew that she might never get the chance to question Albrellian like this again.

'The ability to regenerate flesh and control pain have the hypnocontrollers. Few injuries would actually prove fatal, and if died a carrier then the hypnocontrollers to what had happened would alert us. To wherever the body was would travel one of us, the meta-cobalt and hypnocontroller would remove and reimplant in another human,' Albrellian said off-handedly. 'Everything thought of we.'

Vicki opened her mouth to say something, but a wave of darkness suddenly swept over her. This time she did not dream.

Shakespeare's head was in a whirl as the three of them were hustled along a path through the jungle by the stick-men. What brave new world could have such . . . such *creatures* in it – more devils than vast Hell itself could hold? Truly this was all some phantasma, or a hideous dream. A fever-dream, perhaps, caught from some old salt who had passed him by in the street. Soon he would wake up and find himself under a table in a tavern in Cripplegate, or lying on a lawn in Richmond. These things could not be happening – not in a sane, rational world. There is something in this more than natural, if philosophy could find it out.

A bony finger poked him in the centre of his back. He turned, and found himself staring into the mad red eye of one of the stick-men. If it *was* a dream, t'were one done well.

The path opened out onto a flat plain of grey stone at the base of one of the lofty towers. Ferns and trees rose up all around, giving the area a secluded, claustrophobic feel. A man was waiting for them. He had a lean and hungry look – although compared to his minions he was positively Falstaffian – and he wore spectacles. His hair was straight and mouse-brown, and it fell in a slight curl over his eyes.

'Doctor,' he said as the party halted in front of him,

'I'm sorry that this little reunion has to take place in such a manner, but needs must when the devil drives.'

'Braxiatel, my dear chap!' The Doctor strode forward and shook the man's hand. 'Good to see that you followed my example and left them too.'

Braxiatel. Shakespeare's confused mind hung on to that name. Kit Marlowe had used it back in Venice. Braxiatel had been the man whose cellar Kit and young Steven had investigated: the man whose name the Doctor had reacted so strongly to. He was obviously a prime mover in this nightmarish conspiracy, and perhaps a link to whatever negotiations were going on with this mysterious empire of which Marlowe had heard.

'Oh, they allowed me to leave,' Braxiatel replied, 'and I've spent most of my time since trying my best not to follow your example.'

'So,' the Doctor said, 'tell me about these aliens flying around Venice, and the spaceships you have on the moon.'

Braxiatel sighed. 'Please, Doctor, not in front of the locals.'

'These aren't just any locals,' the Doctor snapped. 'This is Galileo Galilei —' he indicated the Italian '— and this is William Shakespeare.'

Galileo just nodded curtly, so Shakespeare executed a courtly bow. 'I am honoured, if puzzled, to meet you,' he said in a voice that shook less than he had expected. 'My lord and master, King James of England, commends me to convey his best wishes to you, and bids me —'

Braxiatel dismissed him with a glance. 'Did you have to bring them with you, Doctor?' he said as Shakespeare subsided. 'I have been trying to keep this thing quiet.'

The Doctor raised an eyebrow at Braxiatel. 'If you had told me that you were behind all this,' he said waspishly, 'then I wouldn't have had to involve anybody local at all.'

Braxiatel sighed. 'I did tell you, Doctor,' he replied with the air of a man who has rehearsed the matter in his mind for some time, 'but our people wiped your memory. You were on a mission for them.'

'I was?' The Doctor appeared surprised. 'How strange. Tell me more about this mission.'

Braxiatel raised a placating hand. 'There are rules about this sort of discussion, Doctor, and we are infringing them merely by meeting like this. Suffice it to say that our people gave their blessing to my asking you to chair an arms limitation conference of galactic races here on Earth, and that you agreed. Unfortunately, your memory was wiped and I've ended up with another chairman.'

'The invitation, of course,' the Doctor mused. 'It was programmed to bring me here.' He shook his head. 'This is all academic. My companion – Vicki – you have her in safe keeping?'

'I did, but she's been kidnapped again by one of our envoys.'

Envoys. Shakespeare held on to that word. There *was* a meeting going on. Representations were being made, and he had to make his contribution. He hadn't travelled all the way around Europe to be dismissed by someone who had the lean and hungry look of a man who thought too much.

'That envoy would be Albrellian?' the Doctor asked.

Braxiatel nodded. 'Well done, Doctor, you're picking the situation up nicely.'

'And the boats headed towards this island? What of them?'

'I wouldn't worry.' Braxiatel glanced at one of the stick-men, who nodded. 'If they are carrying weapons, our security precautions will prevent them from landing. If not, the Jamarians can frighten them off.'

The Doctor raised his head and gazed down his nose at Braxiatel. 'You always were over-confident, Braxiatel, even as a child. The people on those boats are all suffering from some sort of radiation sickness. Given that people of this time cannot refine radioactive materials, has it occured to you they might have been supplied with fragments of some material that is inert normally, but when brought together in large quantities becomes radioactive and, when the quantity is large enough, will explode? And has it occurred to you that such a device would circumvent your security procedures, because the weapon would not actually *exist* until the people all arrived in the same place at the same time?'

Braxiatel, Shakespeare thought, was beginning to look a little pasty.

'No,' the Doctor continued grimly, 'I don't suppose it has.'

'Surely we can't hold a duel in a church!' Steven said, pacing across the room that the Doctor had been given by the Doge. He passed a hand across his forehead, hidden beneath the holographic image of Galileo's forehead, and wasn't surprised when it came away moist with sweat. His first instinct when Tomasso Nicolotti challenged him had been to steal a boat and head straight for the TARDIS, but caution had prevailed, and he had sought out Marlowe for advice. Not that Marlowe was looking too concerned now, as he lounged against the window frame, paring his fingernails with a slender knife.

'We can and we must,' Marlowe replied. 'The Church of San Trovaso lies at the boundary of the territories controlled by the Nicolottis and the Castellanis. It's the only neutral place to hold a duel. On the rare occasions in which a Nicolotti boy has married a Castellani girl, or vice versa, the two families enter and leave by doors on opposite sides of the church. Will Shakespeare used the story of one such marriage in his little entertainment *Romeo and Juliet*, and I believe that mountebank Francis Pearson did the same in his triviality *John and Jill*.'

'But what about the sanctity of the place? What does the priest have to say about it all?'

Marlowe shrugged. 'Perhaps the priest is being paid by both sides to keep his eyes shut when he prays. Clerics have never been averse to more money. Or perhaps he is tied up elsewhere. I neither know nor care, and neither should you. The Castellanis have refused to turn up, on the basis that they disown your actions, but we can't disappoint our Nicolotti hosts.'

'Look,' protested Steven, indicating the hologuise generator strapped to his hip, 'can't we just turn off this device and pretend that Galileo has slipped out of Venice?'

Marlowe shook his head. 'They'll have guards stationed at all the landing posts. They'll know that he couldn't have "slipped out", and they'll torture us until we tell them where he is. Not that they would believe the truth, of course, so we would probably die. No, there is only one way out of this. I will have to fight the duel for you.'

For a moment, Steven thought that his ears had deceived him. 'You? But it's *me* they challenged.'

'No, it's the Paduan Galileo Galilei that they challenged,' Marlowe corrected gently. 'You merely happened to be borrowing his form. I could just as easily fill it – he is corpulent enough.' Marlowe reached out to ruffle Steven's hair. 'And which one of us would last the longest against the head of the family, eh? Take it from me, Tomasso Nicolotti has done this sort of thing before. Fortunately, so have I, and I cannot – will not – see you skewered upon his sword.' He held up the knife with which he had been cutting his fingernails. 'And I have this small stiletto. If Tomasso gets too close, he'll feel my sting.'

Steven opened his mouth to protest, but shook his head instead. Marlowe was right – he would have no chance against any swordsman, expert or not. Marlowe at least might survive. Reluctantly he switched the device on his belt off and handed it across to Marlowe.

'If I believed in God I would call that the work of the Devil,' Marlowe murmured as he slipped the device into his jerkin and switched it on. He shimmered, and suddenly Galileo Galilei was standing in his place, bearded

186

and arrogant. 'Does it work?' he said, his voice jarring with his new form.

Steven glanced up and down the image. Apart from the tips of Marlowe's grey mane sticking up from Galileo's hair, the camouflage was perfect. 'You look wonderful,' he said, his mouth dry.

Marlowe smiled. 'You say the sweetest things.'

Vicki awoke to find the pins-and-needles feeling was ebbing away. She could move her limbs again. Albrellian's toxin seemed to be wearing off. Not that there was anywhere to go. On the viewscreen she could see the sterile lunar plains rising up towards the skiff. They seemed to be heading towards one particular ship with an iridescent red hull that was all curves, like a venomous beetle. Yellow insignia on its back looked almost like the outline of a huge pair of wings.

'Light-years away within a few minutes can be we,' the arthropod muttered, its attention divided between Vicki and the controls. 'And have to be will we. If the meta-cobalt device on schedule explodes, to be a long way away want do I. Braxiatel's people knowing that I had anything to do with it want do not I. Stories about what they do when they're angry have heard I.' His claws fiddled with the controls of the skiff, and they drifted gently down towards a hatch that was opening like a flower in the hull of the Greld ship.

'What about the other Greld?' she said. Her voice was slurred, and speaking was an effort, but at least she could make herself understood easily.

Albrellian's eyestalks dipped. 'The suspicions of Braxiatel or his Jamarian cronies cannot afford to rouse we. Until the bomb goes off will stay my friends.'

'And you're running for it?' Vicki sniffed and turned ostentatiously away. 'I don't know why you ever thought you had a chance with me. You're just a coward.'

'You little fool,' Albrellian laughed. 'With you in love was never I – just to get you to the island wanted I so that, when the time came, easier to kidnap you it would be. With my friends, dying gloriously at the culmination of twenty-year plan our, would rather be I, but the chance to bring one of the fabled Doctor's companions back to the Greld Commonwealth is too good to miss!'

'Even if your companions think you're scared?' Vicki asked. Albrellian did not reply. As the skiff settled to rest in the dark curves of the Greld ship's bay, Vicki thought over what Albrellian had said. 'Does this mean you don't like me?' she said in a plaintive voice.

'Vicki,' Albrellian said, 'how to break this to you know do not I, but a naïve and rather stupid brat are you. To mate with you would not I if the last sentient creature left in the fourth galaxy were you.'

'Oh.' It took a moment for that to sink in, and it hurt. 'So – so why *are* you kidnapping me? You said you were under orders.'

A clang from outside and a flashing pink light presumably indicated that the hatch had sealed shut again, and that the atmosphere was breathable. Albrellian released the safety catches, and the skiff's door rose up revealing the bay outside. Vicki could smell a strange, alien smell, like a cross between cinnamon and tar.

Albrellian scuttled for the doorway. 'Just think,' he said, 'what for our business could do you. With knowledge of which wars will be fought when, and between whom, possessed by you, expand our market share immensely could we. Suppliers of quality weapons to people who be needing them realize do not we could be.'

'That's sick,' Vicki snapped.

'That's business,' Albrellian said. 'Come on, or the toxin again use I will.'

Vicki exited the skiff and looked around the bay. Like Albrellian, it was a combination of bowed surfaces and sudden spiky bits. Various bits of high-tech equipment ranging in size from a hand-held multi-quantiscope to a zeus plug five times the size of the TARDIS. Other small ships – Greld shuttles and one-arthropod fighters, she assumed – were lined up along the sides, and three more of Braxiatel's discus-like skiffs were sitting in a cluster in the centre. Albrellian gave them a curious glance as he passed by.

'I won't cooperate,' Vicki said.

'Will you,' Albrellian replied, heading towards a hatch in one wall. 'Promise I.' He stopped beside a large multi-tubed device that was lying on the gently sloping floor. It was about fifteen metres long and three metres high, and one end looked like it had been wrenched from a socket of some sort, complete with trailing wires and pipes. The other end terminated in a series of parabolic dishes. 'That is not right,' Albrellian muttered. 'This thing was not here when left we, swear would I.'

'What is it?'

'A terrawatt beam generator – one of products our.' Albrellian ran a claw along the device's surface. 'It is used for short range ship to ship battles. Fitted to the ship's exterior them have we.'

'So it's a weapon?' Vicki said.

'Yes,' he hooted, 'it's a weapon. And still fitted in the weapon bays it should be, not here in bits where just walk off with it could anybody.'

'Not anybody,' said a thin, vicious voice from the doorway. The open doorway, Vicki realized with some dismay. Five thin figures were standing in it, their horns almost brushing the ceiling. The look in their eyes was one of unalloyed triumph. 'This ship, and all its weapon systems – especially its weapon systems – have been appropriated by the Jamarian Empire.'

'The *what*?' Albrellian growled, rising up on his front walking claws. 'An Empire have not got the Jamarians.'

'We have now,' the leading Jamarian said.

The long narthex of the Church of St Trovaso stretched away from the group of men towards the altar. Sun-light streaming in through the stained glass windows cast a multitude of colourful but insubstantial diagonal buttresses across the aisle. Motes of dust drifted lazily into them, sparkled briefly like fireflies, and then were gone. It was a timeless, beautiful place.

'Ho, Paduan!' a voice called, 'are you ready to die?'

Marlowe stuck out his hand. Steven shook it firmly. Marlowe held on longer than Steven expected, turning the handshake into something like a caress. 'If I had words enough, and time,' he murmured, and Steven could have sworn that he caught sight of the man's intense grey stare through Galileo's dark brown eyes for a moment. Marlowe turned to where Tomasso Nicolotti was essaying some practice thrusts and parries, his blade hissing through the air, and said loudly, 'Ho yourself, you Italian fop. You have come to the right place to meet your Maker.'

The two men advanced to the centre of the church, and the Nicolotti family made a rough semicircle around them. Steven stayed where he was, near the font.

Tomasso flicked his sword towards Marlowe's face. Marlowe parried and brought his blade whistling back to cut through the space where Tomasso's head had been moments before. His opponent had stepped back and Marlowe took a step forward, lunging at the man's chest. Tomasso intercepted the tip of Marlowe's sword with his own and, while taking two more paces back, guided Marlowe's sword in a quick circle in the air. Deftly he pushed it out to one side and slashed back at Marlowe's neck. Marlowe was forced to take two stumbling steps back to avoid injury, and Tomasso pressed him hard with a series of short jabs which Marlowe had to deflect with his hilt, they were so close.

The clash of metal echoed from the roof and the stone walls, making it sound to Steven as if the church were filled with invisible fighters. He clenched his fists, wishing there was something he could do, but he had no choice but to play the hand he had been dealt, however catastrophic it was for him, or for Marlowe.

The balance of power had shifted again, and Marlowe was on the offensive, taking short steps towards Tomasso and flicking his sword up towards the man's eyes from underneath, trying to make him nervous. Tomasso was deflecting Marlowe's blade with the minimum force necessary, and twice Steven thought that the edge caught his ear, nicking it. Seeing the trickle of blood, Marlowe again took a step forward, lunging at Tomasso's chest, and again the Italian intercepted the tip of Marlowe's sword with his own and manoeuvred it in a quick circle in the air, while retreating at the same speed with which Marlowe was advancing. As before, when the swords had almost completed their circle, he used their momentum to push Marlowe's blade out to one side while slashing back at his neck. Marlowe, anticipating the trick, stepped to one side and let the razor-sharp edge whistle harmlessly through empty air while he jabbed at Tomasso's thigh. The Italian stumbled back to avoid the crippling blow, and almost lost his footing. Marlowe followed up with an inelegant but powerful overhand hack at the crown of Tomasso's head which the man could avoid only by throwing himself to one side and rolling. The spectators quickly cleared a space for him while Marlowe's blade sent sparks flying from the granite flagstones.

Steven realized that he had been holding his breath, and released it in a long exhalation. He could feel his heart pounding against his ribs. He knew that he would have been dead by now, but there was a smile on Marlowe's borrowed face as if he was enjoying himself.

Marlowe waited until Tomasso had regained his balance, then reached out to the full extent of his sword and batted the tip of Tomasso's blade a few times, taunting him to advance. Tomasso snarled and stepped forward, knocking the sword aside with his hilt and then bringing his elbow right back, giving him just enough room to jab into Marlowe's stomach. The Englishman stepped forward as well, colliding with Tomasso and trapping the man's blade between his arm and his body. Tomasso brought his knee up as Marlowe released his pressure on

191

the blade and stepped back. While Tomasso was off balance he again executed what Steven assumed was his favourite manoeuvre – lunging at the centre of Tomasso's chest. Again Tomasso parried in the same way – deflecting the tip of Marlowe's blade in a complete circle while backing away. Marlowe, knowing that Tomasso would push the blade out of the circle and slash at his neck, tried to pull his blade back, but this time Tomasso continued to push the blades around the circle while reversing his direction. As he stepped forward, Marlowe automatically stepped back. The blades cut through the air and Tomasso, in what must have been a move that he had been planning since the beginning of the duel, pushed Marlowe's blade *down* and out of the circle as Marlowe's foot passed underneath. The tip pierced Marlowe's boot and his flesh, and the sound of it grinding against the flagstone was almost covered by his involuntary cry.

Before Marlowe could pull his blade from his foot, Tomasso Nicolotti's own sword was emerging, streaked with gore, from Marlowe's back.

Fourteen

Galileo gazed around with something approaching awe. The hall that the group were standing in was made entirely of something that looked and felt very much like blue marble, and yet its arches soared so high over their heads that clouds hid the apex. That shouldn't be possible: not without some form of flying buttress or other load-bearing structure. Galileo had seen the Sistine Chapel in Rome, and he had seen the Basilica of Saint Mark in Venice, and he had studied the art of structure until he sometimes dreamed about columns and domes, and he knew – *knew* – that there was no way under God's heaven that a marble arch so high could support its own weight.

He swallowed. It was beginning to look as if this Braxiatel fellow could teach Galileo Galilei a thing or two, and that wasn't a comfortable feeling for Christendom's foremost natural philosopher. Not a comfortable feeling at all.

A snort from the Doctor brought Galileo's attention back to the little group. Braxiatel was shaking his head, and the Doctor had his thumbs hooked behind his lapels and was looking down his nose at the tall man. Behind them and slightly to one side, William Shakespeare was eyeing the horned stick-men as if he couldn't decide what was worse – the possibility that they might be the product of some insane delirium or the possibility that they might be real.

'It's impossible,' Braxiatel said. 'Building a weapon like that would require years of planning. Who would attempt such a thing?'

'Who has just left this island of yours in some haste, hmm?' the Doctor snapped. 'Your friend Albrellian would appear to be the prime suspect.'

'But – but the Greld are –' Braxiatel paused, and considered. '– Are just desperate enough and clever enough to try it,' he said, sighing. 'Why did I ever bother arranging this Convention? I should have known that an envoy would try to sabotage the whole thing. I mean, there's always one, isn't there?'

The Doctor smiled slightly, and shook his head. 'This isn't helping, Braxiatel. No, it isn't helping at all. We should be evacuating the island. Yes, we should be evacuating.' He wagged an admonishing finger at Braxiatel, who just shrugged and reached into his pocket.

'You should know me by now, Doctor,' Braxiatel said calmly. 'I prepare for any eventuality.' His hand re-appeared with a rounded object that appeared to be made of a dull metal. Small objects like gemstones were set into its surface. He pressed one, and a circle of air in front of the group seemed to solidify, like ice, and suddenly Galileo found himself gazing out across the choppy lagoon at the oncoming boats. It was as if the air itself had become a window. As Braxiatel and the Doctor moved closer to the view, Galileo took a few steps to one side. A stick-guard moved to intercept him and he waved it away irritably. The circle was almost invisible when seen from the side: all that Galileo could see was a slight haze, like the air above a stone that had been left out in the sun. Truly a wonder. It was almost as if . . . Almost as if the view from a spyglass had been projected across a distance and made visible to many. Yes! A feeling of elation spread through him, and he couldn't stop himself from smiling. These things were wonders, but they were not beyond human comprehension. Once it was known that they were possible then they could be duplicated, just as Galileo had duplicated Lippershey's spyglass based upon nothing more than a garbled description in a letter from Paolo Sarpi. Duplicated and improved.

He moved back to a position behind the Doctor, rubbing his hands gleefully. Oh what wonders he would perform as soon as he got back to his workshop in Padua.

Through the round window, Galileo could see at least twenty vessels ranging from gondolas to fishing boats heading towards the island. The sky was grey and stormy above them, and the wind was whipping the waves up. The sails of the fishing boats alternately billowed and sagged as the wind gusted against them, and the lines whipped so violently around that Galileo could almost hear the whipcrack noise as they pulled taut. Three of the smaller, faster vessels were already drawn up on the sand of the beach, and a group of drab Englishmen were milling around as if unsure of their purpose now that they had arrived on the island.

The wounds on their faces were red and raw. Bile rose in Galileo's stomach as he realized that two of them had no eyes left – just curdled white lumps in their sockets.

'Whatever it is that you have prepared, dear boy,' the Doctor murmured to Braxiatel, 'I would be grateful if you would reveal it now, yes I would. The radiation levels are rising, and if the remainder of those people arrive on the beach and join their companions then you might find your Convention ending with somewhat more of a bang than you had anticipated.'

Braxiatel smirked, and pressed another of the dull gemstones on his metal box. Nothing happened for a moment, and then a shudder ran through the room. The stick-men rocked on their feet and glanced around suspiciously. Galileo gazed upward, hoping that the marble arches weren't about to prove his conjecture about their strength right, but they were as stable as the Dolomite mountains.

When Galileo glanced back at the circular window, he noticed immediately that the view had changed. It seemed as though they were looking down upon the ocean and the boats from a distance of some twenty feet or so, or the ocean had receded from the beach. And that was the odd thing – the beach was unchanged, with its three small hulls and confused group of people. The window still showed them as if they were only a step away, but the ocean was definitely lower.

Or, Galileo realized with a sublime insight, the island was higher. That was the logical corollary. The island was rising into the air, quitting the ocean for the sky. Well, why not? Was it any more impossible than the things he had already seen?

'Tolerably impressive,' the Doctor murmured. 'It will probably suffice to put enough distance between us and the components of the bomb. I had wondered why the island was called Laputa.'

'My little joke,' Braxiatel smiled.

'Let's hope it won't be your last laugh,' said the Doctor as he turned away.

Albrellian didn't have a jaw to drop, but his palps visibly quivered. 'What mean do you, ship and all its weapon systems appropriated have you?' he hissed, hoisting his shell up at the front until it was almost vertical. 'Cannot that do you: an envoy of the Greld am I!'

Vicki cast a quick glance to either side. They were surrounded by Jamarians – etiolated figures that had emerged from the shadows of the ship's hold to encircle them. Most of them were carrying devices that trailed wires behind them, as if they had just been removed from the ship's hull.

The lead Jamarian stepped forward from the group in the doorway. 'The Greld, the Greld, the all-powerful, all-arrogant, all-greedy Greld,' it snarled. 'When the revolution comes, your sort will be first up against the bulkhead.'

'What is your name?' Albrellian said. 'About this will hear Braxiatel.'

'My name is Szaratak,' the alien replied, and spat on the ground between Albrellian's front pair of claws. 'Do what you will — Braxiatel is nothing to us. He has served his purpose. We don't need him any more.'

Vicki felt a pang of sadness. She had liked Irving Braxiatel. He had believed that what he was doing might actually help, and now it was going to come crashing down in flames around his ears. Poor man.

'Purpose?' Albrellian reeled backwards. 'What purpose?'

Vicki reached out and patted his shell. 'Mr Braxiatel brought all the envoys together, didn't he?' she asked, directing her comments more at the Jamarians than at the Greld envoy. 'And he persuaded them to leave all their ships unguarded on the moon as a gesture of good faith. Their heavily armed ships, ready to be taken apart for their secrets.' Something suddenly occurred to her, and she turned to the Jamarian. 'It was you that tried to kill Galileo, wasn't it? He was the only person capable of seeing that you were going to and from the moon. Braxiatel just tried to stop him from seeing anything, but you tried to kill him.'

Albrellian was silent for a moment. 'Very clever have been they,' he said finally in a very quiet, very flat voice. 'Badly underestimated them did we, and that is not something often do the Greld. Too paranoid they were, thought we, too psychotic ever to amount to anything in the universe. Scrabbling around in their play-pit of a planet, them watched we, no two of them ever agreeing with each other for long enough to form an alliance, and at them laughed did we. It was not even worth selling them weapons, knew we, because nothing to offer us apart from their obsessive fascination with detail and their amusingly vicious natures had they. When using them to arrange this Convention Braxiatel was heard we, that he'd stopped them squabbling for long enough to get them to do anything amazed were we.'

'*Psychotic?*' Szaratak screamed, its little red eyes glinting with madness. 'I'll show you psychotic!' Dipping its head until its rapier-like horn was pointed directly at

197

Albrellian's palps, it lunged straight at the arthropod envoy.

As Vicki stepped back out of the way and into the lee of the huge zeus plug, the other Jamarians started cheering and clapping. Szaratak's thin legs propelled it at Albrellian so fast that the sound of its feet hitting the deck was a continuous rattle and the air whistled past the sharp point of its horn.

And when Szaratak was about to plunge its horn deep into Albrellian's mouth, the Greld reached out with his second set of claws and calmly snipped the Jamarian's knob-like head off. The Jamarian dropped to the floor, spouting blood from the stump of its neck.

'Quick!' Albrellian yelled to Vicki as the shell of his back folded open and two massive fans of leathery skin burst forth. 'To the skiff run!' The last thing she saw as she turned away and ran for the flattened disc behind them was Albrellian buffeting the Jamarians with mighty strokes of his wings. Light streamed from the open doorway of the skiff, its welcome glow pulling her on like a magnet. Her feet echoed like gunshots against the metal deck. From behind her she could hear what sounded like a pavement being thrashed with a lot of sticks but which must have been the Jamarians jabbing at Albrellian's hard shell with their horns as he ran. Time seemed to break into fragments which whirled confusingly around her in no particular order, and she couldn't tell whether she was running, safe or dead.

And then a nightmarishly thin figure reached out of the shadows of a fighter ship and wrapped its bony fingers around her head. She screamed, and the sound seemed to go on for ever, echoing throughout eternity. Nothing was real but the insane glint in the Jamarian's eye, and the way its muscles moved like eels beneath its warty skin, and the gut-wrenching stench of its breath emerging from its perpetually pursed lips.

A pair of claws grabbed her shoulders and wrenched her from the Jamarian's grasp. Before she could register that she was flying through the air, Albrellian had landed beside the skiff and was bundling her through the door and into a seat. Ten seconds later, as they rose like a tossed stone away from the deck and the crowd of flailing Jamarian limbs and towards the hatch that was opening its petals far above them, she could still feel those thin fingers, cold and moist against her skin.

Shakespeare watched with awe as the magic mirror reflected scenes of another place. The mirror hung unsupported in the centre of the marble hall, and the view it reflected was one he recognized: the beach upon which he, the Doctor, Steven Taylor and the arrogant Italian had been washed up less than an hour before. A small group of men were churning up the sand as they moved aimlessly around, the sores on their hands and faces painfully evident. Boats were approaching the golden strand, their bows cleaving through the waves like so many ploughs through soil, and men were throwing themselves into the water in their frantic efforts to arrive at the island and join their compatriots.

Less than an hour. He had been here less than an hour. Shakespeare groaned inwardly as he realized how his wits had turned to sand in that scant time. Had someone told him, as the mists parted and the island was revealed, that he would be standing beside demons watching a magic mirror then he would have called them mad. Now he was debating whether or not it was he who was mad.

The view was slanted now, as if the mirror was suspended above the waves. Shakespeare could have sworn that there was a rim of grey metal between the beach and the receding water, and sand was trickling over this rim and vanishing from sight. Some of the men had thrown themselves full length on the beach and had extended their arms over the edge towards the nearest swimmers.

As far as Shakespeare could see, there were three possible explanations for what was happening to him.

The first was that the mirror was devilish work – the creation of some dark-working sorcerers or soul-killing witches. He glanced over at Irving Braxiatel, trying once again to evaluate the man. Braxiatel stood calmly next to the Doctor, a slight frown upon his face. He had the demeanour of an honest, God-fearing person, that much was true, but he certainly associated himself with the spawn of Satan.

Shakespeare caught the errant thought, and cursed. Just because these creatures were not pleasing to the eye, it did not mean that they were evil. In nature there was no blemish but the mind: none could be called deformed but the unkind. He kept telling himself that as his eyes strayed to the skeletal figures of Braxiatel's assistants.

As Shakespeare watched, Braxiatel pressed a small stud on the box in his hand. A ripple crossed the mirror, and the reflected view shifted. Now they were looking across the water and towards the island. The curved hull of a small fishing boat obscured the vista to one side, and Braxiatel nudged at another stud until the mirror's view shifted sideways by a few feet. The swimmers' heads were dark blobs silhouetted against a grey metal cliff that rose some thirty feet or more from the water until it was capped by sand. More and more of the cliff was revealed as the water withdrew, or the metal rose, a smooth expanse of a dull substance that was not iron, or bronze, not copper or brass.

Perhaps he had become brainsick. That was another possibility. Perhaps his wits had become estranged from themselves and he was indulging in turbulent and dangerous lunacy. Had he not himself known men who believed that they were being followed by fabulous beasts, or women that talked to invisible companions?

The distance between sand and sea was increasing as the island reared up like an emerging kraken, but the swimmers were throwing themselves from the water and clinging to the metal surface, finding purchase on patches of barnacles or clumps of seaweed and scuttling like spiders up to the sand where their friends pulled them over.

It was also possible, Shakespeare considered, that he had eaten of the insane root that took the reason prisoner. Such plants were known of, and Shakespeare had eaten hurriedly of some strangely flavoured vegetables since arriving in Venice. Did they not say that men caught in the thrall of such food would find fragments of nightmare scattered through their waking lives like plums in a plum duff?

Looking upward to the beach, which was now fifty feet or more above the churning waves, Shakespeare could make out a mass of people, fifty or more, all standing together. The last few swimmers swarmed up the metal surface to join them. They waited, silent and still, all gazing inward to the towers and halls of Braxiatel's palace. Shakespeare wasn't sure, but he thought that they were holding hands. Somewhere beyond them was the blue of the sky, and Shakespeare thought for a fleeting moment that he saw something drop from the sky towards the island – a flattened disc with lights set equally around its circumference.

There was a fourth possibility, of course. It could all be true. Men from another star: islands that could rise from the water: people with rocks in their heads that gave them the plague. Yes, it could all be true. And Shakespeare himself might be King Sigismund of Denmark.

Shakespeare sighed. At the end of the day, did it matter whether he was bewitched, mad, dreaming or sane? Would it affect what he did? What he said? What he had to do?

'I don't understand,' the Doctor was saying to Braxiatel. 'They are all together now. If my theory that they are all part of one huge explosive device is correct then I am at a loss to know why they haven't exploded.'

'Don't sound so disappointed,' Braxiatel replied. 'Perhaps they're not all there. That was the point of raising the island – to leave a lot of them bobbing on the ocean, too late for the party.'

'I think you were too late for that, my boy.' The Doctor nodded sagely. 'If I am not mistaken, everybody from the boats is now standing on that cliff. And they're not waiting for Christmas, hmm?'

Braxiatel shrugged. 'Then perhaps there's something missing – a fuse of some kind that they require, an arming mechanism. Something that is supposed to turn up at the last minute to ensure that they don't go off when they pass each other in the street.'

'Perhaps.' The Doctor sounded unconvinced. 'But if so, where is it, hmm? Where is it?'

The late afternoon sun shining through the stained glass windows of the Church of St Trovaso cast a jigsaw-puzzle of coloured light across Christopher Marlowe's face. Steven had turned the hologuise off to see how badly Marlowe was injured. The rest of the church was in shadow, and in the darkness Steven could hear Tomasso Nicolotti's triumphant laughter as he and his cronies left. Within a few moments, they were alone.

Marlowe's head was cradled in Steven's lap. If Steven hadn't known that the playwright and spy had been wearing a white shirt, he would have sworn that it was made of scarlet cloth. Whenever Marlowe shifted, the blood from the exit wound in his back sucked glutinously against the cold flagstones.

'While I had expected that you and I would end up in this position,' Marlowe gasped, 'I had not anticipated that it would be for this reason. So does life imitate bad art. Too many times have I written duels not to be struck with the irony of dying in one.'

'You're not going to die,' Steven said tightly. 'I'm going to get you through this.'

'You should never lie to a professional liar, Steven.' Marlowe smiled, then winced as a pang of pain shot through him. A stain of bright arterial blood bloomed against the cloth of his shirt. 'Marlowe, the scourge of God, must die, but did it have to be in His house?' He leaned

202

back, his eyelids fluttering and his breath coming in short gasps.

Out in the shadows of the church a door opened, spilling glowing light across the flagstones. A priest entered, his face floating above his black robes. When he saw Steven and Marlowe he crossed himself and withdrew, muttering.

'Maybe if I bandage the wound, or put stitches in it, or something,' Steven muttered, 'it might help.' Carefully he pulled at the tacky fabric of Marlowe's shirt, peeling it away from his body until the torn skin was revealed. He winced. Tomasso Nicolotti had twisted the blade viciously in Marlowe's stomach, turning a simple slash into a gaping hole through which he could see the taut membranes of Marlowe's guts and –

And a flash of red-slicked silver. Steven bent closer to look. Gingerly he pushed at a fold of intestine with his forefinger, moving it out of the way. Behind it was a smooth metal object with patterns incised into its surface, part of a larger device apparently hidden within Marlowe's lower chest.

'Well, I guess you didn't escape from the aliens at that colony after all,' he murmured. 'They've put something inside you.'

'If my body fascinates you that much,' Marlowe whispered, his eyes still closed, 'then I pray you undress me further.'

'Don't you *ever* give up?' Steven snapped.

The ghost of a smile fluttered around Marlowe's lips. 'Indulge the last wish of a dying man,' he mouthed. 'Kiss me, Steven.'

'Well,' Braxiatel said, clapping his hands together, 'shall we repair to the refectory for drinks?' He collapsed the image field with a quick motion of his hand and, glancing over towards one of the Jamarians, he snapped his fingers. 'Tzorogol! Take a party outside and bring the locals in. Try not to panic them. We'll need to do a full medical scan, so

203

alert the infirmary. Oh, and you'd better split the group into three and keep them apart, just in case the Doctor is right.'

'Yes, Braxiatel,' the Jamarian said as Braxiatel looked away. There was something about the tone of its voice that made him look back, an underlying sense of repressed anger and barely concealed hatred, but there was nothing on its face to suggest there was anything wrong.

Somewhere overhead, up in the cloud-enshrouded heights of the Great Hall, he could hear the distant sound of wings. Either one of the envoys in the Armageddon Convention was taking a comfort break or a pigeon had got in, and if it was a pigeon then he would have to have it removed before it defecated on the marble. There was always something going on that he had to deal with, and all he had to work with was the Jamarians. 'Are you sure you can manage to remember those orders?' he asked Tzorogol, 'or would you like me to repeat them for you?'

Tzorogol didn't answer for a moment. Its small, red eyes glared at Braxiatel with almost physical force. He had to keep reminding himself that it was part of the Jamarian's physiology: they couldn't help looking like that. It wasn't as if Jamarians meant to be threatening.

'Yes,' Tzorogol barked finally, 'I can remember. I can remember very well.'

The flutter of wings suddenly intensified, and a great shadow fell over them all as Envoy Albrellian settled dramatically where the image field had been. He was carrying Vicki in his claws, and as soon as her feet touched the ground she ran to the Doctor's side. Braxiatel was less concerned with their fond greetings than he was with the envoy's actions. 'Albrellian, he snapped, 'you've gone too far this time – kidnapping one of the Doctor's companions. Action will be taken.'

'Too much action around here already going on there is,' Albrellian said, glancing over at where Tzorogol still stood. 'What your precious Jamarians are doing, know do you, Braxiatel? Our ships up on the moon gutting are they,

204

the weapons out of them stripping are they! Stripping all the ships parked on the moon would not be surprised to learn I.'

'They're what?' Braxiatel exploded. 'But that's —'

'Absolutely true,' Vicki said from the shelter of the Doctor's arm. She gazed at Braxiatel sadly. 'I'm sorry, but it's all absolutely true. I saw it, and I heard them talking about it. Albrellian and I have just come back in a skiff.' She shot the arthropod a nasty glance. 'Albrellian didn't want to, because he's planted a bomb somewhere on the island, but he can't escape now that his ship is in the hands of the Jamarians. The rest of the Jamarians are following us in another skiff. We abandoned ours in mid-air and Albrellian carried me here.'

'Only be a matter of seconds before the meta-cobalt bomb explodes, it must be,' Albrellian cried, his eye-stalks almost fully retracted in agitation. 'All the pieces are assembled!'

'Not quite all.' Braxiatel indicated the virtual screen. 'According to the Doctor, there's a piece missing. Some kind of fuse, he said.'

Albrellian perked up a bit. 'Is it possible that to the island carrying the fuse did not make it the carrier?' he asked. 'That could only have happened if the hypnotic controller had from the brain been removed. Perhaps a chance after all have we — but only if those carriers off the island can get we.' He shot a venomous glance at the Jamarians. 'But first with your revolutionary little clerks to deal have we.'

Braxiatel turned to the Jamarians. 'Tzorogol, there's obviously been some sort of —' He stopped abruptly when he became aware that the Jamarian was shaking its head firmly. 'Tzorogol, what's got into you?'

'Power,' Tzorogol snarled. 'You took a race without any influence or prestige, you put them in charge of technology that it would have taken them millions of years to build for themselves, and you didn't expect them to take advantage of it? That sort of arrogance verges on stupidity.' Tzorogol's little scarlet eyes flickered back and forth over the stunned group. 'We know what other races say about us. We know the sort of snide jokes that are made behind our backs, and you're all wrong, do you hear me? Wrong! We're as intelligent as any of you!'

Braxiatel felt as if the ground was swaying beneath his feet, and he was having trouble distinguishing the Jamarian's diatribe over the sound of the blood rushing through his ears. How could he have been so ... so monumentally stupid? 'Look,' he said finally, 'this has gone far enough –' The words sounded fatuous as he said them, and he stopped in the middle of the sentence, rehearsing the possible conversations that could spool away from that point in time. None of them got him anywhere. The natural order of things had suddenly reversed, and the underdogs had the upper hand. Nothing he could say would change that. He shrugged. 'Yes,' he said simply. 'I've been arrogant and foolish.'

'And not for the first time, hmm?' said the Doctor superciliously. He stepped forward. 'Now that you have this information,' he said to Tzorogol, 'you realize that it is useless? Your species has neither the infrastructure, the resources or the knowledge to exploit it. You're in the position of a child holding the blueprints of a house: you may understand them, but you can't do anything with them.' He clasped his hands behind his back and smiled. 'It will still take generations of effort for you to climb out of your playpen. You may think that you have built your-selves an empire, but it is an empire of glass, a pretty bauble, too fragile to last.'

Tzorogol's horn flicked downward, as if it was thinking about running the Doctor through, but a disturbance at the back of the hall distracted it. A group of Jamarians rushed up to Tzorogol, glaring at Vicki and Albrellian.

'They killed Szaratak!' one of them exclaimed. 'We tried to catch them, but –'

'Did you get the information?' Tzorogol snapped.

The Jamarian nodded, and handed Tzorogol a small control unit made out of curved metal and green glass.

'Every weapon has been dismantled and scanned, and every computer databank downloaded. All the information is in there.'

'You underestimate us,' Tzorogol snarled at the Doctor. 'We're aware that it's knowledge we need, not information, so we're going to auction the information we've collected, sell it to the highest bidder – and we have all the potential bidders gathered here, at the Armageddon Convention.' It held up the control unit. 'Everything we've learned is in here – details of every weapon system and every stardrive in every ship on the moon. Every single scrap of information. We'll sell it in exchange for ships, and weapons, and defensive systems, and we'll take our revenge for all of the slights, the insults and the insinuations. We'll show everyone that we don't just serve drinks and do accounts and run bureaucracies. We're going to be a force to be reckoned with from now on!'

The Doctor gazed at the object with interest. 'A telepathic storage unit,' he said. 'Very interesting: at the touch of a button, all the information contained in the unit is instantly transmitted into the mind of whoever is holding it. I seem to recognize the design as Vilp – I presume that you stole it from an envoy's room here at the Convention. I congratulate you – it appears that you have thought of everything.'

'Not quite,' a hesitant voice said from one side. Before anybody could move, William Shakespeare pushed past Braxiatel and snatched the control unit from Tzorogol's hand. Tzorogol lunged at him, but he backed out of the way. The other Jamarians weren't sure what to do. Two of them lowered their horns, ready to skewer Shakespeare. He, in his turn, gazed wildly around the hall, his hair plastered across his sweaty brow. 'Ignorance is the curse of God: knowledge is the wing wherewith we fly to heaven,' he cried. Holding the unit to his forehead, he pressed the button.

The Jamarians stood stunned for a moment: just long enough for Shakespeare to drop the telepathic storage unit and run out of the hall. The Jamarians looked at each other and then, with a blood-chilling scream, ran after him. As their footsteps died away, peace settled once again on the hall. Braxiatel stepped forward to retrieve the telepathic unit.

'Are there any more surprises waiting to spring on us,' the Doctor asked eventually, 'or is this it for the time being?'

Fifteen

The carved prow of the gondola lurched to the left, and Steven desperately waggled the long oar to straighten it out before the boat hit the side of the canal. The sun had dropped below roof level, and the water was mostly in shadow, making it difficult to steer into the waves which seemed to spring up out of nowhere and ricochet between crumbling walls and around corners before knocking the gondola sideways. Steven was having problems steering straight anyway: the effortless motions of the oars that he'd seen other gondoliers demonstrate eluded him completely, and even without the waves his progress along Venice's watery arteries was a bit haphazard. His muscles were aching with the strain of constantly heaving the thing back and forth, and the stench that rose from the water as he disturbed it made him want to throw up. If he did, he wouldn't be making the canal any less sanitary than it already was.

He glanced down at Christopher Marlowe. The man was propped up in the bows, looking for all the world like an aristocrat out for a quiet trip, rather than a dying playwright and spy with a silver machine in his chest cavity.

Marlowe must have realized that Steven was looking at him, for he turned back and winked. He coughed, and a small trickle of blood escaped his lips. Dabbing at it with a handkerchief, he smiled apologetically.

Someone had told Steven that there were twenty-eight miles of canal in Venice. Was he going to have to heave the gondola along all of them before he found what he was looking for?

They were coming up to a large church. The canal split in two, each branch hugging the church's walls, and Steven realized with a shock that its roof was lined with distorted winged figures. They were leaning forward, watching the gondola approach. Desperately he pulled on the oar, trying to turn the boat around before the aliens could do anything, but the figures weren't reacting. As momentum took the gondola closer, Steven saw their grey skin and their smooth, weathered features, and noticed with surprise that some of them were pointing their tongues out at him.

Gargoyles. He relaxed, feeling angry and ashamed at his panic. They were just gargoyles.

'Saint Stephen's church,' Marlowe muttered.

'What?'

'Saint Stephen's church. I thought you might like the irony.'

'Yeah, thanks,' Steven snapped, 'but I've got more things to worry about than a coincidence in names.'

Marlowe half turned to stare at Steven, the strain of moving evident on his face. His shirt was a patchwork of maroon and scarlet. 'There's a channel beneath the church,' he muttered. 'It's navigable at low tide. I think the house we want is on the other side. I remember noticing the church when we left.'

Gazing ahead, Steven could just make out an arched entrance in the wall of the church, black against the dark brick. 'Is this low tide?' he said. 'I can't tell.'

Marlowe chuckled. 'What have we got to lose?' he said.

Under the disapproving gaze of the gargoyles Steven heaved at the oar, and the gondola sloshed from side to side as they approached the arch.

William Shakespeare leaned back against the blue marble (*a synthetic polymer lighter than balsa wood but possessing a higher tensile strength than steel*) and took a deep breath. His lungs felt as if they were on fire, and his heart was beating so rapidly that he could hear nothing apart from its hammering. Acid surged into his mouth from his churning

210

stomach and he swallowed convulsively, trying not to throw up. He bent double, hands on knees, the air catching in the back of his throat as he tried to recover. Sweat trickled warmly down his bald forehead and dripped to the marble floor. What a weary reckoning this was. He could hardly move another step, let alone make it to the landing area for the skiffs (*small atmospheric and exo-atmospheric craft powered by quantum field fluctuations and capable of flying from England to far Afriq in a matter of minutes*). He needed rest, and no matter that he might be caught by the stick-men before he could move again.

After a few deep breaths the giddy feeling and the sickness in the pit of his stomach passed away, and he found that he could straighten up again. A breeze cooled his brow and, gazing around for its source, he caught sight of a nearby window. He staggered closer, braced his hands against the wall to either side of the opening and gulping the pure, salt-tanged air. Barely a few feet below him were the tops of Laputa's trees, and in the distance he could just make out the circle of grey material that he knew must be the landing area for the skiffs. Beyond that, the light blue sky and the turquoise water met at a line directly ahead of him and impossibly distant. Glancing downward he could see the circular shadow of the floating island (*held up by a repulsive force acting against gravity and produced by anti-neutrons circling in a distronic field*) against the white-capped waves. A seagull floated close to the window on steady wings, eyed him for a moment, then glided away. Oh for a horse with wings, that he could fly home to England in safety with his prize.

Still weak, he leaned back against the wall and glanced both left and right. The airy corridor along which he had been running was empty. There was no sign of any pursuers. Now that the rush of blood in his ears had subsided he strained to hear any sound behind him, but there was nothing. Perhaps he had thrown them off the scent with his constant twisting and turning down side corridors and through empty halls.

Shakespeare let the breath whistle softly from his mouth and closed his eyes for a moment. Just a moment, and then he would head for the landing area. The marble was cool against the hot, moist skin of his palms, and he could feel the raised golden veins (*quasi-organic structures responsible for maintaining the condition of the marble substrate and replacing damaged sections*) pulsing slightly beneath his fingers.

Quasi-organic structures? Quantum field fluctuations? Synthetic polymers? What was happening to him?

After the echo of Shakespeare's hurried footsteps and the frantic rustle of the Jamarians' limbs died away, there was silence in the great marble hall for a while. Vicki gazed from Braxiatel to the Doctor and back again, waiting to see which one of them would be the first to speak. Braxiatel was gazing along the corridor, down which Shakespeare and the Jamarians had vanished, with the faintly disturbed expression of a man who had just found a fish in his coffee percolator. The Doctor was smiling superciliously and staring up into the dizzying arches of the hall, and it struck her for the first time how similar the two men looked. Both of them had aristocratic features, and both of them found it easier to look superior than sympathetic.

'Well?' she said when she couldn't bear the silence any more. 'What do we do now?'

Braxiatel's face didn't alter, as if he hadn't heard her, and the Doctor just glanced pityingly over at her, then at Braxiatel, then away again.

Angry now, Vicki turned to where the others were standing in a small group, wondering if one of them was going to suggest something. Galileo was busy gazing around as if he was trying to memorize everything in sight. Catching her enquiring glance he looked over at her and shrugged slightly. He seemed content to take his lead from someone else. It was, after all, not a world that he was used to. Albrellian looked the picture of misery: his leathery wings were folded around his shell, and his stalked eyes had retracted until they were almost invisible. Vicki didn't blame him: his plans to escape had been turned on their head within a few minutes and he had been forced to return to an island that might blow up at any second.

Feeling the anger simmer within her, she turned back to the Doctor and Braxiatel and opened her mouth.

'Well,' the Doctor said before she could erupt, 'here's a pretty kettle of worms to come to pass, hmm?'

'Shut up.' There was no emotion at all in Braxiatel's voice. 'Just – just shut up.'

'Don't worry, my boy.' Vicki could tell from the expression on the Doctor's face that he was enjoying himself immensely. 'I've made mistakes of my own, you know. Not of this magnitude, I have to confess, but mistakes none the less.'

'I had such hopes for the Armageddon Convention,' Braxiatel said quietly, almost to himself. 'I actually thought that it might do some good in the cosmos. I see now that I was just being naïve. In future I'll just stick to collecting. It's safer and much less trouble.'

'Never try to do anybody a favour,' the Doctor said. 'They won't thank you, and it usually goes horribly wrong.' He clapped his hands together suddenly. Albrellian flinched. 'We should clear this mess up now, before things slide any further. Mr Shakespeare will be heading for England in one of your vessels to fulfil the mission that he talked about earlier – spying for the King. We must stop him.'

'Of course,' Braxiatel said sarcastically. 'And do we save the meta-cobalt bomb for later? Oh, and what about the rogue Jamarians who are running loose around the island?'

'The meta-cobalt bomb appears to be awaiting a final component,' the Doctor snapped, 'so I would suggest that you disperse the carriers before it arrives. And if you use your control box to send all the skiffs away to the moon then the Jamarians will be stranded here for the time being. Now stop shilly-shallying, and get to work!'

* * *

As he slumped down to the floor, Shakespeare's mind was filled with the terrible consequences of what he had done. When he had stood there, listening to the fine speeches of Braxiatel and the Doctor, and Braxiatel's demons, he had grasped one thing: the metal box contained information that King James would want, if he knew it existed. Screwing his courage to the sticking-place, he told himself that strong reasons made for strong actions, and that things done well and with a care exempted themselves from fear, but his hands still shook uncontrollably when he reached out to snatch the box. And now his mind was filled with a whirling mass of facts, each fighting for his attention, as if some little demon were inhabiting his skull and naming everything he looked at. The worst thing was that he understood it all. It wasn't as if the names and the descriptions made no sense. He knew that a quantum field fluctuation was a process by which an intense gravitational field disturbed the energy levels of a vacuum, causing matched pairs of particles and anti-particles to appear spontaneously. He knew that a laser pistol used light as a weapon by causing the individual photons to march in step, like soldiers around the walls of Jericho. Each word in each sentence in each description led him into deeper and deeper definitions, until he felt that the world was just a thin tissue of facts, and that there was nothing tangible at all for him to hold on to.

No. There was one thing to hold on to. He had to get this knowledge, this vista of philosophical discovery, back to England. Shakespeare knew – an intuitive knowledge, not one engendered in him by the control device – that he could change the world. King James' fleets could reign supreme on the ocean with these weapons that he could build, not skulk in fear of Spanish ships. King James' good Protestant armies could march across Europe, subjugating those in thrall to the Pope. King James' benign, enlightened policies could hold sway across Christendom. If only Shakespeare could get to England and to safety.

And the only way to get to England was to steal a skiff.

He knew how to pilot one – the knowledge was there, in his mind, ready to be summoned, like the knowledge of how to bake a cake or build a barn. He didn't even have to think about it – just do it. The stick-men would be combing the building looking for him, and he was unlikely to be able to evade capture by staying inside the building, so . . .

Before he could change his mind, Shakespeare clambered half out of the window and twisted around so that his hands were clinging on to the inside of the sill and his feet were projecting out into the void. Sliding his knees backward until he could feel the lip of the outside sill beneath them, he offered a quick prayer to God, then leaned backward until his knees slipped over the edge and skidded down the outside of the building. His chest thudded against the wall, knocking the breath from his body, and his hands jerked against the inside of the sill. Hanging by his fingertips, he risked a glance downward. His feet were dangling an inch or two from the topmost branches.

Taking a deep breath, he released his grip on the window, and plummeted into the heart of the trees.

'His mission?' Braxiatel was at a loss. 'What mission? I thought he was here by accident.'

'Mr Shakespeare was sent to Venice because rumours of this Convention of yours had got out. It seems that King James had heard that secret talks were being held concerning military treaties, and had commanded Mr Shakespeare to find out all he could. I suspect that Mr Shakespeare has succeeded beyond his Monarch's wildest dreams, and is taking the information so painstakingly collected by the Jamarians back to England even as we speak. We should intercept him before that information can change history.'

'But it won't, will it?' Vicki interrupted. 'The people of this time would never be able to build the weapons or the stardrives. They haven't got the resources or the technical ability.'

215

The Doctor glanced over at her. 'You forget, my dear,' he said, 'that Mr Shakespeare will be taking with him one of the vessels that Braxiatel here has been foolish enough to use on a primitive inhabited planet. I sincerely doubt that anybody on this planet could duplicate the technology, even given Mr Shakespeare's newly acquired knowledge, but they can use it. Protestant England is the most religiously rigid country in the world at this point in its history, and they will treat this information as the gift of God. I would predict that within ten years England will have subjugated most of the world with one flying vessel. Within twenty years Mr Shakespeare's knowledge will be fully written down and widely distributed as being the new Word of God. Within fifty years there will be an industrial revolution which will place the human race in space before it has the maturity to know what it is doing. Humanity will be destructive enough when it gets to the stars under its own steam: if it leapfrogs normal progress by three hundred years then it will carry religious intolerance from planet to planet. We cannot allow that to happen.'

'Look on the bright side,' Braxiatel said, 'they might just assume that he has been possessed by a demon and kill him.'

'Given the positive effect that Mr Shakespeare's plays will have on the thinking of humanity,' the Doctor mused, 'I'm not sure if that wouldn't be worse.'

'So how do we stop him?' Vicki asked. 'I mean, according to you we can't kill him, so how do we make him forget?'

Braxiatel waved his little control unit at her. 'I can use this to move Laputa to England. At full speed we're as fast as a skiff.' He reached into his pocket with his other hand and took out a box that rattled when he shook it. 'I had these pills ready in case any locals got wind of the Convention. They'll wipe twenty-four hours from the memory of any human being. If you can get one of them down Shakespeare's throat, then we're safe. If not –' he gazed soberly at the Doctor '– then you and I had better change

216

our names and get as far away from here as possible, and pray that our people never ever find us.'

The Doctor looked longingly at Braxiatel's control box. 'Can I drive?' he asked.

Under Shakespeare's expert guidance, the skiff emerged from the watery depths and hovered a few feet above the surface of the Thames. As the water cascaded from the viewscreen, Shakespeare rotated the skiff. Green fields and hedgerows lay all around, and he felt his heart lift to see the familiar sights of home. To think that such a journey could be accomplished in so short a time! It had been a bare half hour after leaving Laputa that he had seen England appear on the viewscreen like a precious stone set in a silver sea.

Quickly, he ran his hands across the controls, scanning for signs of life. No boats were within sight, and the proximity detectors could locate nothing more intelligent than voles and foxes within half a mile.

The sunset was the same purple-red colour as it was in Venice, but somehow it was an *English* sunset, unlike any other. The water was the same consistency as the rigid, regimented canals, but somehow it was *English* water: purer and sweeter. He opened the hatch and let the English air drift in, replacing the stink of Venice − rotting vegetables and ordure − with the familiar tang of woodsmoke and flowers. Shakespeare vowed then and there never to leave again, not for any reason. He would die in England, happy and safe, a playwright and man of commerce, not a spy.

The lights of Hampton Court Palace flickered on the horizon. King James was most likely there with his retinue at this time of year, but if he wasn't then it would only take Shakespeare a few hours to locate him in the skiff. How pleased the King would be. How grateful. A man could retire on the King's gratitude and never go hungry.

Shakespeare was about to steer the skiff across the fields and park it in front of the Palace when a thought stopped him. It would be all too easy for some of the more frightened members of the Court to accuse him of witchcraft. King James's opinions on the subject were well known — Shakespeare would be burning at the stake before he could explain that these ... these *machines* came from God, not the Devil. He would be better off appearing on foot and explaining cautiously, with all the skill that his years as an actor had provided him with.

He guided the skiff across the fields to a nearby haystack and left it there, buried in the dry stalks. Before he left, he keyed the security systems to respond only to his voice. Everything about the skiff came naturally to him, just as naturally as writing. He struck out across the fields, taking in the silence, the smells and the sights of home. As he walked, he realized that he was hungry — starving in fact — and he hoped that the King's hospitality would be up to its usual standards.

Within twenty minutes Shakespeare was walking past the tall hedgerows that he remembered so well and up to the great double doors. The setting sun cast his huge shadow across the guards as they lowered their pikes towards him.

'I am William Shakespeare,' he said, 'and I have important news for the King.'

The house was in the alley of St John the Beheaded.

'Is this where Irving Braxiatel lives?' Steven said to the servant who opened the door.

'Are you expected?' the servant said calmly. He was dressed in velvet breeches and a white silk shirt with an embroidered waistcoat. His eyes moved from Steven to the blood-soaked Christopher Marlowe, who was slumped with an arm across Steven's shoulders.

'I don't — look, just announce us will you?' Steven snapped.

The servant was imperturbable. 'May I ask what the nature of your business is?'

Various possibilities flashed through Steven's mind. He could lie, he could bluff, he could force his way in, or ...

Tiredness washed over him and receded, leaving him shaking. He couldn't be bothered. Marlowe had to be healed, and healed fast. There was no time for lies. 'My friend has been injured in a duel,' he said finally. 'We need help.'

'Ah, you're looking for the Doctor,' the servant said calmly, opening the door wider. 'Please come in.'

'Yes, a doctor would be . . . What did you say?'

The servant glanced at Steven. 'You must be Signor Taylor. I have been waiting for you. My master alerted me to your presence in Venice.'

As Steven carried the almost unconscious Marlowe into the richly appointed house, he said, 'How did you know that we would turn up here?'

'Where else was there for you to go?' the servant murmured, leading them down a book-lined corridor. 'After my master discovered that you had been in the hidden underground room, he suspected that you might return.' He turned a corner and stopped by a particularly ornate tapestry between two bookshelves. 'Originally my instructions were to kill you, but he recently changed the word "kill" to "help" after he realized that you were an associate of the Doctor.' Pulling the tapestry to one side to reveal a metal door set into the brick behind it, the servant pressed a set of buttons in its centre. 'My name, by the way, is Cremonini.' The door slid back into the wall and he led the way down a set of white metal steps. Steven followed slowly, with Marlowe almost a dead weight on his shoulder.

Steven recognized the room as soon as they entered: a white metal box with a wide path around the edge of an empty pool of water and a small control panel set into one wall. As he let Marlowe slump to the path, Steven let out a sigh of relief.

'Your friend is close to death,' Cremonini said, kneeling down beside Marlowe and lifting a sodden corner of his shirt. 'I do not know much about mammalian physiology, but I do know that much.'

219

'I'm hoping that the Doctor can help,' Steven said. 'Can one of those shuttle things get us to him?'

'The envoys' skiffs are able to home directly on Laputa.' Cremonini straightened and walked over to the control panel. 'I will summon one now.' His hands drifted over the buttons. 'What is that device in the gentleman's chest, by the way?'

'I don't know.' Steven slid down the wall until he was sitting with his feet dangling in the water. 'But it's been there for a good few years, apparently.'

Cremonini turned and looked over at him. 'I only ask,' he said calmly, 'because it looks to me like the fusing unit for a meta-cobalt bomb.'

Steven turned to look at him, too tired to be amazed. 'Aren't you in the least bit surprised?' he asked.

'I'm a robot,' said Cremonini, 'nothing surprises me.'

A contingent of four guards escorted Shakespeare along the torch-lit corridor. The flickering light made the wood-panelled walls seem to shift disconcertingly, like rippling backdrops. Laurence Fletcher, one of the King's minions, had been despatched to the door to check that Shakespeare was who he said he was, and he now led the way towards what Shakespeare recognized as the Great Hall. There must be a feast going on, or a great entertainment. He hoped that the King would not take his appearance amiss and upbraid him for interrupting the evening's festivities.

A voice echoed along the corridor towards them from the open doorway of the Hall. A great, booming voice that Shakespeare recognized. It was Burbage's voice. Richard Burbage: Shakespeare's principal partner in the company that had started out as the Chamberlain's Men and had, under James's patronage, become the King's Men.

'Say from whence you owe this strange intelligence,' Burbage boomed.

The words struck Shakespeare like cold daggers to the

heart. They were his words. The words that he had written months before when he was preparing the story of Macbeth, who had ruled Scotland six hundred years before according to Holinshead's *Chronicles of England, Scotland and Ireland*. It had seemed to Shakespeare like the perfect subject for a play to put before the King — witchcraft decried, a regicide beheaded and James's own ancestor, Banquo, shown in a good light — but he had fully intended to be there himself and guide the actors through the final rehearsals. This was Act one, scene three of the play, in which Macbeth confronted the three witches on the blasted heath. How long had he been away? Had that bastard Burbage decided to put the play on in his absence? Running now, he outpaced the guards and the royal flunky and reached the open doorway as Henry Condell, playing Banquo, proclaimed: 'The earth hath bubbles, as the water has, and these are of them. Whither are they vanished?'

Shakespeare found himself looking across the heads of the seated audience at the stage. It was built beneath the minstrels' gallery out of planks laid across barrels. A curtain draped from the gallery hid the other door from the hall and provided an entrance and exit from the stage. The boards were bare of scenery.

'Into the air,' Burbage responded magisterially. Shakespeare could see him and Cordell in their borrowed finery gazing around, looking for the vanished witches. Burbage was as bombastic as ever, looming over the slight Cordell.

Shakespeare found himself torn. One part of him wanted to rush forward and interrupt the proceedings, informing the King of his discoveries from the stage, while the other part wanted to remain in the doorway and watch his play unfold for what was probably the first time in front of an audience.

The decision was made for him when a figure standing by the door noticed him. As it rushed towards him, Shakespeare recognized the lugubrious features of William Sly.

'Will, thank the Lord you are arrived. We had not sight nor sound of you for months!' Before Shakespeare could say a word, Sly was pulling him by the sleeve. 'Young Hal Berridge, who was to play Lady Macbeth, was taken ill not ten minutes ago and lies even as we speak in a fever. Will, you must go on in his place!'

Sixteen

'Hmm,' the Doctor mused, 'not a bad piece of piloting, even if I do say so myself.'

Galileo gazed at the strange mirror that hung in mid-air, reflecting a view of a river, some green fields and a distant, mist-shrouded red brick house of impressive mien. 'And this is England?' he asked. 'We were moving for barely long enough to get from one side of Padua to the other by horse, and that at full gallop.' He turned to the rest of the group and shrugged. 'This science of yours is marvellous. Not beyond my mental capabilities, of course, but to lesser mortals it must seem like magic.'

Irving Braxiatel didn't even spare Galileo a glance. He was standing slightly apart from the rest of the group, quietly fretting. Vicki smiled warmly at Galileo, and the crab with the red wings just cocked an eyestalk at him. That crab fascinated Galileo. Judging by the talk he had overheard it was a denizen of another inhabited sphere, and if so, Galileo had some questions to put to it.

'Yes, this is England,' the Doctor confirmed, 'and that building is Hampton Court, where we should find both Shakespeare and King James the Sixth of Scotland and the First of England.'

'How do you know we're in the right place?' Vicki asked.

'Look,' the Doctor commanded, pointing at the mirror. Galileo followed the direction of his finger, and saw a maze of hedges set amid a carefully landscaped garden. 'The maze and the Tudor knot garden,' he continued. 'Did you really think that I would make such a foolish mistake as to

223

take us to the wrong palace? Where is your faith, my child?'

'No, Doctor,' Vicki said placatingly, 'what I meant was, how do you know that this is where Shakespeare was heading?'

The Doctor gestured towards the mirror with Braxiatel's controlling box. The view shifted in the same manner that Galileo had observed when he moved a lens in a spyglass while still looking through it. So, he mused, this mirror *was* just a sophisticated spyglass, tricked up in finery to be sure, but a spyglass for all that. The mirror now displayed a stretch of field with a haystack. The Doctor manipulated the image until they were looking straight down on the haystack from above. There was a glint of metal inside.

'The skiff that Mr Shakespeare stole,' the Doctor said. 'It contains a transponder. We merely followed its signal.' He handed the controlling box back to Braxiatel. 'Thank you, my boy,' he murmured. Galileo strained to overhear. 'A wise move, making this Island and all its systems telepathically controlled.'

Braxiatel indicated the blue marble hall with a flick of his head. 'I didn't want to leave temptation in the Jamarians' path,' he said, equally quietly, 'but I didn't realize quite how far away from the path they would stray.' He hefted the box in his hand. 'I should check on the Convention. It's been suspiciously quiet in there.'

'Indeed,' the Doctor said, nodding, 'and Vicki and I will head for the Palace and intercept Mr Shakespeare. May we borrow a skiff?'

'Of course you may. As soon as you leave, I'll send the others away to stop the Jamarians from leaving. We can deal with them later: their plans are scotched anyway, but they're vicious creatures.'

The Doctor took a few steps away, then turned back. 'Keep a careful eye on those people on the beach,' he said. 'If the fuse for the bomb turns up, the Jamarians and Mr Shakespeare will be the least of your problems. The death of so many dignitaries from so many opposing races could ignite the galaxy.'

'This is odd,' Steven muttered, glancing across the skiff's controls, 'the automatic pilot is taking us away from Venice. Wherever this island is, it's not where it was, if you see what I mean.' He glanced up at the viewscreen, but all it showed was a sky more blue than black at the altitude they were flying at, and a bright star that must have been Venus.

The skiff rocked slightly as it passed through some sort of atmospheric turbulence. The feeling was so familiar that Steven found himself having to choke back a sudden surge of recognition. He let his hands move across the controls: not adjusting or pressing anything, but just happy to know that he could if he wanted to. It had been so long since he had flown a ship of any sort that he had almost forgotten how it felt. The years seemed to slough away from him, and he was eighteen again, piloting his fighter into combat with the Krayt. His fingers twitched as he fired imaginary missiles and avoided non-existent laser blasts.

A groan from behind him broke the spell of memory, and he was once again sitting at the controls of an automated skiff, heading God knew where. He turned to where Christopher Marlowe was laid out across a couch at the rear of the cabin. Marlowe's grey, ironic eyes were fixed on Steven's face.

'Not much longer now,' Steven said. 'Just . . . just hang on. The Doctor will be able to help.'

Marlowe shook his head. 'No, young Steven,' he murmured. A great cough racked his body, and sent fresh blood spilling down his chin. 'And now doth ghastly death, with greedy talons, grip my bleeding heart. My soul begins to take her flight to Hell, and summons all my senses to depart.'

'Can't you just shut up and rest?' Steven yelled. Marlowe didn't reply. He just kept on staring at Steven, a slight smile on his face. Another slight atmospheric buffeting tilted the skiff to one side, and Steven leaned the other way to compensate. Marlowe's eyes didn't move: staring now at an empty bulkhead.

'Marlowe?' Steven could hear the rising panic in his voice, but he couldn't quell it. 'Marlowe, talk to me!'

But Marlowe was dead.

As the Doctor and Vicki vanished through a nearby arch, Braxiatel pointed the box at the mirror. The view shifted again to show a conference chamber that looked to Galileo remarkably like the one he usually lectured in at the University of Padua. Creatures of different aspects and visages lined the seats around the steep walls. Rather than nausea or shock, Galileo felt a sudden and completely unexpected wave of nostalgia wash over him. It took a few moments to work out why, and then he smiled as he realized that the creatures reminded him of nothing so much as the masks and costumes that the Venetians wore during Carnival time.

A man who, at a passing glance, resembled the Doctor stood at a lectern in the centre of the chamber. He appeared to be moderating an argument: several of the creatures were on their feet – or other appendages – and shouting at him. He was smiling.

'Is that Cardinal Roberto Bellarmine?' Galileo asked.

'Yes,' Braxiatel replied. 'Why, do you know him?'

'Our paths have crossed.'

'He thinks he is dead,' Braxiatel said.

Galileo smiled slightly. 'If only he would stay that way,' he muttered.

Braxiatel adjusted the virtual screen to show the beach on Laputa where the humans with the – what had the Doctor called them? – the meta-cobalt fragments had gathered. The sun had set, but the moon was casting its sterile light across the sand. The humans were all huddled together now in one huge mass of flesh and clothing from which limbs stuck out in odd directions and the occasional blistered face peered blindly at nothing.

Braxiatel sighed and turned to where Envoy Albrellian was slumped on the floor. Galileo was astonished to see him kick Albrellian's shell as hard as he could. The envoy rocked backwards onto his rear set of legs. 'Envoy Albrellian! Will you please pull yourself together!'

The arthropod stirred, and extruded an eyestalk. 'The point what is?' he said. 'As soon as the fuse arrives, all doomed are we.'

'Well,' Braxiatel said grimly, 'it's possible that the fuse is going to turn up late, rather than not turn up at all. We need to get these people off this island and separated as soon as possible. With the Jamarians gone after Shakespeare we haven't got enough muscle to accomplish it ourselves. Can we use the device you called them all together with to split them up again and move them off the island?'

Something moving in the depths of the mirror attracted Galileo's attention. 'Forgive me for interrupting this fascinating, if incomprehensible, discussion,' he said, 'but it would appear that one of your celestial chariots is on its way back to the island.'

Shakespeare stepped from the curtained booth onto the stage. His legs shook with strain, and he could taste bile in the back of his throat. The hand holding the letter – just a sheet of blank parchment, but the audience wouldn't be able to tell from that distance – shook so hard that, had anything actually been written on it, he would have been hard pressed to read it.

The flickering torches illuminated the audience of assorted nobility and courtiers who sat on the hard benches out in the Great Hall. On a raised dais at the other end were two rows of padded seats, and in them sat King James and his Danish wife, Queen Anne, along with a few favoured friends such as his astrologer, Doctor John Dee. James's sallow, bearded face was enraptured by the action on stage, and Shakespeare felt a little tingle of pride run through him. The King was wearing a doublet that was padded so heavily against knife thrusts that his head and arms looked ridiculously small sticking out of it. His tongue – too large for his mouth, or so the gossip ran – protruded slightly from between his wet lips.

A slight ripple of eager interest ran through the audience as they recognized Shakespeare standing there in the robes of a lady. The noise roused Shakespeare from his trance, and he raised the parchment as if to read from it. Desperately he tried to recall the words that he had so carelessly dashed off all those months ago. What was he supposed to be doing? Macbeth had met with the three witches who had told him that he would be King, and he had sent a letter to his wife. This was the scene where Lady Macbeth read her husband's letter and realized that, for Macbeth to be King, the present King had to be murdered.

'They met me in the day of success,' he said, his voice hesitant, 'and I have learned by the perfectest report that they have more in them than mortal knowledge. When I burned in desire to question them further, they made themselves air, into which they vanished . . .'

James was nodding now, a thin line of saliva glistening on his chin. The play had been written for him and him alone, pandering to his hatred of witchcraft and his fear of assassination.

'While I stood rapt in the wonder of it,' Shakespeare continued, 'came missives from the King –'

He stopped, for the doors at the rear of the hall, behind the dais, had opened, and two figures had entered. Two familiar figures.

It was the Doctor and his companion, Vicki.

Braxiatel dragged his mind away from thoughts of impending destruction and glanced over at the virtual screen again. A silvery disc was spinning rapidly towards the island. Quickly he manipulated his control box with his fingers and his mind, and the view shifted to the landing area, where he was unsurprised to see a group of slender silhouettes standing and arguing. Two of them were engaged in shoving each other back and forth across the pad, and the whole thing looked as if it might degenerate into a fight. 'There's trouble in the ranks,' he said.

'Do I take it that your plan was for those creatures to be stuck here?' Galileo asked.

'It was,' Braxiatel replied. 'That's why I sent the other skiffs away. One problem at a time, I thought – sort the bomb out first and deal with the Jamarians at my leisure – but if they hijack that skiff from whoever is piloting it, we're finished.' His fingers and his mind played across his control box. 'And unfortunately whoever *is* piloting that skiff has set it on automatic homing mode. I can't override it until it arrives.'

'And is there any way of determining who that pilot is?'

Braxiatel thought for a moment, then touched a stud on his control box and caressed it with a thought. The virtual screen blurred, then cleared to show the padded interior of the skiff. A dark-haired, square-jawed man wearing a brown, embroidered jacket was sitting at the controls with his head in his hands. Braxiatel, unsure whether the man was a native of Venice or a companion of the Doctor, set up a two-way channel directly to the viewscreen in the skiff. Before he could say anything, the man looked up.

'Are you Braxiatel?' the man asked. There was despair in his eyes.

'I am,' Braxiatel replied. 'And you are?'

'Steven Taylor. Is the Doctor with you?'

'Not quite. He's –' Braxiatel suddenly noticed the body slumped behind Steven. 'Who's your friend?'

Steven grimaced. 'His name is – was – Christopher Marlowe. Look, there's some kind of metal device in his chest. I don't know what it is, but it's been getting warmer as we've been getting closer to the island.'

Braxiatel suddenly felt very old and very tired. 'The fuse,' he muttered, 'it had to be, of course. When things can't get any worse, they always do.' He rubbed a hand across his forehead, and was about to say something when Envoy Albrellian pushed him to one side.

'The hatch open, then the meta-cobalt fragment from the man's chest try to remove,' he said, the ruff of hair around his eyes fluffed up with some strong emotion. 'To join you flying out am I. One chance to wrap this whole thing up, and one chance only, have we.' Turning to Braxiatel, he said, 'A lot of your problems caused I, and sorting them out intend I. The hypnocontroller to get the humans with the meta-cobalt fragments to the landing pad will use I. When the skiff lands, Jamarians on board let must you.'

'You mean, let them escape?' Braxiatel snapped.

'That is exactly what mean I.'

'What do we do now?' Vicki hissed.

'A very good question,' the Doctor replied. Vicki watched as his gaze flickered around the torch-lit Great Hall, taking in all the pertinent details. On the stage at the end of the room actors were entering, shouting their lines and exiting again as fast as they could. The whole thing seemed to her to be taken at breakneck speed. Vicki was used to more refined entertainment: she knew that Shakespeare was meant to be a great playwright, but she couldn't follow what was going on at all.

The Doctor's gaze seemed to have halted on a figure sitting on a dais nearby; a tall, cadaverous man who wore black robes.

'Is that the King?' she asked.

'No,' the Doctor murmured, 'the man wearing what looks like a large eiderdown is the King. I don't recognize the man in black, but I have a terrible feeling that I should.' He shrugged and glanced towards the stage. 'No matter. I am familiar with this play, and they appear to be coming to the end of act four. We have to get that amnesia pill into Mr Shakespeare soon. The longer we leave it, the greater the chance that he will spill the beans, as it were.'

'I'm surprised he hasn't already.' Vicki looked at the stage, where Shakespeare's face could just be seen peeking at them through a gap in the curtain at the back. 'If I was him, I'd have made a bee-line straight for the King.'

The Doctor shook his head. 'Interrupting the King's entertainment is as good a way as any to obtain a long-term room in the Tower of London. James was never noted for his tolerance. And, as I recall, there was a story put about by a writer somewhat after Mr Shakespeare's time that Shakespeare was called on stage to replace a dying actor during the first performance of this very play.' He beamed. 'A fortuitous coincidence, and a provoking thought. It gives me hope that somebody up there likes me.'

Vicki glanced up at the empty gallery above the stage. 'Somebody up where?'

The Doctor didn't reply. Vicki turned, and found that she was alone. The Doctor was striding down the aisle along the side of the hall towards the stage, for all the world as if he intended to get up on stage himself.

Steven watched on the skiff's viewscreen as the island of Laputa grew slowly larger. Whoever had piloted it had set it down in the middle of a wide stretch of river, and from above Steven could see the river's currents building up silt around the island as they tried to force their way past its bulk. By the light of the full moon the landing pad was a grey circle in the middle of green trees and bushes, and to one side of it a series of impressive buildings cast pointed shadows across the banks of the river.

A small shape was flying up towards the descending skiff. Its powerful wings beat mercilessly at the air, and Steven could tell that it was tiring. He had never seen a creature like it before, but he recognized Marlowe's description. It was one of the creatures that had attacked the colony in New Albion, although Steven assumed from Braxiatel's words that it was on their side. There was a lot about this whole situation that he did not understand.

As the creature laboured towards the skiff, close enough now that Steven could see the ruff of hair around its eyestalks flattening in the rush of air, he opened the hatchway. The skiff rocked slightly as the airflow around it changed, but continued on its stately course. There was something terribly preordained about the slowness of that descent. Steven knew that it was probably a preprogrammed speed set for safety reasons, but it seemed to him that the skiff knew about the coming explosion, knew that there was no way of stopping it, and was deliberately prolonging the tension.

He moved back into the central section of the skiff and bent down by Marlowe's side. The playwright's eyes were open, but the devilish gleam had gone. Steven reached out and ruffled his hair. 'Goodbye, friend,' he murmured.

The skiff lurched to one side, and Steven turned to the hatchway. The arthropod was pulling itself in, and having to turn sideways to get its shell through the narrow opening. 'The meta-cobalt fragment out yet have not got you?' it asked as its wings furled beneath hinged sections of its shell. 'A minute or so before this thing lands have only got we, and then finished are we.'

'Look,' Steven shouted, suddenly furious, 'he was a friend of mine, and you desecrated his body twenty-two years before he died. He gave his life to save me. Haven't you got any decency at all?'

'None,' said the creature, and reached forward with a claw. Before Steven could react it had pushed into Marlowe's chest and taken a firm grip on the metal device. 'Not too late we are hope let us,' it said, and pulled. The device came free with a sucking sound, like a foot being pulled out of mud, and Steven winced. It was a sphere, about the size of his fist, incised with symbols, and it seemed to be glowing. 'Satisfy my curiosity,' the creature whistled. 'To the hypnocontroller in his head what happened?'

'Removed by a surgeon after a sword fight,' Steven replied tersely.

'Because of a series of stupid little incidents, the best laid plans come to nothing of Jamarians and Greld. If that hypnocontroller still had he, at the island with the rest of them turned up would he have, the bomb gone off would have and happy everyone would have been. Or dead. There must have been some influence left, though, because to Venice at the right time did actually get he.' The creature scuttled towards the hatchway, then turned an eyestalk back over its shell to regard Steven. 'When this thing lands, as soon as possible get out must you,' it said. 'Because one large explosion soon afterward will there be. Oh, and make sure the hatch so that it can't be closed before you go fix you. My hypnocontroller to order the humans carrying the meta-cobalt fragments to congregate on this spacecraft have used I.'

'You want me to *what*?' Steven yelled, but he was too late. The creature jumped out into the air, still clutching the device. Steven saw its wings open wide, catching all the air they could, and then it had soared away out of sight. Turning his attention back to the landing pad, he saw that they were only a few hundred feet away and descending slowly. A group of painfully thin aliens with horns were gathered waiting for it, and beyond them a shambling mass of humans was heading for the touch-down point. Steven quickly ran his hands over the controls, looking for some way of fixing the hatch fully open, but he could see nothing that might help. Turning, he gazed around the cabin, hoping against hope that there might be something lying around that he could use. Again: nothing. He glanced back at the screen. Fifteen seconds perhaps to touchdown. He was close enough to see the mad gleam in the eyes of the thin aliens, and the melted eyes of the oncoming humans. He glanced franti- cally around, but there was nothing, *nothing*, that would do any good. Whatever plan of Albrellian's depended on the hatch being open was doomed to failure, and that meant they were all doomed.

Seventeen

Vicki raced down the aisle of the Great Hall after the Doctor, aware of the ripple of attention that they were attracting.

A small, broad actor was just saying, 'The night is long that never finds the day,' as the Doctor reached the stage. He turned towards the curtains, then turned back and cast a puzzled glance towards the Doctor, who was clambering up onto the stage.

Vicki reached the stage herself in time to hear the actor hiss: 'You can't come up here! We're in the middle of the play!'

'I am a friend of the King,' the Doctor snapped, low enough that nobody in the audience could hear him, 'and he will be most displeased if I am not allowed to participate in this little production.'

The actor cast a worried glance towards the back of the hall, then exited rapidly through the curtain. Vicki assumed that he would be discussing the situation with the other actors. From behind, she could hear people in the audience whispering to each other. The Doctor turned magisterially, hooked his thumbs beneath his lapels and gazed down his nose at them. 'I have two nights watched with you,' he said loudly, his voice echoing around the hall, 'but can perceive no truth in your report. When was it she last walked, hmm?'

There was silence. Vicki risked a glance at the audience, and saw that they were rapt with attention, all eyes fixed on the Doctor.

'I said I have two nights watched with you, but can

perceive no truth in your report. When was it that Lady Macbeth last walked in her sleep?'

There was some commotion behind the curtain, but nobody was coming out on stage. Impulsively, Vicki scrambled up on stage to join the Doctor. He smiled at her in approval, nodded towards the King and made walking movements with the fingers of his left hand out of sight of the audience.

'When the . . . the King . . . er . . . left,' she said haltingly, watching as the Doctor made a rising gesture with his hand, 'I saw her . . . rise? . . .' He nodded, and made an unlocking motion. '. . . Unlock her . . . her closet . . .' As she became more practised at interpreting what the Doctor was trying to convey, her voice gained confidence and she started playing to the audience. 'She got some . . . some paper and wrote on it, then she read it, and . . . and then she got back into the bed, and all the time she was still asleep!'

The Doctor smiled at her, and Vicki felt a little glow of triumph ignite deep inside. She certainly hadn't used Shakespeare's words, but the Doctor seemed to think that she had got his sense across.

'A great perturbation in nature,' the Doctor proclaimed, 'to receive at once the benefit of sleep and do the effects of watching. In this slumbery agitation, besides her walking and her other actual performances, what at any time have you heard her say, hmm?'

Vicki looked for a cue. The Doctor turned his head away from the audience and mimed holding his lips closed. 'Why, nothing that I can report,' Vicki said quickly.

'You may to me,' the Doctor snapped, winking at her in reassurance, 'and 'tis most meet you should.'

'No,' Vicki said firmly, stamping her foot, 'I cannot.'

Hurried footsteps behind her made Vicki whirl around. William Shakespeare had arrived on stage, still wearing Lady Macbeth's robes and wig but now holding a lit candle, apparently thrust through the curtain by his fellow actors. He glared at the Doctor.

'Look, here he — er, she comes!' Vicki cried in surprise.

'How came she by that light?' the Doctor responded quickly as Shakespeare glanced out at the audience.

'Search me,' Vicki muttered when she received no cue from the Doctor.

The Doctor stepped nearer to Shakespeare, who shied away like a frightened horse. 'You see, her eyes are open,' he said, reaching into his pocket for something.

'Yes,' Vicki said, and then when the Doctor mimed waggling a finger at his forehead, added, 'but there's nobody home.'

Vicki heard someone behind the curtain urgently whispering to Shakespeare. With barely concealed ill-grace, the actor began to rub his hands together as if he were washing them.

'What is it she does now?' Taking Irving Braxiatel's amnesia pill from his pocket, the Doctor took another step towards Shakespeare. 'Look how she rubs her hands.' Catching Shakespeare's eye, he whispered, 'Mr Shakespeare, it is very important that you swallow this pill.'

'Yet here's a spot,' Shakespeare cried, glancing down at his hand and reacting as if he'd seen a spider. Casting a sideways glance at the Doctor, he hissed, 'Throw your physic to the dogs, Doctor, I'll have none of it! I have filled my mind with wonders — wonders I shall share with my monarch ere the end of this play.'

'Hark, she speaks,' the Doctor said, turning to the audience and raising his hands high. 'I will set down what comes from her, to satisfy my remembrance the more strongly.' Turning again to Shakespeare, he whispered, 'I implore you, please take this pill. You cannot understand the damage that will be done if you keep the knowledge that you have stolen. Wisdom must be earned. Advances in science must be worked for.'

'There is no darkness but ignorance!' Shakespeare

hissed. Flicking his hand towards the Doctor, he shouted, 'Out, damned spot, I say!' Vicki flinched, waiting for the impact, but none came. 'Hell is murky! What need we fear who knows it, when one can call our power to account?'

The Doctor interrupted in a low tone. 'I must warn you that if you do not cooperate, I may be forced to employ violence!'

'Who'd have thought the old man to have had so much blood in him?' Shakespeare shouted, and Vicki wasn't sure whether he was talking to the audience or warning the Doctor.

Clenching his fists, Steven forced himself to calm down. How could he jam the door open? What could he use? Slowly, painstakingly, he gazed around the cabin again. Everything was fixed down, or moulded into place. Everything was seamless.

Except . . .

Except Marlowe's body. Steven leaped across to him and quickly ran his hands across Marlowe's bloody clothing. It only took moments to locate the stiletto that Marlowe had mentioned, strapped to his ankle in a sheath. With a constant countdown running in his mind, Steven leaped back to the control console and jammed the stiletto blade into the thin crack between the hatch control button and the rest of the console. Sparks fountained and, caught by the air rushing through the open hatch, whirled madly around the cabin.

It would have to do. The skiff was starting to slow down, ready to settle on the landing pad. Without thinking, Steven rushed for the open hatch and jumped. The world outside was a confused blur of green vegetation, grey stone and blue sky. His legs were already scissoring in mid-air, and he hit the ground running. Two of the thin aliens tried to intercept him but, head down, he charged them and knocked them out of the way like skittles. His legs pumped away at the hard ground.

Air whipped at his face and brought tears to his eyes. Marlowe's finely chiselled features and mane of grey hair seemed to float before him as he ran, one eye closed in a knowing wink. Suddenly, out of nowhere, the group of humans appeared before him. Their faces were burned raw and each one had smoke rising from a glowing mass in his or her chest. They weren't concerned with Steven: he just pushed them out of the way and turned, panting with exertion, to watch as they stumbled towards the skiff.

Steven wiped the tears from his streaming eyes and tried to focus on what was going on. The Jamarians had crowded themselves into the skiff, and had presumably regained control from the autopilot. He saw that the hatch was still open; that was a blessing, at least. One of the Jamarians was tugging vainly at the door when it saw the oncoming humans. It yelled something to its colleagues inside, but too late. The humans reached the skiff. Some of them tried to force their way in through the hatch, and Steven saw the Jamarians' horns plunging into the mass of flesh to discourage them, but the majority were clambering up the skiff's sides and congregating on its gently sloping top.

A glint of red light in the sky caught Steven's attention. The arthropod was hovering a few hundred feet above the ground, its slowly beating wings illuminated from below by the light of the device it was holding. The device was glowing red as the rest of the pieces of the meta-cobalt device approached.

The skiff began to rise unsteadily from the ground, its hatch still open and the humans all somehow crammed inside and on top. The Jamarians must have made a decision to evacuate the island and worry about the humans later. Perhaps they didn't know about the bomb.

The skiff began to accelerate. Within moments it would be out of sight, heading for the moon perhaps, or a waiting ship.

The arthropod folded its wings and dived towards

238

the skiff like a hawk, still clutching the device. Within moments it was descending so fast that all Steven could see was an arrow of scarlet light, aimed straight at the heart of the skiff.

The arthropod was still ten feet away from the skiff when the meta-cobalt formed a critical mass. Suddenly there was no skiff, no winged arthropod, no stick-creatures and no humans — just an expanding ball of light that was so intense that Steven could still see it expanding through his closed eyes . . .

. . . And suddenly night was turned into day, Dunsinane Castle was turned into bare boards and a curtain by the pitiless light, and Lady Macbeth's robes were once again just a length of threadbare velvet. The audience rose to their feet and let out a collective gasp of astonishment, as if for a moment they believed this was some effect in the play, some theatrical trick, and not a freak of nature. The Company of King's Men emerged from behind the cur-tained entrance — Richard Burbage's mouth was hanging open, while Richard Cowley, John Heminge and the rest were white with shock. At the back of the hall, King James raised his hands and shrank back frightened of assassination by witchcraft, while his guards just stood nearby, entranced by the spectacle.

William Shakespeare forgot his lines, forgot the Doc-tor, forgot even the audience and turned to where the new sun was shining in through the windows of the Great Hall. From the corner of his eye he saw the Doctor step forward. Before he could react, the Doctor had reached around his head and thrown something smooth and rounded into his mouth. He tried to spit it out, but the old man clamped his hand beneath Shakespeare's jaw, holding his mouth closed, then reached up with his thumb and forefinger and pinched Shakespeare's nose. Shakespeare lashed backward with his elbow, catching the old man in the ribs, but those gnarled fingers held on with amazing strength. He reached back to grab the

Doctor's ear, but the old man squirmed out of the way. Fire burned in his lungs as he tried to draw breath but couldn't. The pill was a hard, chalky lump in his mouth. Desperately he tried to struggle against the wiry arms that pinioned him, but he might have been encased in iron chains for all the good it did. His lungs laboured so hard that his throat closed up and he could feel the pill being drawn back in his mouth. Flailing with his arms, he did his best to fight his way free of the Doctor's grasp, swinging his body to and fro to dislodge the old man, but it was to no avail. Blackness encroached around the edges of his vision and the hubbub of the audience grew distant, as if heard through several doors.

Finally, able to resist no longer, he swallowed the pill. Instantly the Doctor's hands released their pressure, and Shakespeare sank to his knees, drawing in breath after breath of precious, sweet air. He couldn't breathe in deep enough, and he imagined his lungs swelling, like leather sacks full of water, fit to burst.

The light outside began to fade. Whatever had caused that brief, false dawn had also caused it to withdraw. With it, Shakespeare's false memories began to vanish softly and suddenly from his mind, one by one, like potato peelings washing down a drain. The ores that could be dug from the ground to provide heat and light, if they were treated with care – gone. The weapons that threw spears of light – gone. The devices that could carry messages through the very air itself – gone. Tiredness drew its cloak across him, and grief for all the things he had lost, and all the things that England could have been but could be no longer. Like a dull actor, he had forgotten his part. The insubstantial pageant faded; he slumped to the bare boards and slept, and did not dream.

The clamour of voices echoed through the Great Hall of Laputa, and Galileo gazed around with something approaching awe at the assembled envoys. The party was going well, and the wine was the best that he had ever tasted. It was as sweet as honey, but not as cloying, and it had a long, complex aftertaste that put him in mind of nutmeg and vanilla. And even better than the taste was the fact that, no matter how much of it he drank, he wasn't getting drunk.

He raised the goblet to his lips again but missed. The lip of the goblet hit his cheekbone, sending the sweet liquid cascading down his beard. Vicki, in conversation nearby with Irving Braxiatel, saw the mishap and smiled at him. He smiled back. Perhaps he *was* drunk, but he wasn't sure whether it was on the wine or on the company. To think that he was celebrating the successful end of a conference of star-people. His life would never be the same again. The things he had seen – the things he had heard! – would lead him on to greater inventions than any man could imagine. Shakespeare had stolen such information, and it had been taken away from him again somehow, but Galileo didn't need to do anything so clumsy. Having seen these marvels, he knew that they were possible, and knowing that something was possible was half the battle. It might take him years, but he would recreate them and call them his own. His name would go down in history.

Two elderly men clad in scarlet robes staggered past. Blinking, Galileo realized that there was only one man. Perhaps the wine was stronger than he thought. A thin woman whose silver skin seemed to undulate of its own accord was following the man, who turned as if to kiss her. She skipped away, giggling. For a moment Galileo thought that the man was the Doctor, until he realized that it was actually Cardinal Bellarmine, behaving in a most unCatholic way. How could the Church suppress this knowledge, when one of its own most senior Cardinals had seen it all? They had tortured and burned Giordano Bruno to get him to recant the truth, but they couldn't do the same to Galileo. Not now. Not with Bellarmine on his side.

He swigged back the dregs of his glass, and couldn't

help smiling at the taste. If only he could get hold of a case of that wine, he could die happy.

'You like our *rakeshla*?' a voice hissed. He turned, and found a squat figure in leather armour behind him. The creature's potato-like head, which grew straight from its massive shoulders, would not have been out of place projecting from the roof of a church.

'Rakeshla — is that what you call it?' Galileo burped, and wiped the back of his hand across his mouth. 'It is excellent! Truly excellent! Where can I buy some?'

'We do not sell *rakeshla*,' the gargoyle hissed, its lipless mouth stretched into a wide smile. 'It is a drink of victory, a drink of celebration with which we of Sontara toast our returning warriors.'

'And this —' Galileo waved a hand at the various creatures from the stars that surrounded them. 'Do you consider this a victory?'

The gargoyle's entire upper body jerked forward. Galileo reflected that it was probably the only way the creature could nod. 'Indeed!' it said. 'The bargaining was hard, but the Doctor was more reasonable than we had expected. A true warrior prefers to gaze into his victim's dying eyes, rather than wipe out a star-system from orbit, and the agreements we have made here reflect that. A good result, for us all.' Its piggish eyes glinted at Galileo out of deep-set sockets. 'I am Tayre.' The creature slapped a hand across its broad chest in salute. 'I am Colonel in Chief of the Strategic Arm of the Ninth Sontaran Army. What is your rank and designation?'

'I am Galileo Galilei.' He bowed. 'I am an astronomer.'

Tayre nodded. 'Ah, a stellar cartographer. That is good. Accurate maps are a prerequisite for a successful military campaign.'

Galileo nodded fervently. 'If only more military commanders thought the same way you do.' He glanced over at Cardinal Bellarmine, who was entwined with the silver-skinned woman, and said, 'Tell me about your world, Tayre. Which sun does it revolve around?'

'None,' Tayre replied, 'our sun revolves around our home planet.'

Galileo felt as though he had been punched in the stomach. 'You are mistaken!' he snapped. 'That is not possible. Worlds *must* revolve around suns. I know it to be so.'

'Sontarans are never mistaken,' Tayre hissed ominously. 'We have rearranged our solar system more logically. The Sontaran Imperator decreed it.'

'No.' Galileo shook his head. 'Worlds revolve around suns. I say it is so.'

'Are you calling me a liar?' the Sontaran snapped.

'If truth is beauty and beauty truth then your ugliness shows you for the liar that you are.' Despite the fact that it was the wine talking, Galileo was pleased with the insult. His pleasure lasted only for a moment, until the Sontaran's gloved fist smashed into his face.

The TARDIS was where they had left it, on one of the small islands in the Venetian lagoon. Sand had drifted against its base, and dew sparkled on its sides in the early morning sunlight. Steven stepped out of Braxiatel's skiff and onto the pebbly beach. Somewhere above his head, a gull cried out in hunger.

Marlowe was dead. He kept having to tell himself that, because he kept forgetting. Every now and then he would turn around, expecting to find those grey eyes staring challengingly back at him. But they weren't there. They never would be again.

Behind him he heard Vicki jump into the water with a loud splash. A few moments later he heard the Doctor fussing: 'I'm quite capable of getting off this contraption by myself thank you.'

Why did he feel this way? Marlowe had been a decent enough guy, but nothing special. Steven had seen people he had known for years go crashing down in flames beneath the guns of Krayt battlecruisers and felt less about their deaths than he was feeling about a man he had known for a handful of days. Why? What was it about Marlowe that engendered such . . . such feelings of regret in Steven? He would probably never know, and the terrible thing was that there was nobody else on the TARDIS who he felt he could ask. Vicki was too young to understand, and the Doctor . . .

Steven turned around to see the Doctor hobbling up the beach. He smiled when he saw the TARDIS – a small, secret smile that vanished when he noticed Steven watching him.

No. The Doctor wouldn't understand either.

'Happy to be leaving, young man?' the Doctor asked as he approached.

'Ecstatic,' Steven said levelly.

A slight cough from the direction of the shuttle made them both turn. Irving Braxiatel was standing in the hatchway. Vicki was on the beach, holding a pebble in her hand.

'Farewell Doctor, Vicki, Steven,' Braxiatel said. 'I wish I could offer some advice, but too much knowledge is a dangerous thing. Take care of yourselves, and try not to get involved in too many adventures.' He smiled lop-sidedly at the Doctor. 'After all, you're not as young as you used to be, eh?'

'Don't patronize me,' the Doctor snapped.

'Are you going to be okay here?' Vicki asked. 'I mean, what's going to happen to the Armageddon Convention and all that?'

Braxiatel shrugged. 'Cardinal Bellarmine has done wonders – better than the Doctor himself, I suspect.' The Doctor began to splutter, and Braxiatel raised his voice to cover the noise. 'When the party ends, I'll ship all the envoys and their staff back to their ships, and they can all leave peacefully. I've already given Cardinal Bellarmine and Galileo Galilei their amnesia pills and dumped them in Venice, although I had to disentangle them from the Ellillian and Sontaran envoys first. Galileo will blame his lapse in memory on the drink, of course. How the

Cardinal will explain it away I don't know.'

'Mr Shakespeare has forgotten all about the events of the last few days,' the Doctor added. 'And the last we saw had been confined to bed with brain fever. King James was slightly annoyed at the abrupt curtailment of the play, but the free firework display outside the Palace mollified him somewhat. And what about you, dear boy? Has this little adventure cured you of the desire to do good?'

Braxiatel nodded. 'I'll probably stay on Earth for a while, though: I've been building up a little library of suppressed manuscripts which I'd like to find a decent home for. I think I'll stay out of politics and stick to collecting.' He waved self-consciously. 'Goodbye,' he said. The hatch hummed shut in front of him, and then there was silence for a moment before the skiff skipped away from the island, throwing up regular splashes of water like a pebble skimmed across the waves.

'Show off,' the Doctor grumbled, and pulled the piece of ribbon that the TARDIS key was attached to from his pocket. As he fumbled it into the lock, he turned and gazed at Steven. There was sympathy in his eyes, and wisdom, and understanding. 'Perhaps we should get you a key as well, my boy,' he murmured, too soft for Vicki to hear.

'Thanks,' Steven said, surprised at the offer. 'But . . . but why now?'

'Because you've grown up.'

The Doctor pushed the TARDIS door open and gestured Steven to enter. Steven nodded briefly, then turned to where Vicki was gazing off towards the sketchy lines of Venice on the horizon. 'Come on, slowcoach,' he yelled, 'or we'll go without you.'

'The first thing I'll do when I get in,' Vicki said as she trudged across the sand, 'is to have one of those wonderful ultrasonic shower things. I've been dreaming about having one all the time I've been here. What about you, Steven?'

Vicki's head blocked his view of the Doctor's eyes for a

moment, and when he could see them again the sympathy, the wisdom and the understanding had vanished, and the Doctor was just a senile old man again. Had he ever been anything else?

'I'm going to the TARDIS library,' Steven said softly. 'There are some plays I want to read.' He gazed out to sea, trying to get one final look at the towers and domes of Venice, but the mist had closed in around the island. It was as if Venice had never existed, and Steven's time there had just been a dream.

He shook his head, and walked into the TARDIS. There would be other dreams.

Flambeaux illuminated the wide thoroughfare, and their glare made it difficult to see down the narrow alley that parted from it like a twig from a tree trunk. Sperone Speroni cursed. The lapping of water echoed back and forth between the alley's walls, and he thought that he could hear a man groaning somewhere in the darkness. 'Are you sure?' he asked the Nightwatch guard beside him.

The guard was just a youth, and he was sweating with nervousness. 'Yes sir,' he said, his voice catching in his throat. 'That's where they are all right.'

'And one of them is wearing a Cardinal's robes?' Speroni let the scorn in his voice show.

The youngster quailed. 'That's what it looked like to me, sir.'

'And the other was Galileo Galilei, who was killed by Tomasso Nicolotti yesterday?'

'Yes, sir.' The youth's voice was almost a squeak by now.

Speroni rubbed his hand across his bald head. These past few days had been odd to say the least: why should tonight be any different? 'Well, let's get this over with,' he muttered, and followed the guard down the alley. 'I don't know about you, but I'm tired, and I'm cold, and I'm hungry, and I want to go home at *some* stage tonight.'

At the far end of the alley a bridge arced over a small canal. A rat sat on the bridge, washing its whiskers. As Speroni and the guard approached it glanced up and looked them over for a moment before walking slowly in the opposite direction.

'Damn pests.' Speroni spat after it. 'Damned if I know what's worse; rats or Turks. Well, where are they then?'

The guard pointed to a patch of shadows just before the bridge. Speroni crouched down and waited until his eyes adjusted properly to the darkness.

Two men were slumped together in the lee of the wall. One of them was undoubtedly Galileo, although Speroni had five witnesses who said that the Paduan had been killed the day before. Dead he wasn't, but he was snoring fit to wake those that were. His face was covered in bruises. The other man looked at first glance like Cardinal Bellarmine, but what would a Cardinal of Rome be doing slumped, blind drunk, in an alley?

'Did you know I used to build ships?' Speroni said suddenly.

'Sorry sir?' the guard said, but Speroni wasn't really listening.

'Fifteen years I spent working in the Arsenale, man and boy. Fifteen good years. I learned a trade. I was proud of what I did. And then they made me a Lord of the Nightwatch.' He sighed. 'Life used to be so simple.'

The water of the canal lapped against the brickwork. It sounded to Speroni like the distant chuckling of some malign demon whose job it was to make his life as unpleasant as possible.

Before he knew what he was doing, he had risen to his feet.

'What do you want to do with them, sir?' the youth said.

'Do what you wish,' Speroni replied, feeling a fluttering in his chest as if something with wings had been released from a cage. He began to walk away, down the alley. 'I don't care any more.'

'But sir!' the guard called. 'What do you – where are you going?'

'I'm going back to the Arsenale!' he shouted back, feeling a smile spread over his face. 'I'm going to do something important with my life, before I forget how. I'm going to build ships.'

The sun was just rising above the golden domes and stone towers as he walked out of the alley, casting a rosy light across the entire city. He felt as if he had just been released from the deepest, darkest dungeon in the Doge's Palace. He took a deep breath, turned towards the sun and walked away from it all.

Epilogue

April, 1616

'Father, a visitor for you.'

The sound of his daughter's voice from downstairs roused him from a dream full of sound and fury. He found himself in his bed, tangled in sheets that were damp with fever-sweat. For a moment the bedroom looked strange to him, as if the laths were not straight, and the plaster was leaning in towards him. His head ached, and there was a churning in his stomach. It was all he could do to stop himself from rolling over and throwing up, but as his mind cleared he knew that it would do him no good. He had felt this way for three days now, and nothing made any difference — not poultices, nor purges, nor medications of any sort. The inaudible and noiseless foot of time was creeping up on him.

'Send —' His voice was a croak, and he paused to clear his throat. 'Send him up.' A cart rattled past the window, and he could smell hay. Footsteps creaked on the stairs. He levered himself into some semblance of sitting upright, but bile rose in the back of his throat at the effort.

'William Shakespeare?' The man who stood in the doorway was tall and thin, his hair falling across his forehead. Shakespeare knew that he had never seen the man before, and yet there was something curiously familiar about him. He had a lean and hungry look about him, as though he thought too much.

'Yes, I am Shakespeare. I apologize for my condition,

but I have fallen most greviously ill.'

The man nodded. 'My name is Braxiatel,' he said, 'Irving Braxiatel.'

'Forgive me,' Shakespeare said, 'but have we met before? Your face floats most oddly in my memory.'

Braxiatel nodded. 'We did meet, some seven years ago now, in the city of Venice.'

Venice. A dry cough racked Shakespeare's body for a moment, turning his throat to fire. 'I remember little of my time in Venice, good sir,' he said finally. 'I contracted brain fever during the voyage, and awoke to find myself in England again. If I did you injury there, then I apologize.'

Braxiatel shook his head. 'No injury,' he said. 'At least, nothing that lasted. In fact, I may have done you more of an injury than you did me.'

Shakespeare felt a flicker of interest within his breast. 'You intrigue me, sir. Speak on.'

'I come to offer you a bargain,' Braxiatel said carefully. 'I took something from you in Venice that I could return.'

Shakespeare chuckled weakly. 'If I have not missed it for seven years, what use would it be now?'

'I'm talking about your memory,' Braxiatel said calmly, and Shakespeare felt his heart thud hard within the cage of his chest. 'The memory of what happened during those few lost days.'

Another cart creaked past the window. Shakespeare's gaze wandered away from the man's face and drifted across the rough walls. His thoughts grew quiet for a moment, and when he glanced back at Braxiatel he wasn't sure whether he had briefly fallen asleep or not. 'My memory? Even if I believed you, what makes you think that I would want it back?'

'Because you are dying, and you want to die whole. Because that gap in your mind has always plagued you, like a rotted tooth.' Braxiatel smiled briefly. 'I have read between the lines of your plays. I know that it bothers you.'

Dying. The word should have shocked Shakespeare, provoked him to paroxysms of anger, but he had guessed. He *was* dying, and he thought he knew who was responsible. 'Ralegh,' he murmured. 'That whoreson Ralegh. He has poisoned me.'

Braxiatel nodded. 'He was released from the Tower of London five weeks ago. He is here in Stratford under an assumed name and slipped poison into your wine in a tavern.'

Shakespeare smiled weakly. His head throbbed with a sick, hot pain. 'I drew up my will a month ago,' he whispered, 'as soon as I was told of his release. I knew that he bore malice against me. What man would not, after thirteen years of incarceration?' He closed his eyes, intending only to blink, but the call of the darkness almost pulled him in. 'Still, a man can die but once,' he murmured, 'and we all owe God a death.' Forcing his eyes open, he said, 'You talk of a bargain. What have I to offer?'

'You have some manuscripts,' Braxiatel replied, 'plays that did not find favour with the Monarch. Rather than see them lost with your death, I would like to see them placed on display in a library that I am in the process of building.'

'A library? Of my works? Why?' Shakespeare was having to concentrate harder and harder on the conversation.

'The Library of St John the Beheaded,' Braxiatel said quietly, 'is dedicated to preserving works of science, literature and philosophy that would otherwise be lost. Your plays *Love's Labours Won*, *The Birth of Merlin* and *Sir John Oldcastle* might not survive your death if someone does not act to preserve them now.'

'Minor works, they do not deserve to survive.' Shakespeare broke off as a shudder ran through his body. Sweat sprang out across his scalp and forehead, and trickled greasily across his skin to the pillow. 'But you may have them. You may have all my manuscripts. They are in the bottom drawer of the dresser over there by the window.' He tried, but failed, to move his head as Braxiatel walked across to the dresser and bent down. Moments later the man straightened up with an armload of quarto sheets covered with Shakespeare's sprawling handwriting.

'Thank you,' he said.

'And now for your side of the bargain,' Shakespeare whispered. 'I could have counted myself happy these past seven years, were it not that I have had bad dreams. If you have a physic to restore to me that which was lost, I would fain die happy.'

Braxiatel balanced the pile of papers in the crook of his left arm while his right hand reached into a pocket of his coat. When it emerged it was holding a small metal device with a fleck of green glass in one end. He pointed it at Shakespeare's head and pressed a stud on its side.

'Now cracks a noble heart,' he quoted softly. 'Good night, sweet Prince, and flights of angels sing thee to thy rest.'

Shakespeare did not see him leave. In his mind's eye it was as if a curtain had been drawn back, revealing a stage populated with characters and random fragments of scenery. Here, standing by a window, was an old man with long, white hair; there at a tavern table was an older Kit Marlowe with his devilishly beautiful smile. An Italian with a bushy beard quaffed a flagon of wine while, in the background, an island floated above the towers and gilded domes of Venice. Demons stalked the stage too; some with scarlet wings and armoured skin, others like bags of bones. And there was more – so much more – places, people, sights and sounds and smells that crowded at the edges of his mind and jostled for position. Effortlessly he summoned up the remembrance of things past, holding them like pieces of a jigsaw, trying one against another as if to assemble a coherent story from the fragments. And, while so engaged, he did not even notice that he had died.

Acknowledgements

During the writing of my previous mytho-historical
novel, *All-Consuming Fire*, I consulted some thirty
or so books for research. It didn't seem important to list
them at the time, as I was more concerned with capturing
the indefinable flavour of an era than with fitting the plot
between provable historical facts.

This book, by contrast, involves people who once
lived and things that once happened. Galileo was in
Venice when I said he was (although not, perhaps, for as
long), all inhabitants of the Roanoake colony did vanish
mysteriously and Shakespeare did, or so legend has it, take
over the role of Lady Macbeth during the first performance of the play. However, as far as we know, Christopher Marlowe died well before 1609 and Cardinal
Bellarmine was never abducted by aliens. Given this
mixing of real and unreal I thought I'd better list the
books I used as research tools, in case any reader is foolish
enough to want to distinguish between fact, speculation
and downright fabrication.

Charles Boyce – *Encyclopedia of Shakespeare*. All you
never wanted to know about the 'bard' of Avon, and
more, all listed alphabetically. Fanboy Shakespeare, but
a great source of random facts.

Bill Bryson – *The Mother Tongue*. A brilliant discussion
of the way that the English language has changed over
the centuries. It helped inform my decision about how

253

to present the speech of Shakespeare and Marlowe in this book (see below).

Bill Bryson – *Made In America*. A wonderfully anecdotal history of the American language that provides occasional flashes of insight into the lives of the first American settlers, and briefly discusses the Roanoake colony.

Italo Calvino – *Different Cities*. A fictional work in which Marco Polo describes to Kublai Khan the different cities he has visited, but in which they all turn out to be aspects of Venice. Possibly the most beautiful book I've ever read, and thanks to Justin Richards for telling me about Calvino.

Chas Carner and Alessandro Giannatasio – *Venicewalks*. A guide to walking around Venice. Obviously.

Stephen Coote – *A Play of Passion – The Life of Sir Walter Ralegh*. A readable life of a man who does not appear in this book, but has a tangential influence on many of the things that happen in it.

Michael J. Crowe – *The Extraterrestrial Life Debate 1750–1900*. Despite the dates, it does cast some light on 17th century attitudes towards the possibility of life on other worlds, and shows that Galileo did take the possibility seriously.

Antonia Fraser – *King James*. Part of a series of books that Antonia Fraser has written about the history of the period, and quite useful, if a little superficial.

G. B. Harrison – *Introducing Shakespeare*. One of those blue-spined Pelican reference paperbacks on obscure subjects that turn up in every single second-hand bookshop in Britain. Very good on how theatre was actually performed in Shakespeare's day. Reminiscent of a dry, rather ironic history teacher too fearsome to contradict.

Henry C. King – *The History of the Telescope*. In the same week that I was worrying about what Galileo's telescope actually looked like, and when the word 'telescope' was first used, I discovered this book in a second-hand bookshop. This happens to me a lot. Fortuitous, I call it. Expensive, says my wife.

Arthur Koestler – *The Sleepwalkers*. An excellent and thought-provoking book about the history of astronomy. Reading it was one of the factors that provoked me into wanting to write the book you're holding in your hands.

Frederick C. Lane – *Venice, A Maritime Republic*. A scholarly and very detailed history of Venice. As far as I know, Mr Lane and I are not related.

James Morris – *Venice*. The best travel book I have ever read. A wonderful evocation of the more unusual aspects of Venetian history.

Charles Nicholl – *The Reckoning*. A chunky non-fiction portrait of Christopher Marlowe given to me by Paul Cornell. Thanks, Paul.

Graham Phillips and Martin Keatman – *The Shakespeare Conspiracy*. A complete demolition job on all the legends, assumptions and anecdotes that have grown up around Shakespeare: a stripped down version of the man's life that covers 'just the facts, Ma'am,' and comes up with the surprising conclusion that Shakespeare was a secret agent for James I and was poisoned by Sir Walter Ralegh.

Tim Powers – *The Stress of Her Regard*. A fictional fantasy novel set partially in Venice about stone vampires feeding off Byron and his friends. If *All-Consuming Fire* was my attempt to emulate Powers' *The Anubis Gates*, then this book is my *The Stress Of Her Regard*, except that Powers told me he'd never even been to Venice when he wrote it. So, at last I'm one up on him.

James Reston Jnr – *Galileo – A Life*. A recent, lively and detailed biography of the astronomer. Very readable, and the source of many of the anecdotes about Galileo that I've used here.

S. Schoenbaum – *Shakespeare's Lives*. More about how Shakespeare's life has been reinterpreted over the years by various critics than about the great man himself, but it's still a useful source of historical details and little anecdotes.

Gerald Smith – *Galileo, A Dramatised Life*. Half documentary, half novel, and a useful counterpoint to James Reston's book.

Keith Thomas – *Religion and the Decline of Magic*. A description of the fight between superstition and religion in the Middle Ages. A scholarly but surprisingly readable work.

Ian Wilson – *Shakespeare: The Evidence*. A rather thicker debunking of the Shakespeare 'myth' than that written by Phillips and Keatman, but no less readable for that.

A. D. Wraight and Virginia F. Stern – *In Search of Christopher Marlowe*. Yes, but did they look behind the fridge? A very odd book – in some 350 pages the authors don't mention Marlowe's homosexuality once

256

– but it does contain some material about the first American colonies.

A note on dates: it is generally accepted that *Macbeth* was written between 1603 and 1606 and first performed in 1606 – not, as I suggest here, written in 1608 and first performed in 1609. The 'accepted' dating is, however, based only on the fact that a play written probably by Thomas Middleton in 1607 was obviously influenced by *Macbeth*. The first known performance of *Macbeth* was in 1611. My justification, for what it's worth, is that Middleton (or whoever) had talked to Shakespeare about *Macbeth*, or had seen an early draft. In fact, the period between 1608 and 1610 is one of the many blank spots in Shakespeare's sparsely documented life. He could have been anywhere during it. Even Venice.

A note also on language: the elliptical and allusive mode of speech reflected in the plays of Shakespeare and Marlowe is not how 'common' people of the time talked. The private letters and public records are much terser and closer to how we talk now. Given also the *Doctor Who* convention of translating all languages into contemporary English, I have done my best to make Shakespeare, Marlowe and Galileo into real characters rather than period figures. Shakespeare coined around 2,000 new words in his plays. Other words common in his time ('zooterkins', for instance) have fallen into disuse. Had I attempted to write his and Marlowe's dialogue using only the words they would have known, this book would have taken a lot longer to write and would probably have been a lot more difficult to read.

Finally, I would like to take this opportunity to commend the Hotel Savoya et Jolanda on the Riva Degli Shiavoni to anybody wishing to stay cheaply in Venice. It's about three minutes' walk from St Mark's Square and the Doge's Palace. The last time I stayed there, I flew back on the same aircraft as Carol Ann Ford (who played Susan, the Doctor's granddaughter). It's a funny old world.

Available in the *Doctor Who — New Adventures* series:

The next Missing Adventure is *Lords of the Storm* by David A. McIntee, featuring the fifth Doctor and Turlough.